SECRET HARBOR

a novel by Michael J Moore

A HellBound Books Publishing LLC Book
Austin TX

Michael J. Moore

**A HellBound Books LLC
Publication**
Copyright © 2020 by HellBound Books Publishing
LLC
All Rights Reserved

Cover and art design
By
HellBound Books Publishing LLC

No part of this book may be reproduced, stored in a retrieval system, or transmitted by any means, electronic, mechanical, photocopying, recording or otherwise without written permission from the author
This book is a work of fiction. Names, characters, places and incidents are entirely fictitious or are used fictitiously and any resemblance to actual persons, living or dead, events or locales is purely coincidental.

www.hellboundbookspublishing.com

This book is dedicated to my mum, Brenda Murphy

Michael J. Moore

ACKNOWLEDGEMENTS

First, I have to thank God.

Then my partner, Cait Moore, for all the inspiration she's given me.

Our families, my two beautiful daughters, Gabriela and Jazmin, and Cait's three imaginative sons: Carter, Aston, and Dante.

Special thanks to Kat and Tom Richey, who've been supportive of both Cait and I in every way possible.

SECRET
HARBOR

PROLOGUE

Jerry Warden has the demeanor of a used car salesman, and even though he's as transparent as a dinner glass my mom can't seem to see through him. Or maybe she does. Maybe she just doesn't care. It's hard to tell because my view's obstructed by tears. The room's big for an office, but small for a waiting room. It seems to be some cross between the two, with cushioned chairs along one wall and a round table in the center. I know it's nothing more than a set, strategically arranged to convince parents to give away their children.

Over Jerry's shoulder, the late-June sun beams through a window, onto the table, casting a circular shadow on the tan carpet. Traffic passes on a two-lane road, running through Anacortes, Washington. If I thought I could make it, I'd jump through the glass.

I don't mean to cry, haven't done it for as long as I can remember. But as I sit across from the tall, weasely man with missing teeth and greying hair, something grows in my chest. It's like a sickness, only that's not what it is at all and before I have a chance to take charge of it, it expands like a marshmallow in a microwave, overflowing into my stomach, up my throat, and out my eyes and nose.

I hear my stepfather's voice on the other side of my mom. "For the love of God, Tony, you're fourteen-friggin'—years-old. Man up."

My mom says, "John."

Don't 'John' me. We talked about this."

"I know we talked about it, but you don't have to—"

"What? Put my foot down?"

"So the boat leaves in less than forty minutes," Jerry interrupts. When I look up, he slides a pamphlet across the table, stopping just under my mother's nose. She clutches my stepdad's hand so snug that her knuckles are bone white. I imagine water couldn't even seep between their fingers. Tapping the shiny folded paper, Jerry says, "This is the level system."

"Yeah," John replies. "We saw it on the website."

Not missing a beat, Jerry explains, "Everything at Secret Harbor's set up for success. I know what you're thinking Tony, but it's not like that. There're no locked doors in the home. You're not a prisoner. It's all incentive based. We reinforce positive behavior, by allotting privileges to boys who level up.

"He'll begin automatically on level two—well technically, he'll start on level one. They all do. But it's only temporary. A transition period. After two weeks, he'll get his level two and be able to use the phone, go to the activities building—we even have rec equipment." Looking at me, he asks, "You like weights?"

I want to kill him. To punch John in his face. To take my mother by her chubby shoulders and shake her like she shook my little brother when he was a baby. To put my face in hers, bare my teeth, and scream, "How could you do this to me? How could you just send me away to live on some island like an orphan?" But all I can manage, is to put my head down and sit with my own hands in my lap, sniffling and watching tears puddle onto the stained wooden table.

My mom says something about me loving weights. My stepdad snickers, complains about the set he bought me for Christmas being used once then sitting in the yard collecting rust. Whatever else is said, fades out as I think about Karina.

She was there this morning when they picked me up from juvie, waiting just outside the entrance like we planned. We were arrested together, but she was released first because her mom isn't planning on giving her away. I was escorted to the door, and the first thing I heard was my mom's voice, full of venom.

"I want that little—person removed before I pick up my son."

The guard knew Karina because she had been in juvie more times than me. She told my mom there was nothing she could do, and my mom wanted to argue, but she didn't. She just took me by my arm and pulled me outside.

My memories are cruel. My head's a mess. Jerry won't stop talking about the boy's home that he runs. I don't care what he has to say, but there's a finality in his tone and I hate him for it, so I just shut him out.

It was warm already when my mother dragged me from juvenile detention. Still Karina sat curled up on the last step at the bottom of the stairway in a black hoody with her head covered. My mom and my stepfather both took my shirt in one hand and pulled me toward her.

She didn't look up until I was only steps away. Then, when she did, our eyes locked and I remembered why she makes me so crazy. Hers were wide, almond shaped holes in her brown skin. Her short-cropped hair splintered out of her hoody. My heart pounded on the inside my ribcage like a boxer on a speed bag. Not just because I loved her, but because of what we planned to do.

"Tony?" Jerry waves a hand, kidnapping me from my memories, making me aware that my tears have stopped at some point. "You hear me, champ? You like basketball?"

My stepdad laughs. "Tony couldn't catch a ball if he had the plague and it was filled with the cure."

My mom, pretending to care, rebukes him.

"Well," Jerry continues. "There's a lot more to do than just basketball. It's summer break, so you won't have to go to school. The other day all the boys were out in the field playing soccer. You know I coach a team at Mount Vernon High."

I don't want to talk about soccer, or basketball, or weightlifting. All I want is to go home. Before I can stop them, the floodgates open up again and I hear myself crying, begging my mom not to give me away. Promising to be good. To never smoke weed or drink beer, or run away again. Telling her how much I love and need her. It doesn't even cross my mind how ironic it is that just this morning I had planned to kill her.

I'd been planning it since the day I listened to her plead with the judge to send me away. The day he granted her wish and I was escorted back to juvie, where I called Karina and told her when I'd be picked up. Told her to meet me outside with a knife from her kitchen. A big one. To pass it to me so I could stab my mother until she was dead. And if John tried to stop me, I'd stab him too. Not because I hated my mom. I didn't. But because I loved Karina and I wanted to be with her. And it wasn't that big of a deal, because we had killed before. But as I descended the last step, she just gazed up into my eyes—the way she often did when we were intimate—and mouthed the words, "I love you." If there was a knife, it didn't come out. She didn't even stand up.

My mom opened the back door of her SUV and John shoved me inside. I didn't have to check the door to know it was child locked so I couldn't jump out at an intersection. They drove me from the juvie in Mount Vernon, to the office in Anacortes, where Jerry now sits across the table chipping away at any last minute resistance my mom has to giving me away like an old sofa, and asking me about sports, which I have no interest in.

And the boat to Cypress Island leaves in under forty minutes.

* * *

Karina has a Stepfather too, but hers isn't as nice as mine. He burns her with cigarettes and leaves bruises all over her body. Sometimes, I suspect he leaves bruises in other places as well. Places her biological father left them before he disappeared. I can't prove it though, and she never says he does, so I don't ask.

She told me all about her real father and what he did to her. Sometimes we get messed up and she talks about it and cries for me. I'm not good with that type of thing, so when she cries, I just kiss her lips and undress her real slow. She's so tiny, but she's even smaller with her clothes off. I know I won't see her again for at least three months, because that's how long the judge has ordered me to the island.

All the begging in the world couldn't dissuade my mom from giving me away, so I'm driven to a marina in Anacortes and walked along a pier where every different type of boat you could imagine are packed into spaces against private docks. The railings are lined with clear plastic spikes reaching toward the baby blue sky. Jerry tells me that's so birds don't land on them and leave droppings all over the place. The seagulls fly overhead and leave them anyway.

The scent of the sound takes me back to crabbing in the summertime with my Grandpa when I wasn't old enough to even consider killing my own mother. Before he left his own bruises on me. I assume the smell has a similar effect on her, only I spent more time with her dad as a toddler than she has in her whole life, so maybe not.

When we reach a boat with "Sea Wolf" painted on the side, I'm ushered aboard, and handed a black plastic bag stuffed with my belongings, which were packed for me while I was in juvie. Jerry tells me that since I'm behaving so well, he'll allow my parents to ride with me. I'm not sure I want them to, but I don't want to be alone either.

The boat isn't big, but it also isn't small. It has rows of benches like the short buses that kids who wear helmets to school ride. John takes a seat behind me as my mother plops down in my row, so close that our legs touch. She grabs my hand, attempting to interlace her fingers in mine. I pull away, peer out at the water.

"You can go," I say. "I'm not gonna try and run."

"Tony—"

"I can't swim anyway."

"Yes you can."

"Not really. Not good, at least. It doesn't matter though. Look around. There's nowhere to go."

She says she's not leaving me. I turn my head, glance into her eyes. "What about when we get there? Are you gonna leave me then?"

Her lips purse and her forehead wrinkles as she makes a face like she wants to cry. She doesn't really want to, though, because if she did, she would just do it. She's spent her entire life making herself cry and wishing somebody would care. I know I haven't really hurt her feelings, and she doesn't give a damn whether or not she's hurt mine. There's an audience here and she can't look like a bad parent.

"Cut it out, Tony." John retorts.

I ignore him because it's either that or turn around and punch his face and we've been down that route once already. The boat rocks as a short Hispanic man and a fat white guy step on with two boys who might be my age. One's round, with grease in his hair. The other's a black kid. The Hispanic guy disappears into a covered portion of the boat and comes back out with life jackets.

"Here you go, man." He grins as he hands me one. "Gotta wear this." He gives one to my mom and John, then the rest of the crew. The fat kid watches as I put mine on, but he doesn't speak. I pretend not to notice, but the truth is I'm mortified that he and the other one are here because the sickness in my chest has returned and I'm afraid I might cry in front of them. I'm afraid I might beg again.

But begging will do no good. I'll be taken to the island anyway, and then these two boys will have seen me cry and beg like a little bitch. They'll tell everybody else, and that's what I'll be. I've never been to a group home, but don't imagine it's much different from juvie.

I can't become a bitch, which means that I can't be sad. Ever. Or happy. Only anger is acceptable. Red-hot anger, which has been a lifelong friend of mine anyway. So I glare at this kid, open my mouth to ask him what the hell he's looking at. But there's a lump in my throat. He averts his gaze and I don't know if I've ever been more relieved.

Jerry Warden stands at the edge of the dock and watches as the boat comes to life and pulls out. He's smiling. His missing teeth provide a view into his skull and all I can think is that I'm going to kill him the first chance I get.

CHAPTER ONE

I met Karina last year. Even though I'm white and she's brown, people always thought we were brother and sister. Probably because we both have black hair and keep it cut the same length. We had seventh period Math together, but we didn't talk for the first month because I didn't really talk to anybody. Mr. Espinosa made his students sit around tables and work together. One day one of the girls at my table asked me if I was a virgin. My ears burned as I told her I wasn't, and she grinned because she knew I was lying. She never talked to me again.

Karina was one of the cutest girls in school, but she didn't know it so she didn't screw around with the jocks or the rich kids. She sat at the table next to me, and she used to turn around in her chair, and sit with her legs draped over the back rest. The guys sitting with her would always crack jokes and give her crap.

Seventh grade was like an estuary where salt water met fresh water, and kids swam around aimlessly, discovering who they were as they morphed into teenagers. When the year began, I didn't have any friends because everybody I knew from last year went to the other middle school and I didn't have name brand clothes or expensive shoes. It wasn't that my mom and John couldn't afford them—John made enough money as a mechanic to buy us a nice two-story house in a new development—but my mom was in charge of spending it and she didn't think my social life needed to be prioritized. So my clothes mostly came from thrift stores or Walmart. I never complained, though, because so did hers.

I spent my days at Laventure moving from class to class, just as aimlessly as the rest of the fish, only I was alone and most of them weren't. The ones that were, sat against walls, or in corners with their noses stuck in books about dragons and spaceships because I guess it was easier to block out the world than let the world block you out. I just walked the halls with my head down. I've never really been comfortable with eye contact.

Karina ate with the poor white kids, even though she wasn't white. She didn't wear name brand clothes or expensive shoes either, but it was okay because she was a girl and what she did wear, she wore real tight. She was quiet most of the time, but everybody around her was as loud as hell.

I ate by myself, listening to all the noise in the cafeteria. To the spoiled kids, who cleaned their sneakers with paper towels in the bathroom. To the cholos, who carried notebooks under their arms. To the poor white kids, who cut class and smelled like cigarettes. They liked to laugh. All of them. They touched girls and left messes at their tables so people would know they had been there.

I could have sat in corners too—could have walked up to one of the rejects while he had his face in a book and introduced myself, then neither of us would be alone anymore. I didn't though. It wouldn't have been right, because I wasn't really one of them.

Brandon Hope didn't know this, so less than a month into the school year he cut me off on my way into the building with three other eighth-graders and waved a penny in front of my face.

"What's up, sevie? Listen, I wanna conduct an experiment. I'm gonna drop this penny on the ground, and we're gonna see how far you can push it, using only the tip of your nose."

He had obviously seen too many eighties teen movies. I suspected he had only suffered through seventh grade for this very purpose. He had made a point to publicly bully seventh graders on a daily basis since the first day of school. He dropped the penny and it danced on the pavement before coming to a stop.

I could've laughed, because in truth, it was funny. But I didn't. I'm not sure I remembered how. I didn't even look at him. Just kept walking until he put a hand on my chest, shoving me back.

"I don't think you heard me. I said you're gonna push that penny with your nose."

Brandon Hope didn't know that in the second grade, my mom had bought me what she thought were nice clothes, and some kids had jumped me and ripped them, along with my backpack. That they hadn't even drawn blood, but she had when I got home for not fighting back because clothes and backpacks cost money. That my father died in a car accident when I was two, and she had taught me to be a man the only way she knew how, which was with her fists.

Brandon Hope cursed as my knuckles smashed into his nose. He ducked and covered his face. I hit him again. And again. Then somebody pulled on my backpack, and the pavement moved under my feet and came at me as I toppled over. Before I knew it, I was surrounded by eighth-graders. Shoes slammed into my ribs, my back, my face. I just rolled into a ball and saw that none of them wore expensive shoes either. Then I closed my eyes because that's all I could do.

Somewhere in the mesh of grunting and distant laughter, a gravelly voice yelled, "Hey! What the hell do you think you're doing?" Then, all at once, it was over. Rubber smacked the pavement like a drumroll. I looked up to see my punishers fleeing and Ed, the school's janitor standing over me in his grey coveralls with a rag sticking out of his pocket. He yanked me to my feet and said, "You got a death wish or somethin' son?" Then he cursed and asked me what I had been thinking.

The bell rang, but a crowd had gathered around. None of them moved to go to class until Ed yelled and pulled me into the office.

* * *

I never could pinpoint why it was so hard to get the dishes from the sink, to the dishwasher. Or from the dishwasher to the cupboards. It's the only job I had, but I spent hours in our tiny kitchen just trying to get it done.

Nobody ever rinsed their plates before they put them in the sink. In fact, I'm pretty sure they made a point not to. My mom didn't cook, didn't leave her room if she didn't have to, so when John came home from work, he made dinner every night too. He made the biggest messes when he cooked. So big I thought he did it on purpose because he was pissed that he had to cook. But that's how he and my mom kept the rest of the house as well, so maybe not.

Day after day, I came home from school and stood alone in front of the sink. I would put away a couple of dishes, then my mind would wander and thirty minutes later I'd find myself staring out the window daydreaming about some girl at school who had asked me if

I was a virgin, or who liked to sit backward in her chair with her legs draped over the backrest.

They told me when I was younger that I had ADHD, even gave me Ritalin. But I didn't speak much when I was taking it. I just walked around with my head down, or stared off at the sky. So my mom talked to another doctor who told her that I was taking enough to subdue a hyperactive adult and she said I didn't have to take it anymore.

I didn't get in trouble for fighting at school. Ed had seen everything and told the principal I was defending myself. Fighting was the only thing I never got in trouble at home for, so like any other day, I was in trouble for everything else. Mostly, I always suspected, for just being me. Maybe something to do with my biological father as well.

My mom picked me up, then retreated to her room to sit at the desk by her bed and screw around on her tablet. Alex was only six, so he played mostly in the backyard with the dog. Anne was three, and had nursed an unusually long time, so she spent most of her time wherever my mom was. We had the same mom, but John was their father.

Sometimes, When I wasn't staring out the window over the sink or trying to focus on moving the dishes from one place to another, I threw kitchen knives at the wall. I would throw one. Watch it stick. Pull it out. Take a step back. Throw it again. I had broken the tips off a few of them and left tiny holes in the wall that I guessed I would have to pay for eventually, because my mom and John kept a thick leather belt in their closet and knives and houses cost money.

* * *

"I saw what you did to Brandon Hope," one of the poor white kids said to me in the cafeteria the day after the fight. He was fat and wore a green knitted beanie with a metal spike sticking out the top that made him look like a rhinoceros. I had woken up with a black eye and looked like a raccoon which is probably why everybody seemed to be staring at us like we were a zoo exhibit. That and the fact that he had left the poor white table to come over and sit next to me while I ate.

I told him I hadn't done anything to Brandon Hope, but stop his shoe with my face.

"Yeah. And broke his freaking nose."

"Really?"

Instead of answering, he said, "I'm Doug, man."

"Yeah. I know."

Doug said Brandon Hope and his friends were being expelled. I asked him how he knew so much.

"He's my neighbor. I mean, not next door. He lives a couple houses down. I used to bonk his older sister."

"Bonk?"

"Yeah. Brenda Hope. She's a freak, too. She was my babysitter." He laughed and told me that Brenda Hope had a tattoo on her pelvis of Woody Woodpecker pushing a lawnmower through her pubes. Then he asked me why I messed Brandon up.

I told him I was just defending myself and he stared at me for too long before he finally blinked and said, "Brandon's a dick. Brenda told me one time she couldn't find one of her thongs, and then she found out he was wearing it under his pants. It was a white one, too. She told her dad and he beat the crap out of Brandon and tried to give her the thong back, but it had stains in the back, so she just threw it away. Isn't that sick?"

I think I was supposed to laugh, but since I wasn't sure I remembered how, I snickered instead, and said yeah, it was sick.

"Who you got last period?" he asked.

"Seventh?"

"Yeah. What class you got?"

"Uh, Math."

"Mr. Espinosa?"

"Yeah."

"Your name's Tony, right?"

"Yeah. Tony Carpenter. Or whatever."

"You're funny, man. Karina says she sits next to you." He glanced over to the poor white table and I found myself following his gaze. Karina looked up briefly, then took a drink of chocolate milk and shoved some guy who was smiling next to her like he had just made a fart joke. Everybody else in the cafeteria, it seemed, had stopped watching Doug and I at some point and gone back to laughing, touching girls, leaving messes on tables.

Doug asked me if I liked music and even though his questions seemed pointless and I suspected I was falling victim to some prank, it was better than sitting in a corner with my nose in a book or just being alone. So I said, "I don't know."

"You don't know if you like music?"

"I mean—yeah. Doesn't everybody?"

"I dunno. Maybe. What kinda music you like?"

"I don't know."

"Really?"

"No. I mean, I know—I just—I like a little of everything, I guess."

"Even classical jazz?"

"What's that?"

"I'm just messing with you, man. Check it out. You ah—" he pinched his thumb and index fingers together and held them in front of his lips. Before he said the word "smoke" I knew he was asking if I used pot. I didn't. I never had, at least. But everybody knew the poor white kids did. They made a point to let it be known. They didn't have name brand clothes or expensive shoes because their parents couldn't afford them. But they used pot and smoked cigarettes and they were never alone because they were all friends. And even though I wasn't one of them, they looked like me, so I lied and told Doug that I smoked all the time.

He said a few of them were cutting seventh period to go out to the woods behind the school and roast a bowl. He said I should come with. He told me who would be there, but all I remember hearing was Karina.

CHAPTER TWO

We've been in the boat for more than forty minutes and for some reason my mind's played images of a man I left to die in an alley not long ago. I haven't thought much of it until now, so I've been shaking them off and trying to focus on the scene passing on either side of the Sea Wolf.

We've passed multiple small islands along the way with bright green trees and small private docks. Some are only a few hundred feet apart. The fat white guy sticks his chest out, tips his head back like a howling wolf, letting wind fly up his nose as he drives. His thick, dish water hair dances because there's no windshield. The covered portion's just a roof. No walls, no locked doors.

The San Juan's are a cluster of islands that attract tourists, eager to see a family of orcas swimming above the surface of the Puget Sound or seals lounging on one of the aesthetic beaches. There are ferries running from island to island and tourist centers on most of them. I know because before my mom gave me away, I lived just over in Mount Vernon. My class went to a camp on Orcas Island in the sixth grade. I would've gone too, but I got sick. My mom hasn't spoken to me or attempted to take my hand again because there's nowhere for me to run, so she won't have to try and restrain me. The greasy-haired kid continues to glance over, but I've figured out by now that he's not mad-dogging me. He keeps looking because we're the same now, and maybe we'll be friends. The black kid just stares out the other side of the boat at the passing water.

The wind in my face has caused my eyes to water for most of the trip. I've blinked and blinked, but it hasn't helped. I'm doing my best to smile so neither of them think I'm crying. Nobody's said a word for at least twenty minutes. The engine is loud, and I'm guessing nobody wants to lose his voice yelling over it.

We continue along a segment of sound that feels like a river because it's set between two long strips of land, then the boat slows down and another tiny island comes into view at the end of the row. It looks like the scene from the beginning of Jurassic Park, only Cypress Island has a big dock and I'm a prisoner on the Sea Wolf, not a lawyer standing on a raft.

Finally my mom speaks, but all she says is "Tony." I don't respond because she hasn't asked a question. I just scan the island. Past the dock, in the distance, is a huge cabin set on a hill. As we get closer, the smell of the sound fades, replaced by the scent of forest. I see a balcony that runs the length of the cabin and big windows looking out toward the water like an observation deck. It resembles something a rich person might own, or a vacation retreat.

My mom says, "See, Tony, it's beautiful."

Good, I think. Then you stay and I'll go home. But I don't say that. Instead, I just stare because she's right. The entire layout is beautiful. Almost a paradise. Still, as the boat comes to rest against the dock, I begin to panic. Before I can stop myself, I say, "Mom—"

"Kat." John cuts me off before I can get another word out. "Remember, let go."

"Mom—"

"Kat—"

"Please."

"Tony, stop it."

"Mom—"

But my mom doesn't speak. Not one word. Not until I'm off the boat and her and John are still on it. She tells me my blackout period will be over in two weeks and I'll be allowed to call. She'll be allowed to send treats. Letters. Pictures. The two kids who rode with me disappear with the fat staff member and I'm left with only my parents and the short Hispanic man.

My mom makes promises. This is only temporary. Three months, and I'll be home.

"Why?" I ask. "If I'm coming home anyway, why do I have to be here for three months?"

She says, "Tony."

"That's not an answer, damn it! Answer my question! Can't you answer a simple question? Why do I have to stay here?"

The Hispanic guy raises his hand to his face, speaks into a small, black walkie talkie. Almost instantly, four adults step onto the dock, walk toward me. One of them is the fat boat-driver. They want a fight. I'll give them one. I clench my fists, set my feet because I took three months of kickboxing earlier this year.

But when they're close, they walk past me and board the Sea Wolf, taking seats with my mom and John. A tall, skinny man with longish, grey hair raises the trash-bag with all my belongings in it.

"This his?"

John says, "Yeah. That's his."

"Here ya go, bud." The guy tosses it onto the dock.

My mother told me once that she wished I were never born, then she punched me in the mouth and split my lip open. She said she hated me because I ran away from home.

The Sea Wolf's engine revs as it backs up, turns around. John half smirks. My mom is twisted around in her seat, still pretending she wants to cry. She does it so I'll cry again. But I'll never cry again.

The Hispanic man says something that I pay no attention to because I don't care what he has to say. The boat's driving away and my mom's still staring at me as I pick up my bag and turn my back to her. There's a dirt trail leading from the dock to the cabin. Along the trail is a sign that must be six feet wide and four feet high. It reads: Secret Harbor School.

CHAPTER THREE

In kindergarten, Jenny Metcalf used to kiss me and put my hands under her dress. I called her my girlfriend because I loved her. Then I saw her kissing a second grader and putting his hands under her dress and I cried on the bus ride home. When I told my mom what she did, she said, "That bitch."

I kissed girls at least once every year in elementary school. It was friends that were hard to find, so whenever I had one I would follow him around like a lost puppy. That's probably why I followed the poor white kids after seventh period.

They weren't all white. There was Karina, she was Mexican. And Mathias, who was Native American. Mathias had a ponytail. He stayed close to Karina and teased her every time an opportunity arose. David was as white as you could get, with blond hair and pale skin. By the way Doug dressed, he looked like the poorest of them all. Amber was there too. Amber's eyes seemed to be on me constantly. Her hair was curly, and so dark brown that it was almost black and she kept her hands covered with her sleeves. Like Karina, she didn't talk much.

We met behind the gym, and Doug said we had to hurry across the track before somebody saw us and called the cops. It was bright out, but the sun was concealed by a thick layer of grey clouds. I wore some off-brand jacket that my mom had found marked down at one of her thrift stores last year. At Laventure, the social dynamics I had almost finally learned to navigate in grade school were non-existent, so even though I had never had an urge to try weed, and I was as nervous as hell, I hurried across the track with Doug and his friends.

There was an opening in the fence that led to a neighborhood where apartments went on forever. Every building was a different color, and some were much older and more beat up than others. Windows were broken out of just about every car parked along the sidewalk. I knew a lot of the cholos lived here, because I saw them walking to school in the mornings with their notebooks under their arms.

David spit on the hood of a red Honda and Karina told him he was sick. Doug walked a little ahead of everyone else. I stayed by his side because I was a puppy.

"You live in Green Pastures, right?" he asked.

I said, "Yeah. How do you know that?"

"Desiree Burke."

Desiree Burke lived a few houses down from me in a house that looked exactly like mine, only reversed. Like if my house were looking in a mirror. She wore name brand clothes and expensive shoes and screwed around with the jocks and the rich kids. But sometimes, when I was outside cleaning dog crap from my back lawn, she would come and lean over the fence and smile at me. I asked him what about her? He told me she lived in my neighborhood.

"Yeah," I said. "I know."

"Damn, fool. I'm saying that's how I know where you live."

"Oh."

"You're rich."

"Not really."

"Green Pastures is a rich neighborhood."

I said," It's a new development."

"Yeah, that's rich. Desiree Burke is, for sure."

I asked if he had bonked her and he smiled so deviously you would've thought it was April Fool's Day.

"She used to be different. Not so fat, you know?"

Desiree Burke wasn't fat. Doug was fat.

The forest behind Laventure was just a small patch of trees that sat between the apartments where the cholos lived and the trailer park where David and Mathias both lived. There was a bridge that crossed a small stream. The bridge was wide enough that you could've driven a car across it, so they put metal beams into the ground that stuck up to stop you from doing that.

There was a thin trail on the side of the bridge, going into the woods. That's where we went. When we were a few feet back Doug brought out a cell phone and turned on some rap song. I didn't have a phone and guessed none of the others did either. He produced a glass pipe and David stuffed weed into it and handed it to Amber. She looked like a little squirrel as she brought out a lighter and used her covered hands to raise it to her face. It was still red-hot when she passed it to me, and even though I was scared and my hand shook, I took it and sucked on the end.

Then I was doubled over, coughing and choking. Somewhere above me I heard Doug complain, felt him take the pipe from my hand. Everybody but me exploded into laughter because there was a fire dancing in my lungs.

Mathias said, "This fool's never chiefed before."

"You cool?" Doug asked.

I looked up and saw Amber watching me, covering her mouth with her sleeve and giggling. David smiled from ear to ear with an open pocketknife in one hand. Karina had the pipe. She took a long hit, holding it in while the rest of them continued to watch me cough and laugh at me.

* * *

I knew I was screwed as soon as I walked in the house and saw my mom sitting on the couch, instead of in her bedroom. Alex wasn't home from school yet. Anne sat next to her, looking like a porcelain doll in a red dress and matching shoes. Her hair was done real nice.

My mom's eyes didn't look like they were bulging out of her skull every time she got mad. Only when she was mad at me. When I was really young, she would make that face and chase me around the house for fun until I sank into a corner and cried. Then sometimes she would get pissed and hit me with wooden spoons for crying. I never liked that face, but I liked it even less stoned.

She cursed and told me to drop my backpack. Then she opened it and dumped my things onto the floor. "You think you can cut class and I won't find out?"

I mumbled something about just forgetting to check in with the teacher, but before I could finish she threw my notebook and hit me in my black eye. "Get in the kitchen and do your chores. When you're done, go sit in your room until your dad gets home."

I didn't argue. I had never once argued with her or John.

* * *

The leather belt was thick and pliable. John still wore it when he met my mom when I was four. Then, when it was broke in just right, he transferred his Snap-On buckle onto a new one and gave it to my mom so she didn't have to break anymore spoons because spoons cost money. She kept it in her closet, on top of a pile of old dirty clothes.

There was never a shortage of food in our home. All our cupboards were full and we had a big pantry. Once, when I was seven, my mom's sister was babysitting Alex and me and some cans of Campbell's soup disappeared. John held me down while my mom hit me with the belt until I admitted I saw her sister steal them. I hadn't seen her steal anything, but the belt hurt so I admitted I had.

At thirteen the only two people in the civilized world who didn't think I was too old for the belt were my parents, so John left welts all over my back for cutting class and my mom said I couldn't leave the house outside of school for a month. I didn't care because I wasn't allowed outside the Green Pastures neighborhood by myself anyway, so I didn't have any friends to go see.

CHAPTER FOUR

"Ahaha! Check it out. Tony's on his period!"

Mathias was a dick to everybody but Karina. He was a dick to her too, just not as much. He had only poured a little bit of cranberry juice on my pants, but it did look like I was on my period. Daniel Hope never made it back to Laventure. He was expelled and his eighth-grader followers were close-lipped and tranquil without him around. I had been sitting with the poor white kids for over a month already.

I don't think I'd spoken six words to Karina, because she made my voice shake and I had trouble thinking right whenever I tried. She just called everyone bro and laughed at jokes and our eyes seemed to meet frequently throughout the days. She told Mathias he was a dick, then touched me for the first time ever, using a paper towel to wipe the liquid from my crotch.

Doug said, "Whoa. Karina, you gonna let Tony bonk, or what?"

She shoved him, an exaggerated smile on her face, then kept wiping. Mathias got up and left.

After we ate, Doug, Karina, Amber, David and I went out to the woods where Doug passed out cigarettes from a pack he had. He gave one to everyone but Amber.

"Where's mine?" she asked.

Doug smiled, said, "What are you gonna do for it?" After a while, he gave her one too.

I didn't like cigarettes, but the poor kids did and I liked friends so I smoked whenever they did. I didn't mind the pot. I liked it, in fact. David brought out his knife and threw it at a tree. It sprung back and landed by my shoe. I picked it up and threw it at the same tree and it stuck like my mom's kitchen knives did in the wall at home.

"Not bad," Karina said.

David pulled it out, his cigarette sticking out of his mouth.

Amber smiled at me, then covered her own mouth with her sleeve. Doug said he had some weed at home. His mom wasn't there, so we could ditch the rest of the day and go to his place. Everybody thought it was a good idea. So did I, but I said I couldn't.

Karina touched my arm. "What? No way, you're coming with."

"No. I have something I have to do. I'll probably stop by later."

"Do you know where Doug lives?"

"No."

"Then how are you gonna stop by?"

"I'll call and get the address."

"Do you have a phone?"

"No."

"Then—"

"Damn Karina," Doug said. "Let the fool breathe. Mathias ain't here and all of a sudden you're swinging from Tony's pant leg. It's all good, Tony. My mom'll be home later anyway. Next time?"

"Next time," I said. "Cool."

"Yeah. Cool."

They didn't say goodbye, just turned and stalked off toward the trailer park. I stared after them for a while, then jogged back toward Laventure before I ended up late for class.

* * *

"Mathias' got hands," David said one morning as we stood behind the gym before school drinking beers that I had stolen from my mom and John.

"What?"

"He got hands. The fool can fight."

When I was barely out of diapers, my mom worked two jobs. When she wasn't working, she was in bars looking for somebody to love her the way that my Grandfather didn't. He loved me though, so she left me with him most of the time, which was okay most of the time, but not always.

My Grandfather liked beers. From noon, to nine, he washed them down, one after another. Even though I was only three, he left me a drink in each can when he sent me to dispose of it and fetch him a cold one. Sometimes, as the years went by, I drank with my mom until the rooms would spin, so even though stealing was pretty new to me, alcohol wasn't.

I asked David why he was rambling about Mathias.

He chugged from his can, said, "I dunno," and belched.

We talked about a high school girl who stood at the entrance of the trailer park all summer in boy shorts and got into cars that pulled up. He said she had a Mexican boyfriend. He said he tried to get her to go into the woods with him once and she spit on his shoe. He said he threw a water bottle and hit her in the side of the head. Then he asked what was up with my jacket.

I looked down at it, then back up at him. "What do you mean?"

"Where'd you get that thing?"

"Uh, my mom picked it up at some thrift store. I don't know."

"Value Village?"

"Yeah. How'd you know?"

"I didn't. I was just guessing. That's where I jacked this one from." He pulled on his own coat.

"Shouldn't you be wearing North Face or something, though?"

"What? Why?"

"Cause you're like rich." I told him I wasn't rich.

"You live in Green Pastures."

"That's not rich. It's middle class or whatever."

"That coat sucks. It's ugly."

"Tell my mom that," I said.

"Man, come to my house. I got some clothes for you. They should fit. Doesn't Desiree Burke live in your neighborhood?"

I said, "Yeah. Doug bonked her."

"He what?"

"Bonked her."

"What does that even—? No he didn't. Doug's a liar, in case you haven't noticed. Only thing he's ever screwed is his cat."

I tried not to picture Doug screwing his cat.

The bell rang while we were still drinking, but I had a pretty strong buzz already so I just ignored it. When all eight cans were empty, we left them on the ground behind the gym and cut through the track slowly because we were drunk and didn't care if anyone called the cops.

* * *

There were actually two trailer parks. They were right next to each other, and they both went in circles. They sat by a big field where I imagined there would someday be another trailer park. David lived in a single-wide that smelled like cigarettes and fish-sticks. When we stepped inside, it was quiet, aside from the sound of rain beating on the roof. He said his mom was at work and his younger sister was at school.

I had been in the trailer park before. When I was young, John and my mom were in a program that helped you build your own house, so they used to drop Alex and me off at a day-care here. We always brought top ramen because the trailer it was in didn't have any food. David's didn't look like it had much either.

His room was in the very back. He rummaged through a pile of clothes in a tiny closet and tossed me a couple pairs of jeans and some t-shirts. They were all old and wore out, but they were name brand. Then he gave me a jacket and a pair of dirty sneakers and told me to change.

"See? They got nice stuff at the thrift stores too. You just gotta jack it because it's more expensive."

He told me he went into the changing rooms and acted like he was trying them on, then put his clothes on over them and walked out like he owned the world. I changed into my new clothes, stuffed the rest into my backpack.

"You like knives?" he asked.

"I dunno."

"You don't know if you like them?"

"I guess I do."

"Here." He tossed me a folded blue pocketknife with red flowers on the handle.

"Thanks."

"I think my mom has some weed in her room. Wait here."

He disappeared down the hall. I opened the knife. It had a thick blade and a heavy handle. I wondered if it would stick in the wall in my kitchen. I wondered if it was sharp enough to cut through my mom's belt. I wondered how soon she would receive the call informing her I had cut class again. Then David reappeared with a metal pipe and I folded it shut and slipped it into my pocket.

* * *

I could've gone back to school. I didn't have to sit in David's living room, smoking and watching TV all day. Maybe my first period teacher wouldn't have noticed or reported me. I also could've gone home that night, and faced the consequences, but instead I hid under the pile of clothes in David's closet. His sister shared the other room with his mom, so neither of them knew I was there. I lay in there for hours, with only my head visible, while he sat on his bed and whispered to me. He even brought his dinner into the room and shared it with me.

Later in the night, there was a knock at the front door. Since the walls in the trailer were so thin, we could hear the police asking about me. David told me to hold still, threw a sweater over my head, then went out to talk to them.

I kept thinking they would scare him so bad he would rat on me. He didn't though. His mom told them they could come in and look around, and heavy footsteps shook the trailer. The door opened and I heard a voice coming out of the cop's radio, so I tried not to even breathe. Then he was gone. They thanked David's mom, and as soon as the front door shut, she yelled at him.

"You skipped school again?"

He said, "So what?"

"I told you to cut that out, didn't I?"

"And I told you I don't care."

"Do you know where that kid is?"

"Of course not. How the hell would I know that?"

"You've been taking my weed again."

He told his mom she was an idiot, and a drug addict.

She said, "You better not bring that runaway into my house."

So I guess I was a runaway.

* * *

It rained again, but not as heavy as yesterday. It was a light sprinkle. David went to school, so I wandered about in the rain, wearing my new clothes. The jacket didn't have a hood, but looking like a kid from the trailer park was better than looking like a lost orphan.

It occurred to me that if the police saw me walking during school hours, they might pull over and question me. They would probably even recognize me, so I found my way into the woods behind Laventure where I threw my new knife at trees and thought about what I would do with my life now that I was on my own.

David showed up at lunchtime with Doug to smoke cigarettes. Doug said I could stay at his place tonight. David said he had planned on turning his shed into a house for me because his mom never went in there. Doug laughed, said, "Naw. He can just come to my place. It'll be cool."

* * *

"Why did you run away, anyway?" Ben asked. Ben was Doug's older brother. It was night-time and we were at the skateboard park. One of Ben's friends was there too. It was cold out, but it wasn't raining anymore. We didn't care that it was cold, because we were passing around a pipe and we were already stoned out of our minds. Doug held his cell phone in his hand, and some rap song played from the speaker.

He said, "His mom's a dick, fool. She beats him with broomsticks and crap."

I had never talked about my mom to Doug, and he didn't actually know anything about her, but I didn't correct him. Ben said she sounded like a real dick. He was in high school, and fat like Doug. He dressed like a skateboarder, talked like a surfer.

"That's whack," Ben's friend blew out a cloud of smoke. "Broomsticks? For real? That can't hurt too badly. They're not very thick."

Doug told him to shut up. "You're gonna have to change your name," he said. "You know that right?"

I nodded.

Ben said, "He can't. He can't change his name legally till he's eighteen. Unless he gets emancipated."

Everybody thought that was a good idea. I should get emancipated.

"Doesn't he have to be at least sixteen to do that?" Ben's friend asked.

Ben said, "That's right. I think you're screwed, Tony. Unless—"

"Unless what?" Doug asked.

"Unless he gets a fake ID."

"Can we find him one?"

Ben and his friend locked eyes.

Ben said, "Russell."

His friend said, "Russell."

Doug said, "That's right, Russell."

I said, "Who's Russell?"

"Russell can get you a fake ID," Ben said.

"I don't have any money."

"Dude, he won't charge you. All I gotta do is smoke a bowl with him."

"And he'll do it for free?"

"Yeah."

"But doesn't he have to pay for it?"

"I'm telling you, he won't mind. He's got the money."

"Then why can't he buy his own weed?"

Ben said I asked too many questions. People would think I was a cop, so I stopped asking questions.

Their house wasn't much smaller than mine, and the neighborhood it sat in was just as nice. Even though he looked like the poorest of the poor white kids, Doug wasn't actually poor. He was just white. We sat in his room and played Xbox most of the night, while his mom stomped around the house because she was pissed I was there.

Ben said he'd call Russell tomorrow and get me sorted out. He asked what I wanted my name to be. I asked what he thought I should go with.

"You look kinda like a John to me. What do you think, Doug?" Doug said I looked like a John.

I said I didn't want to be a John.

"Not John?" Ben said. "How bout Carl?"

I said Carl sounded fine.

So it was decided. I would be a Carl.

* * *

A big part of being a poor white kid was walking. I had only been a runaway for two days and had probably put in more miles following them around
than all my previous years combined. The poor white kids trucked around town because they were allowed outside of their neighborhoods, so that's why they had friends.

My legs were sore and there were blisters on the bottom of my feet. I didn't care though. I liked the freedom. It was evening on night three and I was walking to the trailer park to sleep in David's shed because Doug's mom had had enough of me in her house. I had dumped my school supplies in the woods behind Laventure because I didn't plan on going back.

My backpack was stuffed with my new clothes and I was thinking about what my fake ID would look like when a Dodge hatchback pulled up next to me and my heart jumped into my neck.

My mom's friend Sharon rolled down the passenger window and said, "Tony. Hey, Tony. Come on. Hop in."

Her husband was tall and thin like a chopstick, and they looked funny together because she was the exact opposite. He looked past her from the driver's seat briefly, then returned his gaze to the road. I ignored her, just kept walking and the car moved again, following me.

"Tony. Where you going, buddy? Come on. It's okay. Get in the car."

But there was no way I was getting in that car, so instead I started jogging. The car picked up its pace and coasted along next to me.

"Tony, stop. Don't run. You're gonna be okay. We have to get you home. Your parents are worried sick about you. Your sister went to the hospital."

And that's all it took, because even though I couldn't remember a time when my mom and John weren't mad at me for something or the other and it was hard to believe that they'd be worried about me, my sister went to the hospital. I stopped jogging and said, "She did?"

"Yeah. She did."

"Is she okay?"

"Just get in, Tony. I'll tell you all about it."

"Just tell me now."

"Tony—"

"What happened to her?"

"Tony, you're gonna have to trust me. Get in the car and I'll tell you."

The chopstick had his phone to his ear, and I knew he was either talking to my parents or the police. If I ran, he would chase me in his car and tell them where I was. I already knew I wasn't going to run, though. I needed to know what happened to my sister, and maybe Sharon was telling the truth. Maybe my mom and John had been worried sick. So I pulled open the back passenger door and climbed in, and before I even had it shut the car was in motion.

Chopstick said, "Yeah. Yeah, right here. Yeah."

I asked again about my sister. "You'll find out soon, Tony."

I said I'd changed my mind. I wanted out of the car.

"Just relax, Tony. Okay. You're gonna be all right. I promise."

But I wasn't all right because as soon as we pulled up to my house John burst out the door and ripped me from the car. My mom stood in the doorway, her arms crossed over her plump bosom, her eyes bulging from her skull. I lost my balance and almost hit the sidewalk, but John pulled me back up, through the front yard, up the steps, and threw me through the door. My mom bared her teeth and punched me in the head on my way in.

"Where'd you find him?" she called.

Sharon said, "He was just walking through the trailer park on College Way. Didn't even see us pull up."

"Surprised he didn't run."

"Oh he almost did. I managed to talk him down."

"John! Get him in the shower, now! Clean his filthy ass!"

I banged every wall on the way, then I was in the bathroom and my mom was yelling about my new clothes, that I smelled like cigarettes and drugs and sex. John ripped them off me and threw me naked into the shower. My mom turned on the cold water and when it hit my body I found myself gasping, trying to breathe. I yelled, "Please!" and she mimicked me, then hit me in the face with the shower nozzle.

I hiccupped, and I gasped, and my body convulsed, and I was sure if I didn't get out of the ice-cold water I would die. John was too strong, though. Every time I tried to push past him, he shoved my head into the wall. So I lay down and curled up into a pale, naked ball and tried to breathe, listening to my mom tell me that she hated me and wished that she could kill me and get away with it. It was the first time I could remember her ever telling me how she felt about me.

Eventually, the water stopped and one of them dropped a towel on my shaking body. John said, "Dry yourself off. Now."

My mom said, "John, burn those stinking clothes. No child in my house is gonna dress like a gang member."

So I didn't get my fake ID.

CHAPTER FIVE

We marched like soldiers through the halls of Laventure, and nobody paid us a second glance. School wouldn't start for another twenty minutes. That gave us plenty of time to go behind the gym and fight the cholos. Why? Because they challenged us. Why? Because they were cholos and even though we weren't all poor, we were poor white kids. Why? Because they were angry with the world and so were we.

It had been a couple months since I ran away, and things were pretty much back to normal at home. After I climbed from the shower, my mom held me down while John hit me with the belt until my back bled. Then they burned all the clothes David gave me and John put my pocketknife in his top dresser drawer because I guess he liked it. A few days later, my friends at school came together and gave me more clothes they had jacked from the thrift stores, so I threw away every other piece of linen I owned.

My mom's eyes bulged from her head when she found out, so I prepared myself for the belt, or the shower, or her fists, or whatever she had for me. Nothing came, though. So that settled it. I dressed like a poor white kid and poor white kids fought cholos sometimes. It's just the way it worked.

I still wasn't allowed to have a social life outside of school and I still spent most of my time in the kitchen, cleaning filthy countertops and trying to get dishes from one place to another. Throwing knives at walls when I got too bored. Karina and Mathias were dating now. I was dating Amber. Amber had dated every guy in our circle so I was the last to date her.

None of the girls were with us as we stomped through the back door and headed out behind the gym. There were at least seven of us and Doug led the way.

The cholos were already there, waiting with their notebooks under their arms. When they saw us, they dropped them and held their hands out to their sides.

One of them whose name was Bobo, said, "How you wanna do this?"

"How you wanna do it?" Doug asked.

"It's whatever."

"It's whatever then."

"What's up then?"

"I dunno," Doug said. "What's up?"

There were seven or eight cholos. Some of them had shaved heads. Some slicked their hair back. We all wore jackets because it was cold out.

One of them, Emilio, said, "What's up fool? We gonna just stand around and talk about it all day, or what?" and because he was right, I threw my backpack down, ran up, and pushed him into one of his friends.

Then it was on and sneakers squealed as they slid in wet grass and there was movement everywhere. Cholos and poor white kids grabbed each other around the waists and threw punches at each other's bodies, but nobody swung at anyone's face, so neither did I. I hit one of them in the back, then grabbed another by the arm and swung him around as another one punched me in the side. Another kicked me in the ass, and it went on like this for what seemed like way too long. I looked over at one point and saw Mathias throwing body-blows at three of them and holding them off like it was nothing, and it occurred to me why Karina liked him.

Eventually we were all out of breath, against the wall huffing and puffing. The cholos said we could do it again whenever because they weren't afraid of nobody or nothing. We agreed that it was whatever, then we slapped hands, and talked about how much we respected each other. They left first and when they were gone, we picked up our backpacks and headed back into the cafeteria to recount to the girls how bad we had messed them up.

* * *

Mount Vernon wasn't very big. It wasn't some little hick town either, though. You'd have to see it to understand. Certain parts were more developed, active with traffic and businesses everywhere. Others were little more than gigantic fields with houses spaced a quarter mile apart, and two-lane roads with no sidewalks.

Riverside Drive was a wide road. In some places, it had four lanes, in others five or six. It crossed a big bridge that hovered over the Skagit River and took you into Burlington. Once you were in Burlington, it wasn't Riverside Drive anymore. It turned into Burlington Boulevard.

On the left of Burlington Boulevard, fields went on forever and in those fields were little wooden sheds where migrant workers slept. There were clotheslines running between them because there wasn't enough room inside for a washer and dryer, or even a sink and a toilet.

Everybody knew that agriculture brought so many immigrants to Mount Vernon and the neighboring towns that people like my stepdad liked to refer to the area as "Little Mexico." He had words he liked to use for them, too. Most of the cholos weren't immigrants, though. Their parents were, but they had mostly been born in the U.S.

The poor white kids didn't fight them because we didn't like them, and I don't think they had a problem with us either. We just needed someone to fight, so that's what we started doing at least once a week before school. Sometimes we did it more often.

One afternoon in Mr. Espinosa's class, one of the guys who usually sat at my table was absent, so Karina sat there instead and said she'd heard I'd messed one of them up pretty bad that morning.

We still weren't hitting in the face, and it was all just good fun, but I said, "Yeah. I guess."

She didn't say anything else, just half-grinned and gazed down at her schoolwork. She wore tight blue jeans and a black shirt. Mr. Espinosa kept looking at her funny whenever he came over, but he didn't hassle the Mexican kids much, so he didn't say anything. I didn't say anything else to her either, because she made me as nervous as hell. I just focused on my own work. It was a bunch of Math problems in a textbook. I knew I'd never use algebra again after school, but I tried to learn it anyway because I didn't know any better than to just do what was expected.

But I could feel Karina staring at me out of the corner of her eye. When I looked up, though, she turned away before I could catch her. I went back to my work and felt her eyes on me again. This time I didn't glance up, and she said, "You're not very good at Math."

I peered with only my eyes and saw her staring down at my paper. "No," I agreed. "I suck."

"Bro, you really do. Here, copy mine." She slid her paper to me. I scanned it, seeing that all the answers were done and asked her how the hell she had finished so fast.

She chuckled, said, "The answers are all in the back of the book. Didn't you know that?"

"Yeah. Of course I knew. How did you copy them so fast?"

"I didn't. I did it last night."

"But how? We're not allowed to take the books home."

"Yeah? I snagged one."

"Aren't we supposed to show our work, though?"

"You ask a lot of questions. What are you, a cop?"

"No."

Some guy at the other table called her name and she turned around in her seat, threw her slender legs over the backrest. Her shirt came up just enough for me to see a blue thong climbing up her lower back. I looked for longer than I meant to as they talked about a movie I had never heard of. Then a girl at my table grinned at me, shook her head, and I quickly averted my eyes. I hadn't talked to her since she had asked me if I was a virgin earlier in the year.

When Karina turned back around she said, "Hey, Tony, you know how to confuse a gay guy?"

"Uh-uh," I said. "How?"

Everybody at our table burst out laughing, and at first I didn't get the joke. Then I did and I felt my ears heat up.

Karina said sorry. She was just messing with me. Everybody went back to what they were doing, as she looked down at my paper. "Jeez. Slow much?"

"What?"

"Are you gonna copy the work, or what?"

"Oh, yeah." I picked up my pencil and went to work.

Mr. Espinosa walked over at one point and I was sure he knew what I was doing, but I played it off anyway. When he left, Karina flashed a plastic egg at me from down by her lap.

"What is it?" I asked.

She cracked it open and stuck it under my nose. It smelled like a skunk. Like a runner's armpits. Like a new deck of cards. It smelled like weed. She told me it was weed. From California. Her cousin brought it back from Disneyland. The girl who had watched me check out her thong smiled and said it smelled like fun. Karina brushed her off and asked if I wanted to go to her house after class.

The problem was that I wanted to, because Karina was one of the cutest girls I had ever seen. The problem was that I couldn't, because my mom's belt hurt on more levels than I wanted to endure. The problem was, I still couldn't think straight when I tried to talk to Karina. The problem was, she was with Mathias. So I told her I couldn't.

She stuffed the egg into her backpack and said, "I heard your mom's a real dick."

"Who'd you hear that from, Doug?"

"Yeah. How'd you know?"

"Just a guess."

"Is that why you ran away?"

"I don't know. I just didn't wanna go home, I guess."

"You shouldn't a got caught then."

"Yeah. I mean, I didn't mean to. I just—"

"Got caught."

I said, "Yeah," because there was no way to argue against that logic.

"Bro, you should a left. I mean, like 'left' left, you know? Like left the state. Or at least the town."

"Doug was supposed to get me a fake ID."

"What?" she asked. "How?"

"From Russell."

"Who?"

"I don't know."

"Whatever, man. I'm telling you. Next time you gotta get away. Like far."

I said she was probably right.

She said, "I'd be down. You know, to leave."

I said, "Yeah. Totally." Then I finished copying her math work.

* * *

Fighting with the cholos started becoming more frequent, and the fights seemed to get a little rougher each time, until one morning I felt Emilio's chain catch on one of my fingers and snap. He reached down, picked up a small silver cross, and stuck it into his pocket. Then he punched me in the ear, and because I hadn't been expecting it, I just ducked and covered my face.

"You wanna break my grandma's chain?"

I didn't wanna do that. It had been an accident, but I didn't tell Emilio that because he didn't care. He punched me, and he punched me, and he kicked me in the mouth because, as if I didn't know how to fight, I was hunched over. Then the blows stopped and I looked up to see Mathias, Doug, and another poor white kid named Greg kicking the crap out of Emilio who lay curled in a ball on the damp grass.

A cholo punched Doug in the back of the head and Doug cried out, clutching the point of impact. A second later, I saw the brass knuckles lining his hand. Everything else that happened was kind of a blur because we weren't playing anymore, but everyone from both sides attacked like a scene from some medieval war movie. Fists were flying and there was grunting and panting and I just swung as hard and fast as I could, eating blow after blow simultaneously.

Then all at once, everybody backed up in different directions and the crowd thinned like a drop of water expanding on a wooden table. There were gasps as Emilio bent down, clutched his side, his mouth open like a beached fish. He straightened up and looked at his hands. They were both dark red.

He yelled. Cursed. Coughed.

David held an open pocketknife at his side. His eyes were wide, and for a second I thought he would stab him again, but Doug shouted, "Jesus! Run, fool!" and David ran. He sprinted through the track and before I had time to process what I needed to do, the rest of the poor kids picked up their backpacks and followed. The cholos swarmed on their friend. A few of them eyed me as they did.

I watched my comrades disappear through the opening in the fence, knowing what had to happen next. I picked up my own backpack and ran back toward the school. I hit the door so hard I almost smashed my face into it. I ignored the geeks reading and a couple making out in the hall. I flew into the cafeteria where all the poor white kids who hadn't been in the fight sat at our table laughing.

Amber stood up and asked if I was okay. She was my girl, but I had never even kissed her. I told her I was fine.

I told Karina I needed to talk to her. Amber watched as we walked away together.

Once we were around the corner, standing just outside the boy's bathroom, I said, "Are you still down?"

"Down for what?" she asked. But her eyes shone with recollection of the comment she had made in Mr. Espinosa's class only weeks ago.

Still, I said, "To leave."
Without hesitation, she nodded. "Yeah. Sure."
So I told her we needed to go now.

CHAPTER SIX

Secret Harbor School doesn't look like any school I've ever seen, because it's not really a school. I know that's just a title they use since they don't say orphanage anymore. Secret Harbor's a group home for only boys and it's on an island so you can't escape.

The trail leading from the dock goes uphill for about an eighth of a mile, which isn't long, and soon I get a much better look at the lodge. It really is nice. Like a ski-resort. I've never been to one, but I've seen them on TV.

Next to it, I see what looks like a small apartment building in the middle of the woods and the Hispanic guy says, "See? Looks just like apartments." I know his name's Jesus because he introduced himself, but everything's such a blur that I can't remember when.

I nod and fake a smile because the time for crying has passed.

He can tell I'm faking though. He knows that if my mom hadn't left on the Sea Wolf, I'd be breaking down and crying again for her to see, because somewhere in what's left of my heart, I believe she'll make everything better if she just sees me cry hard enough. Somewhere, there's a sliver of hope that she actually cares. I know Jesus can tell because his smile isn't fake. So I want to punch him in his face. But even though he's short, he's older than me and stocky, so he can probably tear me limb for limb.

He says, "You'll drop your stuff off there when we figure out what room you're in."

I say, "Okay," and we walk around the back of the apartments, and ascend a flight of stairs that leads up to the balcony on the lodge. It's connected to the apartments by a wooden bridge.

For a second, I entertain Jerry Warden's claim that I'm not a prisoner. That Secret Harbor is the paradise that it looks like. But before I can spend too much time hosting this lie, I start thinking about Karina, and what she must be doing right now. I've been in Juvie for a month and she's been writing just about every day since she got out three weeks ago. She got somebody to set up an account so I could call the phone we shared, but calls from juvie are expensive, so I've only been able to talk to her a couple times a week.

Karina doesn't change. She hasn't since I met her. She's as crazy as hell and everybody wants to be her friend. She knows a lot of guys so she's probably with one of them right now. In fact, that's probably why she didn't bring the knife this morning. One of them probably talked her out of it so I wouldn't be around and he could have her all to himself. Maybe it was Mathias.

The steps are wooden. Everything here is, it seems. I wonder if they're made of cypress, because that's the tree the island's named after. But no. I don't think so. I don't know much about trees, or what type of wood they used to build things, but for some reason I doubt they used cypress.

Once we make it to the top, we walk around the balcony and in a door where the smell of Pine-Sol fills my lungs. Everything's bright, which reminds me of the psychiatric hospital I spent my fourteenth birthday in. The ceiling's so high I don't even know if I could throw a ball and touch it, but that's probably just because I've never had a strong throw.

I'm in a short hallway where I can hear conversations coming from somewhere close by. A whole crowd of conversations. Somewhere in the cacophony of noise, somebody calls somebody a bitch. We take a few more steps and emerge into a big, open room. It's so big it's not hard to imagine people throwing balls in here. It might even be the size of a basketball court. There are a few foldout tables set up on a tiled floor, where kids sit gripping handfuls of playing cards. A skinny boy with a baseball cap swipes a mop in a figure-eight. To my left, chairs rest in front of a television which is mounted in the corner where the wall meets the ceiling. A huge black man in sweats and a dark T-shirt reclines in one with a remote control in his hand. To my right is a patch of brown carpet with two old couches against one wall. The darkest kid I've ever seen sits alone on one of them. Every eye is trained on me as I stop walking and take in the whole scene.

It's a pointless gesture, because I don't plan on staying long, but I can't help it, because it's all so beautiful. It's beautiful and I hate it. I've spent the past year running, and I don't plan to let this facility slow me down. As soon as I figure out a way off Cypress Island, I plan to run again because I have to be wherever Karina is.

The big guy heaves himself up and you can tell it's not an easy task. He's not just tall. He's fat. He can't weigh under three-hundred pounds. The bright lights reflect off his shiny bald head as he approaches, eyeing me disapprovingly.

Jesus says, "Is your name Anthony?"

"No," I say. "Tony."

"Yeah, I know. But is it short for Anthony?"

"No."

"Is it short for anything?"

"No."

"So it's just Tony?"

I tell him it's just Tony.

"Oh. I'm just asking because his name's Anthony." He nods toward the approaching giant of a man. "But sometimes he goes by 'Tone.'"

When Anthony's so close that he's towering over me, he stops and says, "Sup."

"Sup," I say.

"You Tony?"

"Yeah."

"Tony Carpenter?"

"Yeah."

He looks at the trash bag hanging at my side and shakes his head. "You in room three, up top. Go put yo' things in there an' come on back. You out in the common area till after chow."

I say, "Yeah. Okay," even though I'm not sure I fully understand what he's telling me. Then I turn and walk back the way I came. Everybody seems to have decided I'm nothing special and went about their business playing cards, watching TV, and mopping floors.

Jesus calls after me. "Hey! Hey! Hey! Where you going, man?"

I say, "Room three, up top."

"Naw man, you can't just go out there unescorted. You're in the common area till after chow."

"I thought he said—"

"It's all good, man. Come on. I'll take you."

So I guess I'm not allowed to go to my room unescorted.

* * *

My room's pretty big, with a wooden floor and two beds—one on each wall. Mine's the one by the door. Between the beds, there're two large cabinets and two nightstands. One has a digital alarm clock on it, which reads, 2:32. The walls are light brown, and it smells like forest even inside. The apartment building has two stories, and probably more than ten rooms on each floor. I'm in three, up top. There's a bathroom halfway down the row of dorms.

Jesus stands in the doorway, his hands pressed against the outside wall, leaning in and looking around as I toss the trash bag onto my new bed. I ask if I can just stay here and he tells me I can't.

"You gotta be in the common area during the day, man. That's the rules. Unless you're sick."

I tell him I'm feeling a little sick.

He smiles, says, "Come on, bro. There's lots to do in the common area. You play cards?"

"No."

"Chess?"

I think about when I was young, and my mom taught me to play chess. How she used to relentlessly checkmate me when I was five with a smile hanging from each ear. I tell Jesus, no. I don't play chess.

"What about soccer? A bunch ah the guys were just out playing the other day, man. Went till almost dark. It was tight. You see that big field when we were coming in?"

I say, "Yeah," even though I hadn't been paying attention.

"That's where they played. It worked good. They got the AB too. That's the activity building. You'll be able to go out there in a couple weeks. Come on, bro. Let's get outta here."

So we walk back into the common area and a few meandering eyes focus on me again, but nobody makes a move to talk to me. I guess there must be about twenty guys in here. Some are my age; others are younger or older. Because I don't have any friends yet, I stroll over to one of the two couches and take a seat. Across from me, is a whole wall of huge windows looking out on the long balcony. The black kid looks over at me from the other couch, opens his mouth to say something, then closes it again as Anthony stomps over.

"Up," he says.

"Excuse me?"

"Come on now. Off dat couch. You can't be here. Dat's the rules." So I stand up and ask where I can be.

"Anywhere in'na common area, but here." He points with his remote control to the kid on the other couch. "He in trouble." Then he huffs back over to the TV room and plops down on a chair that I imagine would cry if it could.

So this is it. I don't know anybody. I'm not allowed in my room. I'm not allowed on the couch. I have no clue what to do, so I make my way across the tiled floor, past the kid who's still mopping, and out onto the balcony where there are a few wooden benches and low seats. I go to the rail and look out at the field Jesus was talking about. It is pretty big, but it's on a hill that would make soccer pretty awkward.

From here, there's a view of the water as well. I wonder what else is on Cypress Island. How far away is the town? How close is the nearest resident? There must be a ferry—otherwise how do people get on, and off the island? I need to make some friends pretty quick so I can figure these things out.

* * *

We're allowed in our rooms before dinner. Actually we're ordered into them. Anthony sits in a chair at the edge of the forest, right in front of the apartments, looking down at his cell phone.

My roommate's a red-haired kid named Mike. He reminds me of the geeks who sat against walls at Laventure reading about dragons and spaceships. He's a year older than me, but has a squeaky voice. He tells me he likes to play Xbox. I ask him if they have an Xbox here, and he says they don't.

I ask, "Why's Anthony sitting out there?"

Mike says, "He has to. There has to be someone there whenever we're in the dorms."

"Even at night?"

"Yep."

"So he sits out there all night when we sleep and just watches our doors, or what?"

"Well it's not always him. Actually, it usually isn't. He works during the day, but I guess he's working a double shift today. He's mean too, especially when he has to work a double."

"That must be boring," I say. "Sitting out there alone all night."

"The cats keep them company."

"The cats?"

"You'll see." Mike smiles. "You like RPGs?"

"What's that?"

He seems to deflate as he says, "Never mind," and I can already tell Mike and I won't be friends.

* * *

When we're let back into the common area for dinner, the tiled floor's covered in foldout tables, and kids are taking seats. There are more than twice as many here now. Probably more than fifty, and a female staff member who almost looks our age. She's blond and wears black leggings. She's attractive, reminiscent of the spoiled kids at Laventure.

I follow Mike, and sit at a table with the skinny guy who was mopping earlier, and a couple of others who aren't talking. I get the impression none of them like each other much, because the other tables are active with conversation.

Out of the corner of my eye, a dark-haired kid with olive skin passes and takes a seat with a group of laughing boys. Anthony storms over, says, "Get up."

The dark haired kid says, "Why?"

"I ain't gonna ask again."

"Why? What's your problem with—"

Before he can get another word out, Anthony reaches down, pulls him from his chair and slams him face down on the tiles. The kid screams, kicks, flails, but Anthony wrenches his arm behind his back and places a knee on his face so he's pinned like a file under a paperweight. Jesus and the female staff member run over and maneuver his limbs into awkward positions as he curses and cries for them to get off him. Jesus has one arm, a female staff member takes both legs, and soon he's spread out like Jesus Christ on the cross, only face down on a tiled floor with his legs bent back and his palms facing the ceiling. Aside from his screams, the huge room has fallen silent. Every eye watches—most of them shining with amusement. I know it's wrong, but I can't seem to peel my own eyes away either.

The kid yells, "Aaahhh! My arm! My arm! Get— Come on! Please! I didn't—"

"Stop strugglin'," Anthony growls. "You done? You done yet?"

But he isn't done. Or maybe he is. I can't tell if he's still fighting to get up, or just fighting against the pain of having his limbs nearly ripped off. It's ten minutes before they finally let him up and start serving dinner.

CHAPTER SEVEN

So we ran. Karina and me. We didn't go to class, didn't even go back into the cafeteria to tell anyone we were going, just walked to the end of the hall and out the door. When we made it to the street, we cut onto a back road and headed toward Westside Mount Vernon, where she lived.

Along the way, I told her what happened behind the gym. She said, "Bro, that's crazy. What was he thinking?"

"Mathias?" I asked.

"What? No. David. Why the hell would he stab that kid?"

"I don't know. Everything was crazy, so it just kinda happened."

"Just kinda happened?"

"Yeah. I mean—"

"Where we going?" she asked.

"Your house, I thought."

"Yeah. Yeah. But after. I mean where we going after that?"

I hadn't thought about that. I hadn't thought about much actually, aside from leaving with Karina, and going as far away from my mom and her belt as I could get. I told her I didn't know, asked if she had any ideas.

"I don't know," she said. "Seattle's pretty big. We could try Seattle." Seattle was an hour away by car, so I asked how we would get there. She said, "That's easy enough. We just hitchhike."

I said, "Cool," even though I had never even thought about hitchhiking before.

She lowered her eyebrows and said, "It'll be okay, Tony. You're gonna be good. We just gotta get you outta here before you get popped. What if that guy died?"

I said, "I don't think he died."

"Are you sure?"

"No. I mean, I don't know. But he was standing when I left."

"Was he bleeding?"

"Yeah. Of course. He got stabbed."

"Was the knife big?"

"Yeah."

"Then he still might've died. Even if he was standing. If the knife was big enough, it could've punctured something important like a lung, or a kidney or something. Sometimes it doesn't happen right away. There could've been some type of internal bleeding. If he died, Tony, you're screwed, you know that, right? It'll be okay, though."

I wasn't sure if it would be okay, or not. I wasn't sure if I cared. The thought of jail wasn't nearly as menacing as the thought of facing my mom and John. Maybe because I was familiar enough with the one to know how much I hated it.

The sun had begun to appear and the clouds were already dissolving, so Karina stopped in a residential neighborhood to slip out of her hoody. She was wearing a black-tank top, and the sweater pulled on it so I could see her stomach for a second. I looked away before she could catch me. Then she stuffed the hoody into her backpack and we walked some more.

The tank top had little straps that hung from her shoulders and there was a big bruise on her arm. She did catch me looking at that. She told me her stepdad punched her because she called him a bitch. She said he'd been to prison and in prison that's the worst thing you could call someone so he punched anyone who called him that.

I said, "Did you know that before you said it?" She said she'd known.

"Then why'd you do it?"

"I don't know. He's just a bitch, so I called him one. Know what I mean?" It made sense, so I told her yeah, I knew what she meant. But the bruise was big, and Karina wasn't, so I think I was supposed to feel something toward her Stepfather. I didn't though. Not at the time, at least. There were cuts on her arms too. Not a lot, but they were big enough to notice. I didn't ask about them.

We walked for about a half-hour before we crossed the Westside Bridge, which went over the Skagit River, and Karina asked me if I knew what 'Skagit' meant. I told her I didn't.

"It's an Indian word," she said. "Skagit County's named after this river, obviously, but the river's named after the tribe that used to live along it."

"Upper Skagit?" I asked, thinking of the reservation two towns over, in Sedro Woolley.

"And Lower Skagit," she said. "They're split up into two reservations because there were two tribes that used the name. Upper Skagit, and Lower Skagit. It means 'People who run and hide.' Isn't that whack?"

"That's what Skagit means?" I asked as we deposited off the bridge and passed Riverfront Park on our left.

"Yeah."

"Yeah. That is whack."

"That's kinda what we're doing, though. Running and hiding."

"Uh—yeah. I guess. You don't think we should do it?"

"No. I think we totally should. You need to anyway after what happened this morning. Otherwise you're screwed."

I said, "Listen, if you don't wanna come with, I understand."

Karina stopped walking and took my wrist. I came to a halt just inches from her and she smiled. Not just with her lips, but her eyes narrowed and almost seemed to curve into tiny crescent lemon slices. She said, "Bro, get outta your head. I'm here, aren't I?"

"Well, yeah, but—"

"Tony, I'm coming with you."

"Okay."

"Okay?"

I said, "Yeah. Okay."

"So you're good?"

I told her I was good, then we walked the rest of the way to her house.

* * *

Karina's stepdad was a big white guy, which surprised me, because she's Mexican. I don't know why I didn't expect her mom to be with a white guy, but maybe that's just some programmed thinking on my part.

His clothes looked like they came from the thrift store. If I had seen him on the street, I would've just assumed he was homeless. He had a glass tube in his mouth when we walked in the door, and he didn't make an effort to conceal it, just said, "Why aren't you in school?" through a long stream of smoke.

Karina didn't answer. She took my hand and pulled me down the hall and into her room. She slammed the door, let her backpack drop, and said, "Bro, I hate him so freaking much."

When my eyes traveled automatically to the bruise on her arm, she said, "Do you know what he was doing out there?"

I told her I wasn't sure what she was asking. Her room wasn't big. A queen-sized bed took up most of it, leaving space to walk on either side, but the floor was littered with clothes.

She shook her head like I had something disgusting on my face and said, "You didn't see the pipe?"

"Yeah. I saw it."

"Do you know what he was smoking?"

Even though I hated always being the naive kid who never seemed to know what was going on in the poor white circle, I said, "Uh-uh."

"It was freaking crack."

"Oh. Wait, really?"

"Uh-yeah."

"Why would he—"

"Because he's a crack-head. He promised me and my mom he was done. Ugh! I freaking hate him, bro. You can take your backpack off."

So I took my backpack off and sat on her bed while she dumped her school supplies onto the floor and began stuffing clothes and other random items into her own bag. I still wondered why anybody would want to smoke crack. Then I wondered what was so bad about smoking crack. I suspected somehow it tied in with Karina's bruise, but didn't ask.

After a while, she disappeared out the door, then returned with a small plastic bag. She tossed it into my lap, told me to hold on to it. "My mom always tries to hide her weed from me."

"Cool," I said.

Karina dug around in her closet and found a small hatchet. She said, "Think we'll need this?" I asked what for and she shrugged and hummed the tune that usually accompanies the words, "I don't know." She tossed it on the bed and told me to put it in my backpack.

* * *

Edgewater Park had a beach. A playing field. A playground with a jungle gym. It even had a big concrete stage where they hosted events in the summer. But it also had a forest. We followed a hiking trail for a few minutes, then Karina moved a bush on our left to reveal a much smaller path. Like a deer trail. It was mid-afternoon and sunny, but still humid and the leaves were saturated with dew.

She said, "Come on," and I followed another minute before the path opened up so wide you could've driven a car on it. There were circular openings on either side with tents planted behind fireplaces. Karina told me we were in Tent-City. There must've been twenty tents here.

We kept pushing until we came to a huge opening with a much bigger fire pit and a homemade shed, constructed by tying a tarp to multiple trees. Pieces of plywood, two-by-fours, and other random object that belonged in a junkyard sat under the tarp. I could hear the river moving somewhere in the distance.

Another trail led to an upside-down bucket, sitting over a hole in the ground. The bucket had a small hole in the bottom. Karina didn't have to tell me it was a toilet. A coffee can sat next to it, presumably with toilet-paper inside.

Tent-City, it seemed, was a ghost town. I asked if people actually lived here.

Karina said, "Yeah."

"Where are they?"

"Most of them don't stay during the day. It makes the place hot."

"Hot?"

"Yeah. It attracts the police."

I asked if we were staying in Tent-City.

She said, "No. We're going to Seattle. Just not tonight. It's better to hitchhike in the morning."

"Then are we staying here tonight?"

"No. I just wanted to check for something. There's another tent that nobody uses. We'll have it all to ourselves. It's in a different spot, so we'll be alone. Come on."

She touched my arm as she moved around me and headed back the way we came. After a second, I followed.

* * *

Everybody has a scent. Some people smell like their favorite shampoo, or perfume, or body odor. Karina didn't smell like any of those things. Even though she loved to smoke, she didn't smell like cigarettes either. She just smelled like her. I can't really describe it; I just knew I liked it.

It got cold at night, so we cuddled up on the floor of the small tent with no blankets or pillows or sleeping bags. Just us. She wore her hoody, and me, my jacket, and it was still cold. Something about her scent seemed to heat me from the inside, though, with every breath. The floor was lumpy, because it was just the ground with a thin layer of fabric over it.

The tent was alone in its own section of the forest. It sat in a small open area a distance away from Tent-City. We didn't hear any of the residents making their way back, but the crickets were pretty loud. Karina had twenty-three dollars and some change, so we bought crackers and cheese in a can, and she took half-smoked cigarettes from the ashtray outside the store, and stuffed them into a small plastic bag. We had been smoking them periodically all evening. And the weed she stole from her mom.

At one point I was so messed up I felt like I was melting into the ground, but having Karina resting on my chest kept me at ease. I asked her whose tent we were in.

She said, "Damien's."

"Damien's?"

"Yeah. You know—Damien?"

"The guy who wears the camouflage jacket?"

"Yeah," she said. "Damien Shepherd."

"Why's his tent out here?"

"He lives in it. Well, sometimes he lives in it. Lately he's been living under the bridge."

"What?" I said. "What bridge?"

Karina giggled. "Westside Bridge. He's been living under it with some old guy. It's like his boyfriend or something."

I told her I didn't get it.

"His dad kicked him out like forever ago, bro. He stays on the street and like eats at the Friendship House. He used to live in this tent, but then he started screwing around with some old guy who stays under the bridge. One night I stayed out here with him, but he wouldn't stop trying to hook up with me. He's freaking gross, too. Mathias beat his ass the next day."

I probably should've been worried about having to fight Mathias too, but I wasn't. I just wondered if Karina had cuddled up with Damien in this tent that night. Then I thought of what it would be like to be kicked out. I'd never have to think about John and my mom and their belt again. Or how strenuous it was just trying to focus on unloading the dishwasher. Or on not being allowed a social life. Instead I would live in tents in the woods, or under bridges with old men.

But before I could follow this thought any further in whatever direction it was headed, Karina said, "Don't you wanna kiss me?" and even though we were cuddled up like lovers, it was the last thing I had expected her to say. And even though I was with Amber and she was with Mathias, I did want to kiss her. And even though I had a feeling she was just messing with me, I told her I did. She said, "Then why don't you do it?"

So I leaned down in search of her lips, and they were already there waiting for me. I kissed her softly, but she pressed into me so hard it almost hurt. Then her tongue was in my mouth, and she was taking my hand and slipping it under her hoody, but over her shirt. I held her chest and we kissed. And we kissed. And we kissed. Then we stopped and she laid her head back down on my chest and sniffed.

She cried and because I didn't know why, or what I was supposed to do, I ran a hand through her short hair and cupped the back of her head. I told her I was sorry.

"For what?" she asked.

"I don't know. Are you okay?"

"I'm not okay, Tony. I haven't been okay for a long time."

I told her everything was gonna be fine and she told me it wasn't. Maybe for me it was, but not for her because when she was just a little girl her father raped her. And her stepdad liked to punch her and burn her with cigarettes when he smoked crack. And her mother didn't care enough to throw him out because she loved him more than she loved her. So sometimes she cut her own arms and for some reason it made her feel better.

Nobody had ever cried in my arms before, so I put my hand back under her hoody and kissed her again. Then I pulled away and looked through the darkness into what I could see of her eyes. I said, "You will be okay. I promise. First thing tomorrow, we're getting the hell outta here. We'll go to Seattle, and we'll start a new life. Together."

CHAPTER EIGHT

We slept maybe a couple hours, then we woke up early and stood by the freeway with our thumbs out. It only took a few minutes before an old town car stopped and let us in. A wrinkly guy with a double chin told us he could take us as far as Edmonds, so Karina sat up front and chatted with him about how we were on our way to a family function in Seattle.

He said it was too bad he had a seminar to attend in Edmonds, or he would've taken us all the way, then he let us out near a sign that read, "Edmonds Whidby Ferry," and Karina said, "What about Whidby Island?"

Cars deposited off the freeway and passed us, and it seemed like they were all headed to the ferry, like wherever the ferry was going was the place to be, so I told her that it sounded like a great idea. Better than Seattle, in fact. I said, "Doesn't it cost money to ride the ferry, though?"

"It only costs a few bucks," she said. "We still have money left. Me and Marvin caught it once and spent the night on the beach in Whidby. It's really nice over there."

I asked who Marvin was and she told me it was her gay friend. She said, "We can just live on the beach. I mean for a while, right?"

"Sure," I said, because living on the beach sounded better than jail or home, and it sounded better than letting Karina be burned with cigarettes.

She said we could dig for clams and catch fish and cook them over a fire at night. We could bathe in the ocean in the mornings before anybody showed up.

"What if it rains?" I asked.

"Bro, don't be a vadge. Are you scared of a little rain?"

I thought about it, then told her I wasn't, but our clothes would get soaked and we'd be cold until they dried off.

"Then we'll take them off. We can just get naked and put our clothes in plastic bags whenever it rains to keep them dry. Then, when it stops raining, we'll put them back on and we'll be warm and we'll be clean too, right?"

It made sense, so I told her it did. Then we followed the trail of cars headed toward the ferry and I kinda hoped it would rain tonight.

* * *

The locals must've treated the birds well on Whidby Island, because one seagull was overly friendly. Or maybe it was just hungry with nothing to lose. Or injured and desperate for help. Maybe it was just old and senile, or young and naive. Either way, we killed it.

Riding the ferry was frightening. Not so much because of the water, but because it was really high. When I looked down at the water, it was like I imagined peering over the edge of a high-rise building would be. It seemed miles away and it caused my heart to race. Then, when we were moving, the wind blew my hair back and gave the impression of flying.

It took me back to one time when my mom forced me onto a rollercoaster and I cried and prayed as it climbed that first hump and click, click, clicked to the top, where I knew I would die once it projected me rapidly toward the ground. Her eyes had bulged from her head, much like they did when she was angry, only she wasn't angry. She was amused for reasons that I never quite understood.

So I didn't spend much time out on the observation deck of the ferry. Karina and I sat inside, across from each other at a table, talking about hunting and killing fish with her hatchet. About sleeping on beached logs that she said looked like they were meant to be beds anyway. We talked about campfires, because we both liked them.

I told her I liked to roast marshmallows and hotdogs over them and make Smores and crap because I had often been camping with my grandparents when I was young. She said she liked to drink and smoke and screw next to them. I told her I liked doing that too.

You could see Whidby Island from the Edmonds dock, so the ride only lasted about fifteen minutes, then we exited and Karina pointed to the beach, and she was right. It was really nice.

"Come on," she said. "There's a store up the street where we can buy some food."

So we trotted up a narrow highway that had neighborhoods on either side that were mostly concealed by layers of trees. It was like a road in the woods, only you caught a glimpse of a house every so often. After about twenty minutes, we came to a store that was just a little bigger than a gas station, with a wide wooden sign out front that must've been carved with a chainsaw. It said something about Whidby Island.

There was a shed next to the store that looked exactly like a tiny house. It was the same size as the sheds the migrant workers in Burlington lived in, and my first thought was that it would be a perfect place for Karina and me to start our new life together.

We used the last of her money to buy a loaf of Wonder Bread and a jar of generic-brand peanut-butter, then we headed back the way we came. Halfway to the beach, the seagull showed up.

It must've been following us for a while, because I didn't hear it land behind me, just happened to turn my head and catch a white spot moving in the corner of my eye, so I stopped walking and turned around. If I didn't know any better, I would've thought it was smiling as it trotted up to us and tilted its head. I glanced over at Karina and said, "You see that?"

"Of course I see it."

"That's crazy."

"A seagull?"

"No. That it's so close. It's not afraid of us."

She was carrying a plastic shopping bag with the bread and peanut-butter in it. She said maybe it could see the bread.

"Should we feed it?" I asked.

"I don't know. I mean, no. What'll we eat?"

"Can we eat that?" I nodded to the bird who stood just a couple feet away from her.

"A seagull?"

"Yeah. I mean that seagull. Can we eat it?"

"I don't know. I mean—I guess."

"Do you know how to cook it? Like over a fire, or whatever?"

She said she did, if I could clean it. I was pretty sure I could, so she set the bag down and the bird's eyes followed it as it took a step closer. Then she slipped off her backpack and dug out the hatchet. She walked over to the seagull and it stared up into her eyes as she swung the back end of the hatchet at its head like a croquet mallet. The bird's mouth opened, and stayed that way like a statue as it plopped onto its side twitching, half on the road, half on the gravel.

I watched it for a few seconds, wondering if it was too late to change our minds. Maybe we could just let it go and it would be okay. Its wings were open and one leg kicked, but not the other. Karina cried. A car came around a sharp corner and missed the bird by about a foot as it passed, and she just stood there crying with the hatchet hanging at her side, so I took it from her and lowered myself to one knee. I raised it over my head and brought the sharp end down as hard as I could on the bird's neck.

Sparks flew on the pavement, I felt the bone snap and the bird stopped moving, but the head didn't dislodge, so I swung again. It took a few tries before the head finally came off and rolled to the side, then I emptied the bread and peanut-butter into my backpack and picked the seagull up by its feet, setting it in the shopping bag. I put the bag into my backpack next to the rest of our food.

Karina had stopped crying at some point, so I smiled and said it was good because we'd have dinner now and we could save the bread and peanut-butter for tomorrow. She said yeah, that was probably a good idea and we both looked down at the seagull's head. The mouth was still open the way it had been before she hit it.

I said, "Let's go," and we turned and made our way to the beach.

* * *

When I was young, my mom decided she wanted to be a bird-breeder. She started with two cockatiels and a cage with a wooden breeder-box mounted on the side. That's where they're supposed to go to screw around and lay eggs. They didn't always do that, though. The cage sat on a cabinet in the living room, and sometimes they would screw out in the open on one of their perches.

Eventually, she got more birds and within a couple years, she had every different kind of parrot you could think of, from parakeets, to four-foot macaws, and the house was so loud that sometimes the neighbors would call the cops.

When I was 11, one of her pairs had a bunch of albino cockatiels, and I became attached to one, so she said I could keep him. I even taught him to fly by flicking him off my finger. He would fly in a circle, then land back on my finger and whistle at me. You could tell he was a boy, because of the yellow spots on his face. I named him Boomerang.

Then my mom's birds caught some Amazon bird plague. Every morning we would wake up and find more of them lying dead in the bottoms of their cages with crust around their beaks. Whenever a live one had crust on its beak, my mom or John would throw a towel over it, take it in both hands and wring it out like a wet washcloth to break its neck. Then they would dump it in the trashcan out back.

So when my mom called me into the living room one summer afternoon while Boomerang was still a chick, to tell me that she found crust on his beak, I asked her as nicely as I could manage not to kill him. She said he would die anyway, and if we didn't kill him now, he would get the other birds sick and they would die too.

I said, "I'll set him free. He can fly away and who knows? Maybe he'll get better, but he won't be around to get all the other birds sick."

My mom said, "No, Tony. These birds aren't bred to survive in this atmosphere. He'll freeze to death in a night. He'll suffer more in the wild. You can't do that to him."

"We don't know that. Maybe he'll make it. Maybe he'll get better and someone'll find him and take him in."

"They don't get better, Tony. The disease he has is incurable."

"Then let him live until it kills him. I'll take him into my room so he's not around the other birds."

My mom shook her head and told me that wasn't an option. If he were in the house, he could still get the other birds sick. So I said again that I would just set him free and hope for the best. But my mom said no.

"But he's my bird."

"This is my house, Tony. I gave you that bird, but everything in this house is mine and you know that. The bird has to die."

And because I knew better than to argue with her, all I could do was ask when.

"Today. Now. It can't wait."

"Fine," I said. "I don't wanna watch though."

"Tony, it's your bird. You have to do it."

Before I could even imagine throwing a towel over my baby cockatiel and ringing him out like a wet rag, my heart dropped into my pants, and my consciousness took a step back, watched out the windows of my eyes from a safe distance. I stuttered as I told her I didn't know how to do it.

She said, "You know the psychic, Sylvia Brown?"

My mother was one of Sylvia Brown's biggest fans, so I said of course I knew who she was.

"Well you know she talks to dead people all the time, Tony. She's so good at it that she even helps the police solve murders sometimes, and Sylvia Brown says that drowning is the most peaceful way to go."

I told my mom that there was no way I was going to drown my bird. She said I had to because she couldn't do it and John was at work, and I needed to be a man for her. And even though I knew she had done it before, the next thing I knew I was standing in the bathroom, filling the sink with lukewarm water and Boomerang stood on the counter glancing curiously back and forth from the water, to me.

I did it how she told me to do it. I made a tiny cage with my hands and lowered it until he was fully immersed, and at first he didn't move because he trusted me not to hurt him. Then he jerked and twitched and fought and started vibrating against my palms. Then he stopped moving and I held him under a little longer.

My mom disappeared around a corner as I exited the bathroom and speed-walked out back with my tiny, limp friend and threw him as hard as I could into the garbage can. Then I started to head back inside, but before I made it to the door, water was pouring out of my eyes the way it had poured into the sink, so I stopped and leaned on the wall, letting my tears run their course before I let my mother see me again. So even though I didn't tell her, I knew why Karina cried when she hit the seagull with her axe.

We went back to the beach which did have logs the size of beds strewn everywhere. Most of them were even hollow so you could crawl through them like tunnels. That's not what we did though. She walked around and found rocks to arrange in a circle for a fireplace, while I brought the bloody shopping bag out of my backpack and set the decapitated bird on one of the logs.

The beach was huge, but deserted. In the distance, traffic drove off and onto the ferry, and people went about their business far enough away that they couldn't see what we were doing as I began to pull feathers from the seagull. It was like moving dishes around in my mom's kitchen, though, and within minutes, I found myself distracted.

When Karina returned with a pile of rocks, she stepped up beside me and we both just stared down at the headless creature until I said, "Don't these things carry diseases?"

"Seagulls?" she asked.

"Yeah. Don't they carry rabies or something?"

"They're scavengers. They could have parasites."

"Like worms?"

"Yeah. Like tapeworms or something."

"Still think we should eat it?"

"No," she said. "Probably not."

So we left the body on the log and found somewhere else along the beach to make camp.

* * *

It rained. As evening set in, the sky didn't turn pink like it does during sunsets in the summer. It grew cloudy late in the afternoon, then just before dark, it started sprinkling, and picked up until it was dumping on us. We didn't take our clothes off and dance in it. Instead we walked shivering back to the store and broke into the shed next to it.

The shed was empty aside from a triangular folding sign that said something about Greek sandwiches, so we hung my jacket and her hoody from it and lay together on the wooden floor. Not like we did in the tent last night—we didn't cuddle—we just lay side by side staring up into the dark and talking, listening to the sound of the raindrops on the roof.

Karina asked me if I was a virgin. I lied and told her I wasn't. She said neither was she, and I told her I knew that.

"What?" she gasped. "What do you mean, you know?" I said, "You're with Mathias, aren't you?"

"Bro, that doesn't mean I screwed him."

"Oh."

"You're with Amber, aren't you?"

"Yeah."

"Well, did you screw her?"

"No. Not yet."

"Not yet?"

"No. I mean—I don't know. I was just—"

"Shut up, Tony."

So I shut up and felt her scoot closer so our sides were touching. She said, "I think we should still try Seattle."

"You don't like the Island?"

"Well we can't just live in this shed the rest of our lives, can we?"

"I guess not."

"Did you ever watch that show about the little flying unicorn who does drugs and goes around killing people with some cop, or whatever?"

I said. "You mean, 'Happy'?"

"Yeah! That show. Have you seen it?"

"Uh, yeah, but I don't think that's what it's about."

"No?"

"No. It's like this little—well the unicorn's this girl's imaginary friend. And she gets kidnapped—the girl does—and the unicorn finds the guy—"

"The cop?"

"Yeah," I said. "Well, he's an ex-cop. Now he's like some hitman for the mob. But he's the girl's dad, so the imaginary friend finds him so he can save her. I think it did coke on accident once, but it doesn't kill people, I don't—"

Before I could finish, her lips pressed against mine, so I cupped the back of her head and put my tongue in her mouth. After a second, she pushed me away. I said, "What made you think of Happy?"

Karina stirred next to me and my ears took in the sound of fabric ruffling. Then plastic crinkling. She said, "I don't know. Don't you wanna get happy?" and I felt my heart beat against my ribs so fast there might as well've been a phone set to vibrate in my chest. I asked her what she meant, and she said, "We still have weed," and I was able to relax again.

I said, "Yeah. Hell yeah. Let's get happy." So we smoked and passed out in the shed.

CHAPTER NINE

"You smoke rock?" is what the old black guy in downtown Seattle asked me, but that's not what I heard because he had no teeth so it was hard to understand him.

We had woken up early, eaten peanut-butter sandwiches, and moseyed out of the shed without anyone ever knowing we had been there. We walked back to the ferry and Karina told a woman we were headed to a family function in Seattle and managed to get twenty dollars from her. Karina was really persuasive.

We took the ferry back into Edmonds, then caught a bus. It was early afternoon and sunny when we arrived downtown. For as long as I could remember, I had loved Seattle. I loved the tall buildings, and the sidewalks that were always active with people. I loved the wide roads, and the smell of exhaust. I loved the way it all lit up the sky at night, so my Aunt Betty used to give me coupons for my birthday and Christmas that I could redeem for a trip to Seattle.

She would take me to the magic shop in the underground tunnel beneath Pike Place Market, then to the Old Spaghetti Factory for dinner. But she never brought me to this part of town, so nobody had ever asked me if I smoked rock before.

He was short and skinny. Smaller than me, but still bigger than Karina, and even though he was asking me, he seemed to be staring at her out of the corner of his eye. I didn't know what rock was, so I thought he said pot, and I told him I did smoke.

He said, "Well, you like ta have people please you, while you smokin'?"

I said, "Please me?"

"Naw, man. I mean bofe a ya'll. You bofe like ta hit'n get yo-sewf pleased at da same time?"

Karina took my hand, said, "No," and pulled me away, but the guy followed us.

"Awe, don't be like dat, girl. I tryin' a get you on. I got people right now, ready ta please you, while you takin' hits. Jus up there." He pointed to an old brick apartment building. "They waitin' right now. They ain't picky, neither. They please bofe a ya'll."

"What are you talking about?" I asked.

"Just ignore him," Karina said. "Come on." She tightened her grip around my hand and picked up her pace until the guy disappeared behind us. He cursed and called her a name, but we kept walking.

I asked her what the hell that was about, and she just said, "Freaking crack-head," and it was a few minutes later before I finally understood what had happened.

* * *

We walked, and we walked and Karina told people that she had a family function to attend in Mount Vernon, so some of them gave her money. Then we found a homeless girl who told us where a teen shelter called the Thomas House was. She told us she didn't sleep there because she liked to shoot speed into her veins and you couldn't do that at the Thomas House. Since we didn't do that, we went there and that's where we slept that night.

The Thomas House fed us chicken and let us watch TV. The only rules were no drugs, and you had to be in by eight or you didn't get a bed. We took showers and they gave us clean clothes to wear. They weren't very nice, but we only had to wear them while we washed our other clothes. The kids at the house weren't friendly. They watched us like we had something they didn't wanna catch, but none of them talked to us.

Except this one couple. The guy said his name was Trouble. He was small and olive skinned and had a fuzzy moustache above his lip. Shay was fat. She had short hair, like Karina, but she wasn't pretty like her, and she smelled real bad. But she was cool to us because she knew Karina had weed. So that night, after dinner, we told the staff at the Thomas House that we were going out for a cigarette, and the four of us went to the park across the street and got stoned.

I sat on a bench, and since Karina had introduced me as her boyfriend, she sat real close to me. Shay was on her other side, and Trouble stood grinning as Karina loaded her glass pipe and passed it to Shay. There was a guy sleeping on a bench a few feet away, but he didn't even seem to notice us.

Denny Park wasn't a park for kids. There were no jungle-gyms or swing-sets, only paved walkways with gardens full of flowers and rhododendron plants elevated above benches. It was almost like one of those Japanese gardens, only with homeless people living in it. Across the street, there was a baseball field with a porta-potty that had hypodermic needles and used condoms all over the floor.

Trouble had eyes kinda like a shark's. He didn't move around a lot, just watched everything grinning. Shay told us we needed nicknames, in case we had to do something illegal. That way nobody knew who we really were.

Karina said, "Cool. I wanna be Tinkerbell." I asked her why Tinkerbell?

She said, "I don't know. I like Tinkerbell. You could be Pan."

"I'm not being Peter Pan."

Everybody but me laughed. Then I laughed too.

Trouble said, "People's gone think you some kinda fairy."

"Bro, I wanna be the fairy." Karina said.

"Naw you don't girl. With a name like Tinkerbell, they gone think you some kinda hoe. A name like Peter Pan, men might pull up fer him too."

Shay told him to stop. "Hey, I'm just sayin'—"

"Troub, shut up." She smiled at Karina. "You could try Pixie."

Trouble said, "There already a girl named Pixie out here."

"No, Pixie's gone. She got picked up a while back, remember?"

"Yeah. That's right. You gone pass that weed, or you babysittin'?"

Shay handed him the pipe and told Karina she looked kinda like a Pixie. Since Karina had a pixie-cut, I told her she did too. She said she wanted my name to be Hollow.

I said, "Why?"

She said, "I don't know. Hollow's a hot name."

Shay said, "Yeah it is."

So we became Hollow and Pixie.

* * *

I stayed on a top bunk in a big room with probably twenty beds, and Karina slept in another one for just girls. They served breakfast at the Thomas House, but we had to go about a mile up the street to the Orion Center for lunch. The Orion Center served dinner too, but so did the Thomas House, so we would be able to choose where we ate tonight.

The Orion Center had a school for homeless kids, but it wasn't like Laventure. You didn't have to go if you didn't want to. Karina and I didn't want to. We walked around downtown until lunch time, then we made our way to the Orion Center and waited in a long line where we met a guy named Trip with a star tattooed on his face, who said he stayed in an abandoned house on Capitol Hill. He pointed to a hill a few blocks away and said, "See that hill right there? That's Capitol Hill. You ever need anything, go there and ask for Trip. Ask anyone. They know me."

Karina said that was cool, and we walked around downtown some more, talking about music and the poor white kids back in Mount Vernon, and taking in the scenery. All I kept thinking, though, was that it was all right. I could do this. I could live this life with Karina, because it wasn't too bad and I didn't want her to go back to cutting herself to deal with her pain. And I didn't want to go back to throwing knives at the wall in my mother's kitchen to deal with the fact that my brain was so broken I couldn't even move dishes from one place to another.

We were sitting on the steps outside of the Westlake Mall, and a guy with dreadlocks was playing the guitar and singing for people to throw money into his guitar case when I told Karina we needed to make a trip back into Mount Vernon. She asked why.

"Because Doug can get us fake IDs."

"No he can't, bro. Doug's a liar."

"Not him though. It's his older brother who can get them."

The guitar player kept looking over at Karina and smiling. Every time he did, she would brush her short hair over her ear and my heart would bounce a little like it were hanging from a rubber band.

She said, "Ben?"

"Russell," I responded.

"He has another brother?"

"No. I mean, yeah. His brother's name is Ben. But he has a friend named Russell who can get the IDs."

"Who? Doug, or Ben?"

"What?"

"Whose friend is Russell?"

"Oh. It's Ben's friend."

She nodded, said, "Then it might be legit."

The guitar player belted out a line that was so far off the note it sounded like one of the crazy cockatoos my mom had before she gave up being a bird-breeder. I said I thought Russell sounded legit.

"So we need to go back?" she asked.

"Yeah. Probably."

"We'll need to get some money first. Do you know how much Russell charges? For the IDs?"

"I guess he doesn't. They said he has money. You just have to get him high."

"Really? If he has money, why doesn't he just buy his own weed?"

The guitar player looked over at Karina again and she turned her back on him, but it was like she was striking a pose, and I decided I hated him because he was older and taller than me and he could play the guitar. I told Karina I didn't know why Russell didn't buy his own weed, but fake IDs would be good to have.

"Yeah," she said. "I know. So we'll go back tomorrow, or what?"

"Yeah. Or sometime soon, at least."

So we decided sometime soon we would go back to Mount Vernon. In the meantime, I wanted to walk over to the guitar player and strangle him with one of his dreadlocks. Or take his guitar from him and stuff it down his throat. But instead, I sat on the steps with Karina burning with a jealousy that made no sense for another half-hour, then we made our way back to Denny Park.

CHAPTER TEN

There are these cats that hang outside the dorms at night like gargoyles guarding the building. Mike says they're feral. That you can't try to pet them, or they'll run away. That if you somehow manage to catch one, it'll claw your eyes out.

They look like house cats to me though. They hide in the woods during the day and sleep just outside our doors at night. They lay under the lights, like maybe they're afraid of the dark, so there's a whole line of cats against the wall who don't stir, or even look up as I walk past on my way to the bathroom. It's one of the stranger things I've seen in my life.

It's past midnight, and the crickets are wide awake, singing somewhere in the woods. The bathroom doesn't have a door to close, and it reminds me a little of a small locker room at an outdoor swimming pool I visited once. There are two showers with metal walls like the ones in juvie, two stalls, and a tiled floor. A black spider's made her home up in the corner in the stall that I use. The mirror is metal and scratched, so I can't see myself well as I wash my hands and exit the bathroom.

A fat white man sits in the chair that Anthony sat in earlier, reading a book. Like the cats, he doesn't look up as I return to room three, up top. Since the building's two stories, there's a room three, bottom as well.

Mike doesn't speak as I climb back into my bed, but I can tell he's awake by his breathing. I still haven't made any friends at Secret Harbor. A couple of guy's asked me questions:

What's my name? Where am I from?

Do I know such-and-such?

Did I come from another group home? But nobody's stuck around yet.

My bed's under a big window, and though there's a curtain over it, the porch lights outside our doors are bright, so they shine down on me from the bottom of the curtain. It doesn't bother me, because I've slept in worse conditions. Much worse, actually.

What does bother me is that I fell asleep around ten thinking about Karina and woke up a few minutes ago from a nightmare about the guy I killed on Capitol Hill.

CHAPTER ELEVEN

The Thomas House didn't even let us back in the front door. A young female staff, named Leti met us outside and pulled Karina to the side, while a guy named Gabe asked me where Leti's car keys were. I asked him how I was supposed to know, and he implored me to empty my pockets, so I turned them inside out. He shook his head and told me I was no longer welcome to stay at the Thomas House.

A couple minutes later Karina walked back over with Leti. Leti, was giving me the dirtiest look you could imagine. She ordered me to leave before she called the police. That was all I needed to hear. I told Karina, "Come on," and since we already had all of our belongings hanging from our backs, we left the Thomas House and never returned.

* * *

The sky was black already when we took Pine Street up Capitol Hill, but Seattle's never dark because the towering buildings are always glowing with blue light. That's probably why they call it the Emerald City. There were a lot of people out wandering the streets, and traffic moving up the hill almost as slow as we were walking.

Karina told me Leti had tried to persuade her to admit that I had stolen her car keys, by promising she could stay if she sold me out.

I said, "But I didn't steal any car keys."

She said, "Bro, I know."

"I don't even know how to drive."

"You don't?"

"No. Do you?"

"Yeah."

"Really?"

"Yeah. I mean, well—you know Marvin?"

"Your gay friend?" I asked.

"Yeah. We used to steal my mom's car sometimes. I mean like at night, when she was asleep. We'd go and smoke out and do donuts or whatever and stay out all night. It was cool, as long as we had it back before she woke up in the morning."

"And you would drive?"

"Yeah."

I said I wondered why Leti thought I had stolen her car keys. She said she knew why.

"Well, why?" I asked.

"Freakin' Trouble and Shay. They said you did it."

Outside a pizza restaurant across the street, a tall skinny guy in dirty clothes yelled something at a passing car, then took off running down a back road. We had planned to eat dinner at the Thomas House and the smell of cooking pizza made my stomach ache. I said, "Why would they say that?"

"Because," Karina said. "They wanted to cover their own asses. Didn't you see the key chain he had last night?"

"Trouble?"

"Yeah."

I told her I hadn't.

"Really? He brought it out like twice. There were like twenty keys on it. Car keys, bro. Freaking car thieves use them to steal cars. He probably took Leti's keys to add to the collection. Or to steal her car later."

"And that's why you think they told Leti I did it?"

"No. I know they told her because she told me they did. Well, she said Trouble did."

I felt my body grow light, like there was nothing inside me because there really wasn't much there, and because I was getting angry in a way that I wasn't used to being angry. It felt like I might float away and maybe a small part of my soul did, because for the first time in my life I was experiencing a betrayal that came with serious consequences. Because Trouble had lied about us, we would sleep on the streets tonight, cold and hungry. And tomorrow? Who knew?

I said, "Why would they believe him?"

"Did they asks you to empty your pockets?" she asked.

"Yeah."

"Me too. Maybe we could've stayed if I could've done it and showed them we don't have the keys. I couldn't though because I still have weed and they would've seen it. We would've got kicked out anyway. Maybe they would've called the cops and I would've got charged with minor in possession or whatever. So I guess it's my fault in a way."

I told Karina that it wasn't her fault. That everything would be okay. That we'd find Trip and stay in his abandoned house with him. I told her everything was still cool and thought about how I could kill Trouble and get away with it.

* * *

Trip was a snitch, but that didn't mean much to me, so when the guy outside the walk-in burger restaurant told me, I just shrugged and said, "Really?"

Karina knew better, though. She snickered and told the guy snitches deserved stitches, and I guess I had heard that too, somewhere, so I said, "Yeah. Hell yeah."

There's a street called Broadway that runs through the part of Capitol Hill where all the restaurants and nightclubs are. When we got there, it was active with traffic, and the sidewalks were packed with people. It was like some kind of a party, only on the street. Every parking lot was full of cars, and you could smell all different types of food cooking, so we started asking people if they knew where we could find Trip.

A guy standing outside of a drugstore sucking on an electronic cigarette laughed, said I was cute. I knew by the way he spoke that he was gay, and that he had no idea what the hell I was talking about, so we just kept walking. It was a few minutes later when we asked the same question to a group of street-kids outside the burger joint and one of them told me Trip was a snitch, and he'd been "eighty-sixed from the hill," earlier that day.

Eighty-sixed meant you couldn't come back. If any of the other street-kids saw you, they would attack you, jump you, stab you, whatever. The guy who told us had long brown hair that was tied into a ponytail. He said his name was Turtle, and he looked a couple years older than us. There were two other guys and a blond girl with him.

They reminded me a little of the poor white kids at Laventure, only they were nothing like them at all. These kids were kinda creepy. You got the impression they had seen things. That if you passed out, or died they would just go through your pockets.

They said they ascertained that Trip was a snitch today, when somebody got out of jail with paperwork that said he was, then Turtle told Karina we could stay with them in an abandoned house up the hill. We needed somewhere to stay, so we told them our names were Hollow and Pixie, and we hung outside the burger joint asking people for spare change for a couple of hours.

Then, when they said we had enough money, and there were even more people out partying on Broadway, we left. Karina had her black hood pulled over her head, and it somehow seemed to accentuate her almond eyes as the streetlights shone into them.

The street-kids bought heroin from a guy behind Jack-in-the-Box and we went into an alley and watched them shoot it into their veins. One of the buildings was a nightclub, and there was loud techno music coming from inside. I tried not to stare, but I had never seen anyone shoot up before. The guys didn't make a point not to stare at Karina, or direct most of their comments at her. I didn't like it, but I kept quiet and that's probably why the guy outside the nightclub noticed me, and nobody else.

We were just coming out of the alley after all the street-kids had shot up, and he said, "Hey you." We all stopped walking and saw him leaning up against the brick wall. He couldn't have been older than thirty, and was clean-cut dressed nice. He pointed right at my chest and said, "Yeah you. What's your name?"

I said, "Hollow."

"Well you're a little cutie, aren't you? You wanna come back to my car with me?"

People were standing around on the sidewalk watching. I felt something dirty stir in my stomach, as I told him I didn't wanna go to his car with him. Karina took my hand, said, "Come on," and pulled me along. But the guy's voice lingered a distance back and I knew he was following us.

"I'll pay you. I have money. You see that car across the street? That's my car."

Turtle walked up next to me and whispered, "Ask him how much he's willing to pay," and for some reason I felt water building up beneath my eyes as I told him it didn't matter how much, because I wasn't doing it.

"Ssshhh. I know you're not doing it. I don't think you're a fruit-loop, little bro. We do this all the time."

"Do what?"

"Roll fags."

"What?"

"Rob em, man. We rob these guys. Find out how much money he's got on him."

So I turned around, and even though the words felt like vomit coming up my throat and out of my mouth, I stopped walking and asked how much he would pay me to go back to his car.

"Two-hundred-dollars."

I said, "No," and resumed walking.

"What? What? Are you serious? Hollow? Slow down. Two-hundred-dollars. Do you even know who I am? I have over a million in the bank."

"Go away!" Karina yelled.

One of Turtle's friends whispered. "Ssshhh. No. Let him follow us. Take a left into that alley."

So that's what we did. We took a left into the next alley, and as soon as we were there, I knew this was really happening because the alley was dark and quiet and I didn't see any cameras. The guy kept yelling about how much money he had and offering more, until the price was up to three hundred, then we stopped by a dumpster and he tried to grab me around the waist. I moved, though, and he was too drunk to keep his balance so he fell face-first onto the pavement and the next thing I knew, I was kicking him in the side of the head over and over again.

Then everyone else was kicking him in the body, and Karina was stomping on his head. He didn't roll into a ball the way that I had when Brandon Hope and his friends had jumped me. His body was limp, sprawled out like the letter "X" as it absorbed the blows from our shoes, one after another.

At some point, Turtle yelled, "Stop! Stop! Stop!" We all stopped and the street-kids started going through his pockets, taking out keys, a wallet, a cellphone. My suspicion that they would do that if you were hurt or dead was confirmed.

Turtle looked at me, said, "He's breathing. He knows your name."

I said, "Really?"

"Yeah, man. You told him your name. Didn't you hear him say it?"

"Oh yeah."

"When he wakes up, he'll call the cops, and you're screwed."

"Well, what am I supposed to do?"

"Whatever you want, man. I'd kill him."

"What?"

"You got a knife?"

"What?"

"Come on man, we don't got time to stand here and talk about this all night! You got a knife, or not?"

I said, "No."

"Here." He tossed me a heavy pocket knife with a black handle, and because we didn't have time to stand around and talk about it all night, I flipped it open and kneeled before the unconscious man, examining his body for the right place to do it.

In the end, I settled for his neck. It wasn't natural, sticking a knife into somebody's neck and my body tried to resist, but I took a deep breath, gritted my teeth and plunged it as hard as I could into the side of his throat with the blade sticking out the bottom of my fist.

He came to life, screamed and rolled over onto his back as I pulled it out. Then I stabbed him again. And again. I stabbed him in his neck, his face, his chest, his stomach. And finally, he did roll into a ball. He screamed and begged me to stop, but he couldn't fight, because every time I stuck the blade inside a different part of his body, that's where his hands would go.

Sometimes it slipped inside him with ease, others it would ricochet off a bone, but I didn't stop because it was too late to stop now. I had never heard anybody scream and cry like that before, and I wanted to cry too. Not because I was stabbing a man, though. I wanted to cry because for some reason, as I stabbed him, it occurred to me how much I hated my life and everything about it.

I clutched the handle as tight as I could but soon my hand was wet and slippery and it slipped over the thick blade, so I shouted, dropped it, jumped to my feet, and glanced over at Karina. She just stared wide eyed from under her hood.

The guy started choking and making hissing and gargling noises that seemed to come from the holes in his stomach as much as they did his mouth. Then he clutched his neck and cried as he struggled to breathe. I knew instantly he wasn't gonna make it.

* * *

So here's the series of events that took place after I stabbed the guy on Capitol Hill:

1. Turtle took a couple steps back, opened his mouth wide and exclaimed, "Damn! Little bro's a savage!" into his palm.
2. He threw the car keys on top of the guy, and we all ran out of the alley and all the way to their abandoned house.

3. They gave me a pair of dirty clothes without blood all over them.
4. I used my bloody T-shirt to clean the cut on my hand. (It wasn't too deep, thankfully.)
5. One of them left to buy more heroin.
6. Karina cuddled up to me like a tiny bundle on the cold floor.
7. She didn't cry like when we killed the seagull.
8. But she didn't talk much either.
9. The blond girl lay next to Turtle on the other side of the room, and we heard them fooling around for a while before they fell asleep.
10. The guy who left never made it back.
11. We woke up the next morning and found out he was picked up for murder and the police were looking for everyone, including two teenagers named "Hollow and Pixie."
12. Turtle freaked out, cursed, walked off without saying goodbye.
13. The rest of the street-kids left us too.
14. Karina said, "We need to leave ASAP."
15. I said, "I know."
16. She cursed.
17. I said, "What?"
18. She said, "Trouble and Shay. They know our real names. If they're questioned, they'll give us up."
19. I cursed.
20. Karina suggested we kill them too.
21. I asked if she was crazy.
22. She said she wasn't the one who had stabbed a guy to death in a dark alley. What was two more?
23. She was right, so it was settled. We would find Trouble and Shay, kill them, and leave Seattle.
24. So we went to Denny Park to look for them.
25. And that's where we were arrested.

CHAPTER TWELVE

Something has changed inside me. I might be broken, because last night I woke up to thoughts of the first person I ever killed, and as soon as I returned my head to its new pillow, I was out again. Only there were no more dreams. Just darkness, which may be all that's left, aside from that flame that still burns for Karina.

She's all I want, and I know that together we're wrong, but it feels so right that I don't care. I wasn't always like this, and my first morning at Secret Harbor, I found myself reflecting on the person I used to be and wondering if he's still alive, somewhere inside me. I suspect he might be. He might be stuffed away, or bound at the wrists and ankles in my subconscious, but then again he might just be dead. I wouldn't know because I don't know much about him. I know even less about the person I am now.

There isn't much to do here, and since we're not allowed in the rooms during the day, and I'm a level one, the only place I can be is the common area. There are tables set up, like yesterday, and guys playing cards, chess, some other games. Others are sitting in front of the TV with Anthony. A tall blond-haired man named Todd took a bunch of guys to the activities building after the community meeting.

'The community meeting happened after breakfast. We all sat at tables, while Todd asked us how everyone was doing and Anthony sat in front of the TV, which I'm beginning to think is his favorite place in the world. Then Todd made me stand up and introduce myself.

During the meeting, I was able to get a better idea of how many guys live at Secret Harbor School. There must be close to fifty. I even know one of them. A blond guy named Curtis, with an unusually long face. He was my roommate at Fairfax, the mental hospital where I spent my fourteenth birthday. He smiled from ear to ear when he said "Hi," but we haven't had a chance to talk, because he left with Todd to do whatever activities there are to do where they went.

I didn't hear much of what was said at the meeting, because I kept spacing out, and wondering what Karina was doing. It wasn't even eight in the morning, though, so I'm sure she was asleep somewhere. Maybe even at home.

Some of the guys left on the Sea Wolf for some kind of a field trip. Others went with Todd. The rest are still here with me, only they're not with me, because I'm alone. So I walk circles around the common area for a while, until Anthony stomps over and tells me, "No walkin' laps in'na common area. Find yo'-self somethin' da do."

The sun shines through the windows, casting gold-colored, square beams on the tiled floor. It's already projecting to be much brighter than yesterday, so I consider hanging out on the balcony, looking out at the water, thinking some more about Karina. There's a group of guys I don't know standing out there laughing, though, and I can tell just by looking at them that I don't like them.

Somebody slams a domino on one of the tables so hard that it echoes around the room as I make my way over to the carpeted area. The black kid sits on the same couch as yesterday. The olive skinned boy who was restrained by the three staff sits on the other. They both eye me as I approach and sit next to the olive-skinned one.

He doesn't hesitate to ask my name. His voice is so nasally that it's almost exaggerated. I hadn't noticed yesterday when he was crying for them to stop hurting him. I think I like him, so I say, "Tony."

"I'm Donny." He smiles deviously, then twitches like something just bit him in the ass.

From the other couch, the black kid says, "Psss. Hey. You know you're not supposed to be here, right?"

I say, "I'm not?"

"No. We're on punishment. You'll get in trouble if Tone sees you talking to us."

I glance over at Anthony. He appears hypnotized by the TV, so I remain where I am until he tells me his name is Tam.

And because I've never heard a name like Tam, I say, "Sam?"

"No, Tam. It's short for Tamarat. It's Ethiopian."

"Are you Ethiopian?"

"No, I'm Irish. My mom was just really into black guys." Donny laughs and Tam tells me of course he's Ethiopian.

I say, "Oh."

Donny asks me where I came from. I tell him Juvie. He says, "No. Ya think?" makes a face that looks like he's chewing on the inside his cheek and asks where I was before juvie.

I say, "Oh. Uh, all over, I guess. Why did they do that to you last night?"

"What? Slam me?"

"Yeah. I guess."

Tam says, "Because he's crazy, and he likes to get slammed."

"Yo, shut up, man!"

"You do, obviously, or you'd at least try to keep your little butt outta trouble once in a while."

"You're in trouble too, you moron."

"Yeah, but that's different and you know it."

I ask why Tam's in trouble and Donny says, "Because he's a queer."

Tam says, "Whatever."

Donny asks me if I've ever fingered a girl. I tell him I have, and he says, "Well Tam likes to finger dudes."

My first thought is that they're going to end up fighting, but then they both laugh, and before I know it, I'm laughing too.

Donny says, "No. seriously, though, he does like to finger dudes," and Tam doesn't argue, so I believe him.

"How long were you in juvie?" Donny asks.

I tell him almost a month, and we get to talking and I think I'm really hitting it off with this guy. He's strange because he twitches and stares off into space a lot, and he never makes eye contact, but there's something about him that's hard not to like.

I learn that he was at another group home before Secret Harbor, and another one before that because his mother's a crack-head. I consider asking about his dad, but decide not to. Tam doesn't appear to be paying attention to us anymore. He's just staring toward the window, half smiling, but I suspect he's listening to every word we say.

At some point, I catch a glimpse in my peripheral of a guy with a backward hat that matches his red shoes sitting at one of the tables and pointing at me. Soon, everybody in the common area seems to be watching, and within seconds, Anthony stomps over. Donny falls silent, just stares up at the massive man until he's towering over us.

He says, "Say man, I done told you already you can't be here! You wanna be one ah them?" He wags a finger at Tam and Donny.

Without thinking, I glance from one of them, to the other, then back at Anthony. I ask him what he means.

He says, "Ah-kay. Dats it," reaches down and wraps his meaty fingers around the top portion of my arm.

The next thing I know, I'm being jerked to my feet and because I don't have time to consider how I should react, I pull away, shove Anthony as hard as I can. But he has the strongest grip I've ever felt. He twists my arm in a way that it's never been twisted, and though there's no pain, my body becomes his slave, throwing itself at the floor. Tan carpet comes at me rapidly, then slams into my face.

I grunt. Yell. Curse.

Try to fight.

But it's useless. Something jabs into the middle of my back, and I crane my neck enough to see that it's Anthony's knee. He takes my other wrist and wrenches both arms behind my back.

"Cut it out now. Stop strugglin'. You jus' gone make it worse."

Now there's pain. It's in my shoulders. My arms feel like they'll pop right out of their sockets if they're yanked any further. I growl like an angry dog, and even though my throat burns, before long I'm screaming at the top of my lungs, calling Anthony every name I can think of. Some I'm not proud of.

What spills out of my mouth next makes me want to crawl under a rock and hide for the rest of my life. I say, "Why?" and it's not so much the word, but the whiny tone of my own voice that kills me to hear. So I guess I wasn't completely dead inside after all.

* * *

Donny Bravo's thirteen-years-old, and he's been at Secret Harbor almost a year. He's lived in group homes since he was eleven. Before that, it was foster care. But he would stuff his favorite clothes into backpacks and run away from every house he was sent to. He never made it more than a couple miles up the road, but eventually they just stopped putting him in houses, and group homes became his life.

At Secret Harbor, the couch is where you go when you're bad. It's like a kind of timeout, only it lasts weeks, months, sometimes forever. For being slammed, I was sentenced to two weeks on the couch. It worked out for Tam, because he was supposed to be there for another two days, but they let him off early so I didn't end up sharing a couch with him or Donny.

You're not supposed to talk to anyone while you're on the couch because if you're there, it means you're in trouble. You can't talk to the other guys who are in trouble, and they even bring your food to you so you don't eat with anybody. You can't have books. Paper. Pens.

I don't care about rules, though, which is why I'm here. So my third morning on my couch, I sit and write a letter to Karina while Donny watches from his own imaginary cage on my right. Like any other weekday at this place, guys sit at tables playing games, while others talk and laugh in groups, or watch TV. The common area's a soup of conversations, all blended together to create a symphony of ignorant banter. You can tell by what you hear whenever one voice manages to distinguish itself.

When Anthony slammed me, another staff appeared out of nowhere. I hadn't even seen him before. He looks like a short version of Todd, and he materialized by my feet, just to drop his knees on the backs of my calves and keep me from kicking.

I stopped fighting pretty quickly, because I'm not stupid and I knew there was no winning. I even yelled, "Okay! Okay! I'm done!" But they didn't care. They pinned me down for what felt like forever, but was probably only a few minutes. Then they dragged me to the couch and threw me onto the stiff cushion. So this is where I've been since. The only times I'm allowed off the couch, are before and after meals, and at bedtime. From time to time, Curtis has passed quickly and whispered questions out the side of his face.

"When'd you get outta Fairfax?"

"How long you got on the couch?"

"Where'd you come from?"

"D'you bring any weed?"

But he's too scared to stop and chat, so whenever we can get away with it, Donny and I talk. I was right, too, because I do like Donny. Even though he says he wants to be a serial-killer when he grows up. His tan skin reminds me a little of Karina's only he's not as dark as her because he's only Italian, and his hair is way thicker than hers.

Donny's a State kid, which I didn't know much about three days ago. A lot of the kids here are State kids. That means they don't have families. That's why they live in group homes. Learning about State kids has made me wonder more and more what the hell I'm doing at Secret Harbor.

Not right now, though. Right now, all I'm thinking about is Karina, so I sit with my feet on the couch, and the tablet of paper resting against my knees, writing to her, even though I know I won't be allowed to send the letter until my blackout period is over. It's okay, because when my blackout's over, I'll just send a whole stack and she'll know I've been thinking of her.

I wanna tell her how much I miss her, and can't wait to see her again, and how I love her so much that it burns in my stomach. But I'm afraid if I write these things, she'll think I'm a pussy. Maybe I am for thinking them. Who knows?

Instead, I call her "bro," and tell her how lame Secret Harbor is. I tell her about Donny Bravo, and how he twitches when he speaks, and wants to be a serial killer. I write, "Lol," but I don't actually find it funny because there's nothing funny, or even fun about killing. I'm convinced I probably know this better than anyone at Secret Harbor.

As I write, I feel the stirring in my stomach that washed up waves of tears on my way onto this island, so I stop, take a deep breath and use every muscle in my face to hold them back. Then a voice appears above me.

"Hey. What are you doing, man?"
And I look up and see Jesus standing over me. He says, "You know you can't have that."

"What?" I ask, even though I know what he's referring to.

"You can't have that." He points down at the paper and pen, then waves his fingers like a fan, directing air at himself. It's the universal signal for the words, 'give me.'

I tell him I'm not doing anything wrong, and I'm not giving him my paper and pen, because I'm just writing a letter to my girlfriend and I have the right to do that. He says I have to give it up, and waves his fingers again.

"No."

"Come on, man. Don't make this harder than it has to be."

"You're the one making it harder than it has to be. I'm just writing a letter, and you're harassing me. Leave me alone."

"Gimme the paper, man."

The conversations in the common area begin to fade as a few eyes point in my direction. I set my feet down on the floor and tell Jesus to try and take it from me and see what happens. A second too late, I wish I would've said something cooler. Like, "If you can take it from me, it's yours," or something like that. But before I have time to consider this any further, Jesus reaches down, grabs my pad of paper, and I fly to my feet like I'm sitting on a spring.

I throw a wild hook, and my knuckles collide with the side of his head. Then I punch him again, only with my other hand. I become one of those toys with a handle and two plastic balls that crash into each other as you shake it back and forth. My fists fly at Jesus, one after another, because I can't stop.

He ducks down, dives for my legs, and because my cousin wrestled for a year, I know to thrust my feet back and try to press him into the floor. Jesus falls on his face and everyone in the common area pops up like jack-in-the-boxes, covering their mouths, laughing, and pointing as I kick him over and over again.

I hear Donny scream, "Yeah! kick his ass!" as Anthony appears in my peripheral. His colossal gut slams into me and I fly through the air, land on my side, and get a rug burn on my face. I'm rolled onto my stomach, then he's on top of me, only not like before. It feels like he's lying on my back, and I think he is, because I can't breathe. So at least I can't scream, or beg, or ask why this time, which might be a good thing.

I'm thinking I'm going to die. I'm thinking I'll be crushed. My neck or my back will be broken. I hear Donny yell for him to get his fat ass off me, and I'm thinking I definitely like Donny. But I'm also thinking I won't know him much longer, because if I survive this, I'll be kicked out of Secret Harbor School for sure

CHAPTER THIRTEEN

I'm woken up so early that it's still dark out and told that I'm going for a boat ride. It's just past five, and it looks like I'm going home. It's a staff member who I haven't met yet, but who sat outside the dorms last night. An older, heavyset woman, in a hat that she probably knitted herself. She seems nice. I ask if I should pack my things, but she says, "No. Just get dressed."

After I was slammed for beating up Jesus yesterday, Anthony and the other guy each held one of my arms out to my sides so I looked like a crucifixion victim and pulled me to my feet. They kept them twisted in a position that hurt like hell, and I think I even squealed like a little piggy at one point. They dragged me into a room in the hall near the entrance to the common area, then sat against the outside of the door so I couldn't open it. They had to do that, because Secret Harbor has a "no locked doors" policy.

It was almost funny, because I didn't try to open the door anyway, just sat against the wall with my knees propped up and tried to catch my breath. Anthony even yelled through the door and asked if I was done fighting. Eventually they moved, but they kept me in that room the rest of the day with nothing to do but push-ups, and sit-ups.

Now I'm leaving on a boat, and I don't know if I've ever been more excited in my life. I try not to show it, though, because if I show it, they might change their minds. Instead, I ask, "Will my things be sent to me later?"

"Just hurry," the old lady says, so I hurry and get dressed.

Mike stirs in his bed, sits up on his elbow, and looks at me through the dark. I tell him I think I'm outta here. He doesn't speak. He did last night, though. Last night he told me that he's been in foster care since he was a baby. That like Donny, his parents are drug-addicts. That when he was real young, there was a tiny bump on the head of his penis and he never thought anything of it. Then one day, a doctor noticed it and he learned that there was a BB lodged in there. That somebody must've shot him in the penis with a BB-gun when he was a baby, because it had been there as long as he could remember.

He also told me that it was crazy what I did to Jesus, because Jesus was some kind of a champion wrestler.

Mike watches me get dressed, then asks if I'm going home, even though he knows as much as me. I can't help but feel something strange, like a tingling in my face, when he says the word "home," because it sounds awkward rolling off his tongue.

I tell him I am and ask him to please pack my things so they can send them to me later. He says sure, he'll do that, no problem. We don't talk much after that, until I say, "Bye," and step out into the cold, dark morning.

The crickets are awake, singing to a rhythm that I've read somewhere will tell you the temperature if you know how to listen right. A grey and black cat gazes up at me as I pass, but I pay her no mind. (I don't know why, but the cats are all girls to me.)

The old woman sits in her chair, sipping a steaming liquid from a coffee mug with a picture of a bulldog on it. Jerry Warden stands next to her. It's the first time I've seen him since the day he stood smiling on the edge of the dock. Today, he's not smiling. He stands stiff as a stop sign, straight-faced, watching as I approach.

Today, I want to smile, because I've won. I've found my way off Cypress Island, which means that Jerry Warden has lost and soon I'll be one step closer to Karina. I don't smile, though, because it's too soon and I could still blow it. So I approach humbly, with my head down, watching him through my eyelashes, and when I'm close, every muscle in his face contracts into a contemptuous frown.

He says, "Ready?"

I just nod.

Jerry tells the woman farewell and we walk side-by-side down the trail to the dock where I was dropped off days ago by the Sea Wolf. A smaller boat awaits, with a guy I don't recognize sitting in front of a steering wheel. The moon reflects off the water, and next to its reflection, something protrudes no more than a foot. Maybe a seal's head, but who cares.

I climb onto the boat and take a seat on a soft bench along the edge. Jerry Warden sits on the other side and says, "You've been pretty busy since you got here, huh?" He still doesn't smile.

I ask him if my mom will be at the dock in Anacortes to pick me up, because in all my life, my mom's never woken up this early, so I find it hard to believe that she will. He tells me somebody'll be there to get me, and I smile inside.

I think, I won't run away again. I can be with Karina without running. We can try to be good and just be a normal teenage couple, because drinking, smoking, living on the streets, and killing people isn't fun anymore. My mom and John haven't hit me since I hit John back—almost a year ago. Maybe we can learn to get along, and before I'm done thinking this, the boat comes to life and pulls away from the dock.

I'll write Donny. Maybe not Mike, because we don't have much in common. I like Donny, though. Even though I've only known him a few days, I feel bad for leaving him, because there was an instant sense of camaraderie between us. Even though he doesn't have a family and I do, neither of us are convinced that any adult has ever cared about us. We never said this, but some things don't need to be said. So yeah, I'll keep in touch. I'll write him or something.

For what may be the longest, and coldest forty-five minutes of my life, nobody speaks, but I think about Alex. About Anne. My mom and John, and what I can say or do to alleviate the tension when I arrive.

Then the boat pulls up to a small dock. Not the one at the marina, though. This one's in a secluded place that looks like somewhere you'd go to dispose of a body. On the shore are shrubs and tall grass, and some kind of an abandoned warehouse stands close by. Someone's on the dock waiting, like Jerry promised. It's a sheriff in a tan uniform.

I begin to panic, and ask, "What the hell's going on?"

The sheriff's a tall guy with brown hair. He leans down, says, "Tony Carpenter?"

I say, "Yeah. What is this?"

"Why don't you go ahead and climb outta the boat, bud."

"Are you driving me home?"

"Go ahead and climb out and we'll talk."

"What do you mean? Talk about what?"

"Listen, Tony. I'm not gonna talk about it like this. Get outta the boat and I'll explain everything." So reluctantly, I climb onto the dock, but my entire body's shaking like the handle of a lawnmower. As soon as I'm standing in front of him, the cop says, "Turn around for me, and put your hands behind your back," and even though I obey, I hear myself as if from a distance asking why.

Once the freezing metal's wrapped around my wrists, he tells me I'm under arrest for assaulting a staff member at Secret Harbor. Now Jerry Warden smiles from the boat where he still sits. He tells me he'll see me when I get back to the Island.

CHAPTER FOURTEEN

The first time I was ever in the back of a cop car, was when Karina and I were arrested at Denny Park. The crazy thing, is that the cops actually showed up there looking for us, because the Thomas House had reported what they thought we did with Leti's keys.

It didn't have anything to do with the murder, though, and Trouble and Shay didn't hang out on Capitol Hill, so they didn't know enough to have outed us. The cops were there because Karina and I gave the Thomas House our real names when we checked in the other night, and I was reported as a runaway. Karina wasn't, but they arrested her too, so they could call her mom to come and take her home.

When they found the weed and pipe in the pocket of her hoody, I started to freak out, because I didn't want her to get in trouble. Weed's legal in Washington, but not when you're thirteen. The cops were chill about it though. They smiled at each other and one of them dropped the pipe in the bag of weed and stuffed it into his pocket. He said he wouldn't report it.

So we sat together in the back of the cop car, and I couldn't help that I was a little relieved we wouldn't be killing Trouble and Shay after all. I hadn't even thought about how we would do it. I'm not sure Karina had either, but she still had the hatchet in her backpack, so who knows.

The seat was made of some kind of hard plastic, and our hands were cuffed behind our backs. I couldn't remember a time I had ever been in a car, traversing the streets of downtown Seattle and my eyes not been drawn to the scenery. But today that wasn't the case, because all I could pay attention to was Karina.

She had this look on her face like she might cry, but she wasn't crying. Her eyes were big and sad, and it brought to mind images of her cutting herself, and of her crack-head stepdad punching her in the arm and burning her with cigarettes, so I told her it was gonna be okay.

She said, "I don't know."

I told her I did, even though I didn't.

She shook her head and looked away. She lifted her legs and slid her hands under them, so her cuffs were in front of her. I tried to do the same and ended up falling over, landing with my head in her lap, and because her legs were soft against my face, I just stayed there. Karina ran her hands through my hair, and the cold steel of her cuffs touched my skin. She said, "Don't you remember why we left?" and I thought of David and the cholo behind the gym at Laventure. So maybe I was screwed.

* * *

I guess holding cells are designed to make you uncomfortable. The one at the police station in downtown Seattle had a floor made of concrete, brick walls, and a thick metal door that you could tell was layered if you punched it. It was cold as hell, too, and they took my shoes, and the jacket I got from the street kids.

For some reason you couldn't wear shoes or a jacket in the holding cell.

I sat against the wall for a while. Then I paced. Then I punched the door, and it opened. A cop told me to chill out. I asked him what was going to happen to us.

He said, "Your folks are on their way to pick you up. Your girlfriend's mom can't make the trip though. Think yours would give her a ride home?"

The truth was, I didn't know. So I told him I thought they might.

He said, "Good. Cause if I can't find her a ride, I'll have to just cut her loose, and she'll be out on the streets alone. You guys're quite a ways from home. Why you decide to come to Seattle?"

I told him I didn't know. It seemed like as good of a place as any. He could call my mom's cell and ask if she'd be willing to give Karina a ride. He nodded, said he'd do that and told me to sit tight. But I kept thinking of Karina on the streets of Seattle by herself and the way the street kids and pretty much everybody always seemed to look at her, so I couldn't really sit tight. Then her voice echoed from just outside the door, but all I could make out of what she said was my name.

I yelled, "Hello?" My own voice bounced off the walls in my cell, and I thought for a second it would go on forever.

"Tony?"

"Yeah."

"Come to your door. Lay down and talk between the crack where the door touches the floor."

So I did, and I was able to hear her clearly that way. She said she was in another cell across from mine. I asked if she was okay.

"I'm fine," she said.

"You?"

"Yeah. I'm good."

"Have you ever been in jail before?"

"No. You?"

"Yeah. Well, juvie. Your parents are coming to pick you up."

I said, "Yeah. How'd you know?"

"The cop told me. My mom's not coming."

"I know."

"He said he's gonna ask yours to give me a ride."

I told her I knew. I didn't think it would be a problem.

She said, "It's cool if they don't. I'll find a way back. Hey Tony?"

"Yeah?"

"You gonna be okay?"

"Yeah. Uh—yeah. Why?"

"I dunno. I mean I know your mom can be kind of a dick. Is she gonna beat you up, or whatever?"

"I don't know. Probably not. Maybe she'll just be glad I'm okay. I don't know."

"Listen bro, I think there's some things we need to talk about when we get back, don't you?"

I thought about kissing Karina in the tent at Edgewater Park. About sliding my hand under her sweater. Her head resting on my chest while we slept. About cuddling in the corner last night in an abandoned house. I thought about her telling the street kids that I was her boyfriend, and there was a warmth in my torso, like one of those heating pads that you plug into the wall. Then I thought about Mathias and Amber back in Mount Vernon.

I told Karina, yeah, there were some things we needed to talk about.

She said, "Tony?"

"Yeah?"

"We almost made it. I mean, we were almost home free, right? Seattle was just a bad idea."

And even though I loved Seattle, I agreed, because now I had killed somebody, and there was no way to ever go back and unkill him. I told her yeah, Seattle was a bad idea.

She said, "We should a just kept going. Like Oregon, or California or something."

I thought about that for a while, then told her she was probably right.

* * *

My mother's knuckles crashed into my lips. Her hands weren't very big, though, so it didn't hurt. I thought I tasted blood, but when I touched my gums, my fingertips came back clean.

Pale. White.

I sat in the back of John's car, and she was turned around in the passenger seat, her eyes bulging from her skull. She told me she hated me. She hated me so much there were no words to describe it. She wished I were dead.

I thought about Little Carter. Little Carter died in his crib when he was a baby. She always called him Little Carter, because Big Carter was my biological father.

My mom was pregnant with me when Little Carter died. She always told me God killed him because He knew she couldn't afford to take care of two babies. I guess that meant it was my fault he was dead. Maybe God should've killed me instead so she didn't have to be so unhappy all the time.

There was no way she was giving Karina a ride home. I didn't even get the chance to ask, because I could see in her eyes that she wanted to punch me when the cop turned me over to her at the station. She waited until we were in the car and a distance away, though, and I knew it felt good for her because she had been holding it in since I didn't show up after school a few days ago.

She said, "That cop called and asked me to drive your little friend home, too. I told him no friggin' way. She's got her own parents for that. Tony, you're in for a whole world of hurting. You can say goodbye to your summer. You're not even gonna breathe without my permission. Do you understand me?" When I didn't answer, she reached back and took a hand full of my hair. "DO YOU? DO YOU?"

She punched me in the back of the head over and over again until finally I cried out that I did. Not because it hurt, or I thought she would be sympathetic if it did, but because if I didn't give her the satisfaction of making me suffer, she would only try harder.

So that was it. She stopped hitting me, turned back around in her seat and told John how much she hated me. He said he knew, in a tone that meant he hated me too, and I just sat wondering why nobody was saying anything about the cholo who was stabbed.

* * *

But they didn't know. The school. The police. Our parents. Nobody knew that David had stabbed the cholo, because the cholo didn't report it. He must've refused to tell who did it, or just lied, because he was still in the hospital the next week when I made it back to school. People were talking though.

Emilio's friends must've really liked him, because the cholos kept giving us dirty looks. We expected them to attack in the cafeteria or something, but they didn't. Just walked around with their notebooks under their arms and pissed off looks on their faces.

School was like a vacation. Home was like a prison. I wasn't allowed online, so my tablet was locked away in my mom's closet next to her belt. I wasn't allowed outside the house unless I was in the backyard picking up piles of dog crap. I wasn't allowed on the phone, and I didn't even know if Karina made it back to Mount Vernon. She wasn't in school, and I had a really bad feeling.

Amber wouldn't talk to me. Mathias tried to play it cool, but I could tell he was pissed. Doug and David had a new bounce to their steps. Stabbing the cholo had changed them. They joked and flashed each other devious smirks in the cafeteria. You got the impression they knew something nobody else did.

At breakfast, Doug had his phone sitting on the table, playing some rap song. He asked me if I had a knife, and I told him I didn't. He looked at David, nodded toward me, then said, "We gotta get this fool strapped."

I said, "Strapped?"

"We gotta get you knife, man. After what happened, it's not a good idea for any of us to be walking around without something. It kinda got real, you know?"

"Sure," I said, because I thought I might know. "David, you got an extra one?"

David said he did, at home. We could ditch class and go get it.

I said, "Naw. I'm not really trying to deal with anymore drama at home." Mathias called me a pussy.

Doug asked David if he could just bring me the knife tomorrow. David said, "Yup."

But that never happened because as I was leaving fourth period, on my way to lunch, Karina showed up in the hall in black leggings with her hood pulled over her head. Under the hood, she wore eye makeup, and it looked pretty good on her, so I wrapped my arms around her waist and asked when she got back. She nudged me away, said, "Bro, chill," and my entire body deflated like a balloon. She said, "You cool?"

And even though I wasn't cool, I told her I was.

She said, "I got back yesterday. I walked to the freeway and hitched a ride as soon as they let me go. Some guy picked me up. He was some kinda creep or whatever. I don't know. How's your mom?"

"What? I don't know. She's cool. Did you just get here?"

"To school?"

"Yeah."

She said, "Yeah. I just got here."

I asked why, and instead of admitting she hadn't wanted to fight with Mathias over leaving town with me, she shrugged and hummed that famous indecisive tune. Then she said we should probably get back to Seattle ASAP. By this time everybody had made their way into the cafeteria, and the hall was clear, but I looked around conspiratorially anyway as I asked, "Really?"

"Yeah." She pursed her lips and seemed to nod with her entire body. "

But I thought we decided Seattle wasn't a good idea."

"Yeah. That's true. That's why we gotta go back, right?"

I had no idea what she was getting at, so I just stared at her, trying to read her face, until she said, "Well we never finished with Trouble and Shay, right?" And when I still didn't talk, she said, "They could still get us screwed, bro. They're the only ones who know that Pixie and Hollow are really Karina and Tony. Like literally, the only ones who know."

And the problem was she was right, because she would always be Pixie, and I would always be Hollow as long as Trouble and Shay were alive. And Hollow and Pixie were wanted for murder. So Trouble and Shay probably still needed to die.

CHAPTER FIFTEEN

John's some kind of Irish Catholic. I don't know if he's actually Irish, because his family talks a lot about him being Polish. It usually comes in the form of jokes about how many Pollocks it takes to change a tire, or mow a lawn or whatever. His Stepfather's Irish, though, and every year when we're over for Christmas he says the same prayer before dinner, and just after he's finished cussing someone out or kicking his dog in the ass.

My mom's some kind of Catholic too, so they've always had that in common. I haven't stepped into many churches in my life, because neither of them actually attend services, or tithe, or do whatever Catholics do, but I've seen movies where people sit in a dark closet and tell a priest through some screen all the bad things they've done, and the priest forgives them.

During the bus ride home, I wondered what would happen if I sat in a dark closet and told a priest the sins I'd committed. There was no way he would forgive me. Especially since I was about to do it all again. He would probably call the police.

Here's the conversation that took place between Karina and I in the hall after we decided we would definitely return to Seattle to kill Trouble and Shay.

ME: David's gonna give me a knife tomorrow. Should we wait till after I get it, then leave?

HER: A knife?

ME: Yeah. I guess everyone's carrying knives after what happened to that guy last week.

HER: Emilio?

ME: Yeah. The cholo, or whatever. You know him?

HER: What? I mean yeah. Well, I didn't know it was him who got stabbed till last night. My cousin Juan knows his older brother. Why would we wait till tomorrow?

ME: So I can get the knife—from David.

HER: I mean you can get a knife anywhere, can't you? Aren't there knives in your kitchen?

ME: Well, yeah, but—

HER: We can't use a knife anyway, bro. Did you see how long it took that guy in the alley to die? You stabbed him like fifty times, and he still wasn't dead.

ME: Ssshhh. Jesus.

HER: I'm just saying, we can't use a knife. You'll stab one of them and the other one'll just run. Or fight.

ME: Not if I stab one and you stab the other. I kinda thought that's how we would—

HER: Well yeah. I mean, yeah, that's how we would—it's just too messy though. We gotta do it another way. You know—something easier, like in and out without leaving a mess or anyone knowing we were even there.

ME: Like a gun?

HER: No.

ME: Well, I don't think there's any other—

HER: Like poison.

ME: Poison?

HER: Poison. I mean we can poison them somehow, right?

ME: Can you buy poison?

HER: No. I mean like, not "poison" poison. But drugs. We need to overdose them on something. Like sleeping pills or whatever.

ME: My mom's got sleeping pills.

HER: Yeah?

ME: Yeah.

HER: What kind?

ME: I don't know. They're some kind of antipsychotics. They put you to sleep, though. Like if you just take a half a one, it'll knock you out for a day. There's a bunch in this drawer in the bathroom that've been there for years. Like whole bottles. I don't even think she'd know if some of them were gone.

HER: No?

ME: No.

HER: That'll probably work. Especially if she won't know you took them, because if she does, and she calls the cops, it'll link back to us—well, to you, right? Just get as many as you can without getting caught. My stepdad has something too. He'll know I took it, but he doesn't call cops. Like ever.

ME: How the hell do we get them to take a bunch of pills though?

HER: I got that. I'll show you when we meet up.

ME: When are we doing that?

HER: After school. You gotta finish the day and go home so you can get the pills, right?

ME: Uh, yeah. I guess.

HER: Then I'll meet you somewhere.

ME: Cool. Are you gonna stay here, or—

HER: Naw, bro. I'll just meet you later. I don't really feel like being here today.

ME: No?

HER: No.

ME: Okay. Sounds good I guess. I'll just meet you—

HER: After school. I'll come back and talk to you before you get on the bus. Do me a favor though, okay?

ME: Yeah, I mean sure. What?

HER: Don't bring Mathias.

ME: No? I mean, no. Of course not.

HER: And don't tell anyone.

ME: I know.

HER: I know you do.

* * *

It was crazy the things Karina knew. Like that if you pour Heat over my mom's little red pills, it takes the color off them. Heat is this antifreeze for your car, but if you put a coffee filter in a funnel, drop a handful of red sleeping pills in it, and pour it on them, the red coating washes off, leaving mostly white pills in the filter. Then you take a razor blade and scrape off whatever color's left. That way, when you crush them up and dissolve them in a liquid, it doesn't turn the liquid red.

My mom was pissed about everything, as always. Maybe she wouldn't have been if she were taking the pills. For years her doctors had been trying to get her meds right. Pretty much since she shook Alex for crying too much when he was a baby. There were so many different prescriptions in the bathroom drawer, that if she hadn't given me the red ones when I had trouble sleeping, I wouldn't have known which ones to grab.

I didn't say 'hi' when I got home, because there was no need to. It's not like she wanted to talk to me anyway. She was in her bedroom, as always, screwing around on her tablet. Alex usually showed up from school after me, so he wasn't home yet. Anne was with my mom. So I just walked in the door, dropped off my backpack, took three bottles of pills from the bathroom, and left quietly.

Karina was waiting at a bus stop up the street. We got the hell out of the area before my mom noticed I was gone and took back roads to a grocery store where she boosted two bottles of liquor.

Another thing she knew was that it's better to poison a clear liquor, because if the victim can see the liquid, they won't suspect that it has sleeping pills in it. So we got vodka. She just walked in like she owned the store, put a bottle in each of her sleeves, and strolled out straight-faced. Not me. I was nervous as hell.

Her house was empty when we got there, so she set one of the bottles on a counter, went into the garage, and came back with the Heat. We turned her kitchen into our workplace, and I learned that she still knew more about killing people that I didn't. After we removed the red coating, she dried the pills in the microwave, used a tiny blender to crush them into a fine powder, and asked if I was sure they were sleepers.

I said, "Sleepers?"

"Come on, bro. Sleeping pills. Are you sure they're sedatives?"

"They knock you out," I said. "They're strong too. I've taken them."

"Let's hope they're strong enough to O.D. someone then."

I told her they were. She tilted her head, squinted into my eyes, but didn't ask. So I said, "My mom killed a kitten with them once."

"Shut up, bro."

"No. I'm serious. She did. She said the kitten was sick, because she was walking funny, or she couldn't balance right, or whatever. So she crushed up a bunch of these pills and mixed them with canned cat food and fed them to her."

"Her?"

"Yeah. The cat."

"What? No. And it died?"

"Yeah. Like a couple days later. After the drugs kicked in, she kept trying to walk, and falling on her face. Then she just passed out, but didn't die. She slept for like a day and woke up and could barely move after that. She was just whining and crying, then the next morning she was dead."

"A kitten?"

"Yeah."

"Bro, what the hell's wrong with your mom? Who would do that to a cute little meow-meow?"

"I don't know. My mom, I guess."

She shook her head, then cracked the bottle open and poured half the vodka into the sink. She said the less liquid we mixed the pills into the better, because it would be less deluded, and increase the chances they would end up drinking it all. She poured the rest into a tiny metal pot on the stove, set it to low heat, and dumped the powder into it.

"Alcohol's a solvent. Know what that means?" I told her I didn't.

"It means things dissolve in it easily. But it depends on like, what you mix with it or whatever. The pills might not be soluble in it, so if you heat it up a little, it'll make them dissolve so you can't see powder residue in the liquid."

I asked her how the hell she knew this stuff. Instead of answering, she bit her bottom lip and put her hand between my legs, and because nobody had ever done that to me, I backed up into the counter. She smiled, said, "Once it heats up enough to dissolve the pills, we gotta let it cool down again before we pour it back into the bottle, or the glass'll break."

"Could we just put it in the freezer?" I asked.

Her eyes lit up and she dashed out of the kitchen. Less than a minute later, she returned with a tiny glass vile and a syringe. "I almost forgot." She used the syringe to draw the liquid out of the vile, then squirted it into the pot. "This is some kinda tranquilizer. My stepdad has these steroids and people who use steroids do tranquilizers too."

"Your stepdad doesn't look like he does steroids."

"He doesn't. He got them from someone. I think he's gonna sell them. Probably just trade them for crack rocks." She used a butter knife to stir the liquid. "We can't put it in the freezer because it'll all separate again. Alcohol doesn't freeze, but the powder will, so it'll turn to like a crystal inside the liquid. You gotta let it cool down slowly."

So that's what we did. She was right, too. Heating it up made the pills dissolve so the vodka turned once again transparent. Then we let the poison cool down and used the black funnel to pour it back into the bottle and I learned not to mess with Karina.

* * *

Tent-city wasn't a ghost-town anymore. There were so many people who showed up at night that it just looked like any other campground. We went there because Damien's tent was gone, and a bunch of us sat around a fire on upside-down buckets smoking weed and listening to this loud, old guy named Bob tell stories about what a bad-ass he was. The real hard-core bums passed a couple bottles of cheap wine and shadowboxed with cigarettes between their lips.

At one point a raccoon with a bunch of babies came out of the woods and ate chips out of Bob's hand. Other than Karina, there was only one other girl. She was older than us and quiet.

Karina knew just about everyone in tent-city, so she wasn't quiet. She joked and laughed with them. Then, when it got late, Bob told us there was an empty tent we could sleep in. We laid a comforter from Karina's bedroom down on the floor and she said, "We need to wrap ourselves in it and cuddle real close."

I said, "Sure. Okay. Yeah."

"You know why, right?"

And because it was pretty cold out, I guessed we needed to share body heat.

She said, "We need to keep the bottle in the blanket with us. You know, the one with the pills. Remember what I said would happen if it got too cold?"

"Yeah. It'll crystalize or whatever."

She said, "Yup," and that's what we did. We wrapped ourselves into a blanket-burrito and cuddled real close with a bottle of poisoned liquor between us like it was our baby. And since we made it together, it kinda was. Karina's hand contracted on my back and it sent this crazy chill through my body. I almost lost it, as she asked how Amber was doing, her face so close that her words tickled my cheek.

"Good," I said. "I don't think we're together anymore though."

"No?"

"No."

"Sorry to hear that."

I told her it was okay because I wasn't sorry. She said, "We almost made it, didn't we?"

"Yeah. Almost."

"You know, I was really excited to do this thing. To just get the hell outta here and never look back. To start somewhere new, or whatever. I ah, I don't—" Her voice shook and she paused, before saying, "You know I have a sister, right?"

I hadn't known that, so I told her I hadn't.

"Yeah. She's older. She moved out a few years ago, and when I told her what my dad did, she said it's not good to tell lies about people. Can you believe that? I mean I know what he did, because he did it to me over and over again, and he did it for years. She can lie if she wants, but I won't. And you know what? He did it to her too, but she still talks to him and pretends nothing ever happened. Like life's just a bowl of freaking cherries. Like our mom's not a loser who's dating a crack-head and our dad isn't a sick child-molester. Like our cousin didn't get shot last year by a rival gang-member, and we haven't been poor our whole lives.

"She just moved out and had kids. You know, a boy and a girl, and one of the dads is in prison. She lives with the other one, and he works at this tire shop over on Riverside. But my sister's smart, you know? She could've went to college or done anything with her life. But she didn't. As soon as she was old enough, she got the hell outta the house and started having kids, because that's all girls like us ever do. We have kids and get married and work at fast-food restaurants until we become managers. Then people tell us how proud of us they are, because we're doing so much with our lives." Karina laughed the saddest laugh I've ever heard, then said, "What about you, Tony?"

"What about me?" I asked.

"Are you happy?"

Twigs snapped outside of our tent and somebody coughed. A zipper buzzed, and liquid splashed a tree in a thin stream. I let her question splash around in my head, and it occurred to me that I wouldn't have known if I were happy or not, because I wasn't really sure what happy felt like. I couldn't remember a time when I wasn't in trouble at home, and I had only started breaking rules this year. I had never been a teacher's favorite student. I didn't know what it was like to be someone's best friend.

But here, with Karina in my arms, there was a warmth in my chest, and it was alive. It was restless. And it was sad. And it felt okay. And it wanted out. I couldn't say that though, so instead I told her I was happy like the little unicorn who did coke and killed people, and she laughed, then pressed her lips into mine. Our bodies tangled up and fit together like Legos, and that sad, restless thing started dancing like a flame in a windstorm. Then Karina laid her head over it and fell asleep to the sound of my heartbeat and whoever was pissing outside of our tent.

CHAPTER SIXTEEN

We had to come back.

I woke up to birds in trees, singing the song of spring mornings. To thoughts of hacking off a seagull's head and drowning a baby cockatiel in the bathroom sink. Of disappearing and spending the rest of my life with Karina. And to the sound of her voice, telling me we had to come back to Mount Vernon as soon as we killed Trouble and Shay. That we had to let ourselves be caught so it looked like we had never even left town. She tore the labels off both Vodka bottles, crumpled them into balls and tossed them just past the tree line.

She said, "There's probably some kind of tracking number on the labels that could link them back to the store they came from. That would link them to Mount Vernon. And us."

Getting to Seattle was easier than it had been the first time. Instead of the Interstate, we walked along Highway 99 with our thumbs out, and secured a ride all the way in a semi-truck. There was a bed behind the seats, so that's where I sat while Karina rode up front and made small talk with the driver. He was coming from Canada and driving all the way to California.

He asked why we were headed to Seattle, and she told him we were just going to kill a couple people. He laughed, and she laughed and said, "No. Me and my brother are actually on our way to a family function."

I wondered silently if we could go with him. Why stop when we could just keep going and disappear forever in California? But I kept quiet, and just past ten we climbed out at an exit in Seattle. As we marched off the ramp, onto the crowded downtown sidewalk, the aroma of food from vendors filled my lungs and kicked the inside my stomach. It was sunny already, but it wasn't warm yet, so we both wore hoodies.

I didn't want to go back to Mount Vernon. I didn't want to let myself be caught, just to be thrown in an ice-cold shower so I couldn't breathe, and whipped until my back bled. But Karina was right, because the whole point was to put a gap between us and a murder, and creating suspicion around two more didn't make any sense.

So I decided I wasn't going to be thrown into a cold shower or whipped, because I was thirteen and I had killed and there was no reason for me to be afraid of anyone. So if my mom punched me in the face again, I'd laugh and tell her it felt good. And if John put a hand on me, I'd hit him back.

On the corner of First and Pike, I picked up a penny that sat heads-up, because neither of us had a cent in our pockets, and I heard stray pennies are lucky if you find them heads-side-up.

* * *

My Aunt Sue died when I was eight, and I played tag with her two daughters at her funeral. We ran over tombstones laughing and I remember fecling a little weird about it. Not because I cared about Sue—I barely knew her—but because something about stumping over graves didn't seem right. I was having too much fun to stop though. I also remember wondering how my cousins could be so happy at their mother's funeral.

But my family didn't give the kids much incentive to care about the adults, so years later I finally got it. Trouble and Shay weren't much older than me, though, so when Karina and I found them waiting outside of the Orion Center at lunchtime, and Shay said, "Wow! Fancy seeing you two troublemakers again," all I could think was, We're really doing this. This is really happening.

The line bowed around the building, into the alley, and they were near the middle, standing on the sidewalk with a group of kids I recognized from the last time we had lunch here. One of them held a cell phone and wore ear buds and he kept singing along to whatever rap song he was listening to. Shay's smile stretched across her face, revealing cigarette stained teeth, and Trouble just grinned, his eyes sharp slits.

If Karina wrote the guide on luring people to their deaths, it would look something like this:

a) Play a role fit for a Hollywood actress, recounting how Leti had grilled you about your boyfriend stealing her car keys.
b) Pretend you don't know your victims framed you for stealing the keys.
c) Whisper to them that you have a bottle of vodka, but don't have enough to share with all their friends.
d) Ask if they know a place the four of you can go to drink.
e) Get them away from their group before they even have lunch.

So that's what we did. Trouble and Shay told their friends they'd meet up later and we left together. As we walked, Trouble asked me if I stole the keys, and any reluctance I had to murdering him drained out of me like he had pulled a cork inside my soul. I might've done it right there if I had a weapon and the streets weren't strewn with witnesses.

They led us to a humongous freeway bridge with a raggedy sofa and a floor constructed of flattened cardboard boxes. It was tucked away so nobody could see, but littered with evidence that people were here often.

Trouble asked where we'd been staying and before I could answer, Karina said, "Everett."

The couch wasn't big enough for all four of us, so Trouble sat on a crate as Karina brought the unopened bottle from her backpack. He sang, "Just a lil day drinkin'. No big deal."

Karina smiled, handed it to him, and asked if he wanted to do the honors. He cracked it open and raised it to his lips, scrunching up his face as he washed the liquid down and handed it to Shay. She did the same, then Karina and me. It burned in my chest and I think if there had been food in my stomach, I would've thrown up.

I didn't talk much as we sat under the bridge and drank. Not because I was nervous about poisoning Trouble and Shay, but because there was nothing I wanted to say, and the vodka was hitting me like a sledgehammer doing a demolition job on my equilibrium. So I smirked while Karina told stories about a mentally disabled brother she didn't really have, and how he got to be the mascot for his high school football team.

Trouble and Shay hung on her every word, nodding like bobbleheads to the rhythm of her lies and the cars passing above us on the interstate. Shay even piped in about some cousin with a disability, and I wondered how long it would take for them to die once they drank from the other bottle. And I wondered how the hell we were supposed to get them to drink from the other bottle. And I wondered if it would be a quick death, or they'd suffer as they choked on their own vomit.

She talked about other things too. Like her cousin who robbed a 7-11 at gunpoint for a hotdog and one of those jalapeño cheese sticks. Trouble paced. He laughed. He said things like, "He must ah had da munchies like a mofo." Shay sat next to Karina and giggled.

When the bottle was half empty, I stood up and walked a distance away to drain some of the liquid from my stomach, and to think more about what we were doing, because what we were doing was premeditated murder. I didn't hear Trouble walk up behind me, didn't know he was coming until he was next to me, fidgeting with his zipper and we were both urinating side-by-side.

He said, "You cool?"

I made a point not to look at him, but told him I was cool as the last day of school.

He said. "Oh yeah? Last day a school, huh? Ah-right. Fo-real though. How y'all livin'?"

I said, "Good. Great. Fine."

Trouble nodded. He seemed to go into a trance as he said, "She beautiful, ain't she? My girl, I mean."

Shay wasn't beautiful, but as I finished my business I told him sure, she was.

He finished his own business and said, "Your girl cool, too. She pretty as hell actually. How you guys gettin' by though? I mean since you got kicked out the Thomas House'n all."

I told him again that we'd been doing fine. Everything was good.

"No it ain't bro. I know it ain't and you know it too, don't you? Look homie, why don't we both cut the crap? I know why we here, and I think you know I know. I ain't runnin' from it neither, am I?"

And because his words caused a chill to run over the surface of my skin like cockroaches fleeing the light, and admitting the truth still wasn't an option, I just stared into his sharp eyes and thought, How the hell could you possibly know?

He said, "Revenge ain't the way lil homie. I learned that the hard way when one a my guys was shot outside the welfare office last month. You know White Center?"

"No." My voice was weak. "Who's that?"

"Not 'who' bro, 'where'. White Center's my neighborhood, in West Seattle."

Behind us Shay called, "Shut up fool. You ain't got no hood. White Center ain't nobody's hood anyway." Then her and Karina laughed and resumed their own conversation as Trouble went on.

"My homeboy was yer age. How old're you, anyway? Thirteen? Fourteen? Spider was about your age and we were going back and forth with these fools from Highpoint. They'd take off on one of us. We'd take off on one ah them. Then one day Spider got caught slippin'. He's at a bus stop by himself and a car pulls up and starts dumpin' on him. Puts seven bullets in him, and now there ain't no more Spider in White Center.

"Listen homie, I know I fouled up when I said you had the keys. I just freaked out, cause they were bout ta search me and my girl, and if they found em on us, we'd a got kicked out. We done been there almost a year now, bro, and we really ain't got nowhere else ta go. I can't do that ta Shay, you understand? So I had to say somethin' just ta get the heat off a me.

"I didn't tell em you had em though. I just said I thought you might. I figured they'd search you, see you didn't, then just drop it. I didn't know you was gone get kicked out, bro. I swear on my momma, I didn't know that.

"But I ain't never run from no fight. So if you really need ta fight me to feel better, we can just go ahead and do it. Or you could accept my sincere apology and I could try'n help you out instead. Personally, I prefer the second option, but it's whatever, ya know?"

It wasn't whatever though. It wasn't that simple. So I smiled, placed my hand on his back, and told him I preferred the second option as well. I told him I wasn't gonna fight him. I told him I forgave him for his imperfections and I knew what it was like to be scared. I told him everything was gonna be okay, and because I was as drunk as hell, I was kinda having fun.

* * *

Karina slipped the half-drunk bottle into her backpack, stood up, and flashed me a smile. "Ready, babe?"

I took her hand and told her I was ready.

I found out later that she had just finished telling Shay we were headed to Idaho because she had family there. She told her we planned to steal a car to get there. Right before we left, she asked Trouble if he knew anyone who might want to buy half a bottle of vodka. Then this happened.

SHAY: Babe, why don't you buy it?

TROUBLE: Cause I ain't got no money.

SHAY: What about those keys?

TROUBLE: What? What about em?

SHAY: They need em more than you anyway. They're tryin' ta get a car so they can get to Idaho. Would you guys be willing to sell it for some jigglers?

ME: Jigglers?

KARINA: They're shaved keys. For stealing cars. What do you say? We do need to get a car if we're gonna make it to Boise.

TROUBLE: Naw. We need em too.

SHAY: Shut up fool! You ain't never gonna use em anyway. You been talkin' bout stealing a car for months now, but you can't even figure out how ta make them things work.

ME: I think it's a good idea.

SHAY: What?

ME: The trade. I think we could trade the vodka for some ah, jigglers.

SHAY: See? Go on, babe. Give em the keys. I wanna keep drinkin' anyway. Don't you want me to keep drinkin'?

And I guess Trouble did want her to keep drinking, because he fished a key chain from his pocket and tossed it to me. I caught it as Karina reached into her backpack and handed Shay the bottle of poisoned liquor, which was identical to the one we'd just been drinking from. Then we left them under the bridge and never spoke about it again.

* * *

I don't think they were dead, or even asleep yet when we managed to hitch a ride out of Seattle. They may have been when we arrived in Mount Vernon, though, just before dark. We tossed the key chain off the Westside Bridge, then sat on a log on the beach and finished the vodka, watching the river flow out of town.

The pink sky would turn black soon, and we decided we should probably figure out a way to be arrested before dark. I told Karina I hoped her stepdad didn't do something crazy, like burn her with a cigarette for taking the tranquilizer.

She smirked and said, "He won't even know it's gone. It's been sitting there so long, when he finally figures it out I doubt he'll suspect me. What about you though?"

"What about me?" I asked.

"You gonna be cool?"

"Yeah. I think."

"Sure?"

I had played the scenario over and over in my head throughout the day, and I was sure I would fight back if John touched me. In fact, I was almost looking forward to it. So I told her I was sure.

She put her arm around me, laid her head on my shoulder, and said, "You know we can't leave again, right?" I took a swig from the bottle and told her I wasn't staying long.

"No, Tony. You have to. We both do. For a while, at least. If we leave again too soon, it could get us caught. I mean probably not, but it's better safe than sorry. Unless you wanna spend the rest of your life in prison.

Running away again will just draw attention to us, and right now that's the last thing we want."

Before she even finished, I heard myself say, "The only thing I want is to be with you."

Her body went stiff against mine. She was like a skeleton leaning against me and I knew I had screwed up. So even though I was still intoxicated, I stuttered as I tried to take it back. But she cut me off.

"No. It's cool, bro. I get it. I like you too, but it's just—it's complicated, you know?"

But I didn't know. I had no clue how it could be complicated. All I knew was that I wanted to be happy and I was pretty sure I could be happy with her. I couldn't say that, though, so instead I just scooted away from her and stared ahead at the passing water.

She said, "Tony—"

"It's okay."

"I just—"

"Really. It's cool."

"No, it's not. I don't know how to explain it, though. You just—you make me happy. You really do, and I like being with you. I like being with you so much and I think we'd probably be really good together. And I'm not just saying that, either. I really do. It's just—I mean, I don't know. Don't hate me, please."

So I told her I didn't hate her, even though I kind of did. And I told her I understood, even though I didn't. And we finished off the vodka and stood outside a bar up the street plucking half-smoked cigarettes from an ashtray until finally a cop car pulled up after dark.

Like before, there was no runaway report on Karina, so she was free to go.

As I was put in cuffs, I asked the cop if I'd be taken to the station, or just dropped off at home.

He said, "Neither, champ. You're going to juvie."

CHAPTER SEVENTEEN

The walls in juvie always seem dirty. Even if you wet toilet paper and use it to scrub them, they still appear stained and gross. You don't want to do that anyway, because they don't even give you enough toilet paper to handle your business, let alone clean your walls. A guard walks around with a roll and wraps a four-foot stream around his hand, then passes it under the door twice a day. If you have a cellmate, you'd better use it sparingly.

The dirty walls may be more due to the color of the paint, though. It's some not-quite-white tint, laid over bricks the size of cinderblocks. In fact, they might be cinderblocks. And they might not actually be dirty, because every so often, a guard named Chuck comes around with a bucket of soapy water and a sponge, and says, "Come on up. Let's get those walls cleaned."

I have sentencing tomorrow, and I already know I'll receive two weeks for beating up Jesus. I've been here close to a month, so once I'm sentenced, I'll be credited with time served and released. I'll be picked up by Secret Harbor staff and returned to Cypress Island, because though I've spoken to my mom every night since I got here, like before, all the begging in the world couldn't persuade her to let me come home. So I stopped begging after the first week.

I have a cellmate. His name's Kenny, and we call each other "cellie," because that's what everybody calls their cellmate. I know Kenny from Laventure. He hangs out with the poor white kids sometimes, and even though he might be the poorest of them all, nobody likes him much because he's annoying. I don't mind him though. Most of the kids who were here when I left, were here when I got back. A couple of them are still here.

The room's not very big. There're two slabs of metal sticking out of the wall that function as beds, with worn-out one-inch-thick mattresses on them. I sleep on the top bunk, and from there I have a perfect view of the girl in the room across from me. One day, when her cellie wasn't with her, she took off her pants and sat on the bunk with her legs spread, smiling at me. Her name's Livia, and she's good friends with Karina.

The door's red. Like a clown's nose. Only thick strips have been carved out of the paint, in lines that form letters, spelling people's gangs and their nicknames and the dates they were here. Above my door, in permanent marker, are huge letters that read, "I love Tony Carpenter." That means Karina once lived in this cell.

I call her every chance I get, but we used all the money on our phone account before I left for Secret Harbor. Still, it's nice to hear her voice when she picks up. She'll say things like, "Hi, handsome." Or, "I love you." Then the automated recording comes on and tells her she needs to use her credit card to add money to the account. The problem is, she's fourteen and doesn't have a credit card. It was hard enough to get someone to add money the first time. She hasn't written this time, though.

So I just call, and listen to her voice in blissful half-second increments, while everybody else watches me and snickers under their breath about how much of a pussy I am.

Sometimes Kenny and I fold our mattresses into the shape of chairs and set them on the cement floor next to each other. We roll tiny pieces of paper up like cigarettes and pretend to lounge around smoking and watching TV. One night we stayed up late and he said we should sleep on the floor. I asked why, and he said, "Cause Carly works tomorrow morning."

I said I didn't get it.

"She'll be dropping off the breakfast trays. You know what that means, right?"

"No. Not really."

"What? Come on, bro. Booty-shot."

And even though I still didn't get it, I slept on the floor next to Kenny. The next morning the cell door opened with a loud, "pop," and an attractive twenty-something-year-old blond guard stepped in with two breakfast trays. She turned around and bent over less than a foot from me as she set them down. Before she straightened back up, she looked back into my eyes, smiled, and said, "Good morning, Tony."

So whenever Carly works, we sleep on the floor.

* * *

I've never met Eric, but he says he works at Secret Harbor. He's shorter than me, and looks like something that might attack you if you try to cross its bridge. Jesus is with him, and his smug smile's nowhere to be found. It's good, because I don't mind juvie, and I had fun beating him up the first time. They meet me at the door, and lead me out into the late morning sun, then into a white van. Jesus doesn't talk the entire ride, but Eric won't shut up from behind the wheel about some clothing brand he wants to create. "Kinda like sports gear," he says. "But hip. Know what I'm saying? Like you won't have to be into sports to wear it. Kinda like Nike, I guess. Gonna be called 'Pure Adrenaline.' P.A. for short. It'll have a real hip logo with the letters P.A. on it."

From time to time, he glances in the rear-view mirror, soliciting endorsement from my eyes. I mostly just listen and stare out the window, daydreaming about jumping out at an intersection and finding Karina. I know the door's child locked, though. They'd be stupid if it wasn't.

Eric asks me questions about what sports I like, and I consider asking if murder's a sport, just for fun. But instead I say, "None really. Well, kick boxing. I took kick boxing for a few months."

Jesus stirs uncomfortable in the passenger seat, and for some reason it makes me feel okay. So I decide to keep talking.

"This instructor came from Seattle and started a class. It was cool, because there's no other kick boxing gym in Mount Vernon. We used to warm up with an hour of these aerobics routines—like kick boxing aerobics—then we'd learn combos and practice on the punching bags and spar and whatever for the next hour."

Eric says, "Kick boxing, huh? That's not quite what I meant. I was thinking more like—"

"I only got to do it for like three months. One of my friends was in the class, though, so we used to take our gloves to school and have matches in the gym. Other people would show up too, and we'd let them box, so we had kinda like a fight club, you know?"

Jesus clenches his fists and purses his lips. He's getting pissed and I can't help that it makes me feel better than I have since I last slept next to Karina, so when Eric tries to stop me, I cut him off again.

"Good thing my parents didn't pay for it though. I got this voucher from my youth at risk caseworker. I guess they thought it would keep me out of trouble, or let me channel my aggression in a positive way or something. Turned out to be a scam anyway. The guy taught three months' worth of classes, then got everyone to sign up for another six months and disappeared with their money.

"I don't think it was a complete waste, though, because I did learn to fight way better. What do you think, Jesus?"

Eric says, "Okay! Enough! That's enough already! Didn't you hear me say that's not what I meant? For Christ's sake," and neither of them speak to me the rest of the ride.

* * *

I wonder what she's doing. I wonder where she is. I wonder who she's with, or if she's wondering about me. She could've come to one of my court appearances, could've called the courthouse and found out when it was, and just showed up. We wouldn't have been able to talk, or kiss, or touch each other, but at least I could've looked into her eyes.

Once the van comes to a stop in front of the office in Anacortes where I first met Jerry Warden, I pull on the door handle and it slides open. It wasn't child locked. I could've run at any time. I could run now. I could run and hide somewhere in town overnight, then catch a bus back into Mount Vernon tomorrow morning.

I don't do that, though, and Eric says, "Come on in and take a seat in the waiting room. They got some DVDs you can check out. Boat doesn't leave for a couple more hours."

So I go inside and an older lady with grey and blond hair eyes me from behind a reception desk. She knows who I am, and what I did to Jesus, but she doesn't speak as I'm led past her and into the room where Jerry talked my mom into giving me away. The round table's gone, and I notice this time that there is, in fact a small flat screen TV, and a stack of DVDs on one wall. I take a seat and stare at the black screen. I can still run. I can probably just walk out. What could they do? We're not on the island yet. Would they slam me here? Maybe, but not if I make it out the door. There are too many witnesses outside. They'd have to just call the cops. Maybe follow me with a cell phone to tell them where I am. I could outrun them though. I've outrun police, so I know I can outrun Secret Harbor staff.

But again, I don't run. Something's happening to me. Like an invisible leash, tied around my soul, or programmed into my subconscious mind. I want to run so bad, but I can't and I don't understand it and I hate it and I want to find this leash so I can use it to hang myself.

Eventually, I do select a DVD. A Harry Potter movie. One of the later, better ones. It occurs to me that Harry was a foster kid. Then, that Voldemort came from a group home. I've seen the movies before, but never put much thought into it, and I don't have time to do that now either, because before the movie's over, I'm told it's time to go.

CHAPTER EIGHTEEN

Dear Tony,
I hope they give this to you. I hope you can read my writing. Marvin came over and we smoked like a whole eighth and I'm pretty faded right now. He left with Jaime about an hour ago. You remember Jaime right? The guy with the gold tooth in front?

It sux out here without you. Everything's the same because nothing changes in this freaking town, but it's different because you're not here. I'm sorry about this morning. I was there and I saw you and I had the knife. I had it in my sweater, and I wanted to give it to you, but then I started thinking and I knew I couldn't. Because if I would have gave it to you and you would have killed your mom, then what? What would we have done after that? Run? Get caught? Go to prison for the rest of our lives?

They would have caught us bro. They always catch us and that's the problem. You're the closest thing I have to a soulmate, and I'm starting to believe that we're just destined to spend eternity trying to be together while the world tries to keep us apart. So we have to play it smart, right?

Anyway, this is kinda ruining my high, because now I'm crying and I kinda want to cut myself. So I'm gonna

end this and send it to you. I really hope you're allowed to get mail in that place. All right then, bye Tony. I love you so much it hurts.
Karina.

* * *

"Well what's it say?" Donny Bravo asks once I finally peel my eyes away from the letter. I tell him it doesn't say anything special. He asks if he can read it. I almost tell him no, then think, What the hell. Why not? and pass it to him. We're at a table in the common area because he's no longer condemned to the couch, and to my surprise, neither am I. While I was gone, it was decided that a month in juvie was punishment enough for what I did to Jesus. My blackout period was waved, which means I can have my mail and I'll be allowed a ten-minute phone call home, once a week. I'm also instantly promoted to level two.

The letter was sent a month ago. The first day I stepped foot on Cypress Island. My counselor must've been holding it since. I've only just met her, and I can tell she doesn't like me. Her office is downstairs, below the common area, and I was taken there as soon as I arrived this afternoon. Her name's Karen, and she was probably pretty ten years ago. She's thin, with sharp features and straightened, black hair.

Jerry was there too. Just waiting in Karen's office, sitting in a chair by her desk looking like somebody spilled ammonia all over his upper lip. He asked me where I saw myself in two years, and I said, "Home."

He said, "You know you're not the first boy to cycle through this place, if you can't tell. I've been doing this job a long time, and Karen's worked with foster kids for years now, haven't you Karen?"

Karen nodded.

I told them I'm not a foster kid.

Jerry smirked and said, "I know. And I saw the tears back at the office the day your parents dropped you off. You didn't wanna come to this place. But unfortunately, this is the bed that you've made for yourself, and now you're gonna have to lie in it a while. My recommendation is that you make the best of it and try and leave with a new perspective on life. But if you wanna cause problems and throw a fit while you're here, we'll accommodate you. We're good at that. It's really up to you, Tony.

"I've been brainstorming with Karen on ways we might help you on your path. She was looking at your file and saw you were diagnosed with ADHD?"

"Yeah. I guess. I don't think I have it anymore, though."

"Unfortunately it doesn't work like that, Tony. Karen's a counselor. She'll tell you. You don't just snap your fingers and get cured of ADHD. If that were the case there'd be a lot of professionals out of a job. Why'd you stop taking your meds?"

"The doctor said I could stop."

"And how old were you?"

"I don't know. Nine or ten maybe."

"Well that's no good, is it?"

"What? What do you mean?"

Karen asked me if I remembered why the doctor said I could stop taking my meds.

I said, "Yeah. They made me like a zombie. I could barely talk to anyone. I just walked around and stared at the walls or whatever. My mom took me to a different doctor and he said the other guy gave me way too much. They tried a lower dose, but it pretty much did the same thing."

"Did it help you focus, though?"

"I don't know. No. I don't think so."

"And that was Ritalin?"

I told her it was and she said maybe Ritalin wasn't right for me. She said there's another drug that might be a better fit. Tomorrow I'd start taking Adderall. Jerry said, "And you'll be going back on your antidepressants. Frankly, I don't know why anybody let you stop taking meds that were prescribed to you by professionals. Tomorrow morning, after breakfast, you'll be at pill line. If you're not there, we'll have to take action to get you back on those meds. Just last week, we had to hold a guy down and stuff his meds down his throat. You know why, Tony? Because he needed them. And so do you, so we can do this the easy way, or the hard way. Your choice."

And at first I panicked because I stopped taking all the pills that had been forced on me for a reason, but then I went back to my room and found the envelope with Karina's name on it and it's all I've able to think about.

So I haven't said much to Donny since we sat down. Once he's finished reading the letter, he looks up, grins with only one side of his face and his lips twitch.

He says, "She sounds hot."

I laugh and ask him what he means.

He says, "What?"

"You haven't even heard her voice."

"Yeah, but—you know what I mean, fool."

"Not really, but thanks."

He slides my letter back to me and I can't stop staring at her handwriting. My eyes follow the lines as they curve and bend, and turn abruptly, forming letters that lead into words that express her love for me.

Why did I come back? Why the hell did I let them bring me back? I had every chance in the world to run, but I didn't. I just sat there like a dog on a leash and allowed them to lead me back to this island, and who knows when I'll see her again now.

"What are you doing?" Donny asks.

"Huh?"

"You're wigging out, man. You're just staring at that letter like it might get up and run away if you take your eyes off it."

"Donny, what's there to do around here?"

"Well, you're a level two, so you can go to the activities building. You can't go by yourself, though. You gotta be escorted. They usually go after lunch and after dinner, so you can probably go tonight."

I ask him if he wants to go there tonight, and he says he can't because he's still a level one for getting in trouble. So I decide I'm not going either. "What else is there to do?"

"I don't know. Just sit around here and think about all the ways you wanna kill all the staff and burn this whole building down. That's what I do."

I look around, then ask him if anyone's ever escaped. He says, "Why? You wanna escape?"

"I don't know. Has anyone done it before?"

"We call this place Alcatraz. You'd have to steal a boat. There's a small dock over by the farm, though, and they keep a boat chained to it for emergencies. I've thought about taking it. It'd be hella easy too. You'd just need a pair of bolt-cutters to cut the chain."

I ask if we can get bolt-cutters and he tells me I'd have to talk to one of the guys who work on the farm, because there are a lot of tools there. So I make a mental note to find out who works on the farm, then I change the subject, and Donny and I spend the next hour and a half talking about how much we want to kill all the staff and burn Secret Harbor to the ground.

* * *

Sergio's kinda like me. He has a family, and they all live together somewhere in Seattle. I'm not sure why they gave him away, and I don't ask, but maybe his story's like mine. Maybe he's in love with a girl who his mom hates. Or maybe his parents just like his siblings more.

Either way, Sergio's been at Secret Harbor over a year now. He's Mexican, and at first glance he looks like he could be one of the cholos at Laventure. Then you talk to him and find out he probably would've fit in better with the poor white kids, like Karina.

Mike has a new roommate, so my new home is room 1, bottom floor with Sergio. Again, my bed's the one closest the door, but I don't mind because it's not a one-inch-plastic mattress on a slab of steel. Sergio's all right, so the first night we lay in the dark telling stories about how bad-ass we are while rap music bumps softly from a small alarm clock by his bed. It's decided that for what I did to Jesus, I take the cake.

At one point he asks me, "You ever been in love?"

"Yeah," I say. "I told you about my girl."

"Naw, vato. That's not what I mean. You ever been in love with another dude?"

"What? Hell no!"

"What about hooking up?"

"What about it?"

"You ever just have casual hook-ups with fools?"

I open my mouth to tell him to quit playing, but I'm so uncomfortable that the words catch on the backs of my teeth and just rest on my motionless tongue. The silence that commences lasts so long that I wish I would've just spit it out, because my hearts beating so hard it feels like it's in my skull rather than my chest. My body grows so light that I might float away, so I summon the will to speak and get ready to tell him instead that I killed the last guy who tried.

But before I can, he laughs and says, "I'm just messing with you, vato. Chillax."

I tell him I'm tired and I'll get at him tomorrow. Then I roll over and think I know now why his family gave him away. It's wrong, and I know this, but I can't help that I kinda wanna get away from him too.

* * *

There's a door on one of the walls in the carpeted area where the couches are. It leads to a room where a bunch of us sit in a circle on the floor with a small karaoke machine. One guy has an electric guitar that's plugged into a small amplifier. He strums chords and screams like he's being burned at the stake while another guy holds the microphone to his mouth.

Todd's in the room with us, sitting between a kid named Casey, and a guy who calls himself Lil Poet. When he tells people his name, be pulls his shirt down and points to a tattoo on his chest that reads, "Lil Poet" in crooked lettering and faded green ink. Lil Poet talks like the cholos at Laventure, but he's white.

Casey's my age and has a lot of nice things, like the karaoke machine. He has a family, too, and I guess they're rich because his dad's a doctor. They live somewhere in California, which is where he lived before they sent him to Secret Harbor.

Once the screaming guitar player's done, Todd smiles from ear to ear, claps his hands. He tells him, "Nice. Very nice. Ever thought of doing something with your talent?"

Next, Lil Poet takes the mic and starts rapping about all the girls he's been with. He uses language that's usually not accepted at Secret Harbor, but Todd doesn't shut him down. Instead, he nods along to the imaginary beat Poet's flowing over. When the song ends, he opens his mouth to praise Poet, but before he can, Casey yells, "Squash the chilly!" and slaps Todd on the crotch.

Todd says, "Oof!" and turns red.

Casey does it again. And again. "Come on everyone! Let's play squash Todd's chilly!" And Todd doesn't stop him, or cover his bump with his hand. Instead, it begins to swell beneath his pants and I grow sick to my stomach as I realize Todd and Casey have likely played this game before.

Poet's mouth opens wide and he lets out a yelping laugh, pointing with one hand at Todd's chilly. He says, "What the hell? Why's it getting hard?" and everyone else joins in.

Todd says, "You guys're just jealous."

And I'm beginning to understand that Secret Harbor may have some secrets other than just in its name. And I'm thinking, *They make movies about places like this.* And I'm thinking, *There's no place I'd rather be than home right now.* And I'm thinking, *I don't like the way Todd's looking at me.* And Casey does it again.

So later I sit in the TV room and tell Donny what happened and he says Casey's a S.O. anyway.

I say, "A S.O.?"

"A sex offender."

"Yeah, I know what a S.O. is. Why would he be here, though?"

He twitches and says, "They have a S.O. treatment program here. That's why a lot of the guys here are weirdos. Mostly the ones coming out of the institutions."

"Institutions?"

"You know, the juvenile prisons."

I nod because I thought that's what he meant. "How many?" I ask.

"How many are S.O.s?"

"Yeah."

"More than half the guys here are. Your roommate's one. He molested his little brother. He was in the institution for like two years, then they sent him here."

"What? Really?" I let that bounce around in my head, then ask why they would send Casey all the way from California.

"Because, he wasn't in the institution. They gave him probation or something, and his parents paid to send him here. That's mostly what this place is, if you can't tell. They mix us with those freaks cause they get funding for having us here. Otherwise it would be just S.O.s, but they need the money they get from housing us to run their program." He seems to be having fun watching me process this, so he says, "Welcome to Secret Harbor."

But I don't get it, because even if Casey's a S.O., he's still a fourteen-year-old boy, and Todd's still a staff member.

CHAPTER NINETEEN

I learned about S.O.s after I was picked up outside the bar with Karina and I went to juvie for the first time. There was this fat one who was there for something he did to one of his cousins. His name was Troy, but nobody called him that. They just called him, "the S.O."

I'm sure there were more of them, only nobody knew that's what they were, and they knew how to socialize better than Troy, so no one suspected them either. Troy wasn't like anyone else in juvie. He didn't walk with his head up, or his chest out. When he spoke, he didn't tell you how hard-core he was, or how many people he'd beat up. In fact, Troy had probably never been in a fight in his life before Adolfo took flight on him.

Taking flight meant you attacked somebody for any reason. It was something the cholos did to each other because they weren't all from the same gangs. But when word started circulating about Troy, and what he'd done to his baby cousin, they forgot about their differences for a while in order to make his life a living hell.

He was scared, and he was awkward, but he tried his best not to be either of those things. He laughed and smiled every chance he got. He was fourteen and seemed to have the mind of somebody much younger.

I tried my best not to talk to Troy, because you're not supposed to talk to sex offenders unless you're threatening them. We worked laundry together, though, which meant we spent two-hours-a-day folding dark-blue, tattered jumpsuits in the dayroom, and because nobody else would be nice to him, he would always use that time to solicit conversation from me.

After I was handcuffed outside the bar, I was led into the back of the cop car where I stared out at Karina. She waved goodbye, then turned and walked toward her house. The cop told me I was a youth at risk, which meant I could be put in juvie for running away now, so they sentenced me to a week, and that's where I met Troy.

He asked me questions about video games, and even though I didn't like video games, I let him tell me which ones he liked because I felt bad that nobody was nice to him. But when the other prisoners were around, I ignored him. The girls were mean to him too—mostly because the cholos were, and they liked the cholos.

Then, one day, they were quiet. They whispered at a table, but nobody could hear what they were talking about, and at lunch, when Troy got in line to pick up his tray, Adolfo punched him in the back of his head. He squealed like a mouse in a snake's mouth. He ducked and covered his face with his hands as Adolfo hit him again, and again, and yelled, "Pinche rapollo!" until the guards slammed him face down on the cement floor. The next day my parents picked me up and took me home.

* * *

I didn't make it back to school that year because the day after I got out of juvie, my mom and John drove me to an inpatient treatment center three hours away. The doors didn't lock, and I probably would've run, but instead I got kicked out after a week because I yelled at one of the counselors.

My parents drove all the way back to pick me up, and on the way home, my mom told me I wouldn't be returning to Laventure this year because she'd worked something out so I'd be able to pass the seventh grade with an "incomplete."

So I spent the rest of the year in the kitchen, throwing knives at the wall. Then, one night early in the summer, John caught me. He dragged me by my shirt into the room he shared with my mom and turned toward the closet to get the belt. That's when I finally did it.

I jumped onto the bed because he was so tall and punched him in his face over and over again while he ducked and covered and the next thing I knew my mom was grabbing me and slamming me down on the bed, laying on top of me. She yelled, "John, call the cops!"

Then I went to juvie again for a month, and John had a black eye the whole time I was gone, but he never tried to hit me again.

* * *

My friends posted pictures online of all the fun they were having, and they messaged me in the middle of the night when they were messed up at parties. I didn't usually respond, because when I did they'd invite me to join them, and I wasn't even allowed out of the house.

Then one morning I woke up and saw these posts on David's page:

R.I.P. Homie. Much love. R.I.P. David.

This is messed up. This is really messed up. He was way too young. David Mayfield, rest in peace. We'll always remember you, and you'll always be in our hearts. Don't worry, we're gonna make this right. I promise. W.T.F?

What happened to him?

He got shot. WHAT???

6 times.

Rest in Peace David. You were a good friend and a kind soul. I know you're in a better place.

Who the hell shot him?

Call me, and I'll tell you what happened.

I don't get it. I've been in kind of a fog all morning. This doesn't make sense, why something like this would happen to a thirteen-year-old child, and all I can keep thinking is what could we have done differently? Where did we go wrong?

I don't have ur number.

I'll message it to you. Hold on. And so on. And so on...

David was shot just outside the trailer park when a carful of cholos were driving by and recognized him. One of them was Emilio's older brother. He wasn't the one who pulled the trigger, but he was in juvie with the rest of them anyway.

At first I pictured this at night, with the barrel of a gun lighting up as six shots rang out. But I learned that the sun was just setting when it happened, and way more than six shots were fired. Only six found their targets, but six was enough. He was hit in the pelvis, the hand, the torso, and the head. But he didn't die right away. He didn't die for hours. He died in the hospital at three in the morning. He died in front of his mom.

So for the first time all summer, I was allowed to be somewhere without my mom or John. I was dropped off at the funeral home and some of the poor white kids were already there. There was Doug, Kenny, Chad, Amber, and a few I didn't recognize. Mathias was there, but not Karina. Even though they were still together, I found myself disappointed.

When I stayed over at their house, I didn't have a chance to notice that David's mom was attractive. Even crying in the pews she was pretty. His sister was young, but you could tell she'd be beautiful when she's older too.

So this pastor told a bunch of lies about how good of a kid David was, then a real sad song played while we lined up to walk by the coffin and look down at his body. Even though he was shot in the head, they managed to fix him up enough for an open casket.

Doug left an eighth of the weed he'd gotten from his brother in David's pocket as he passed, because David was being cremated, and he said David would've wanted to go up in a cloud of marijuana smoke. I heard later that somebody stole it out of the coffin.

* * *

The sun shone through the window above the sink, illuminating dirty dishes and a sponge that needed to be washed months ago. The sliding-glass-door was wide open, because Anne and Alex were in the backyard playing with the dog. They laughed, cars passed, birds chirped, and I held the biggest knife in our kitchen in my right hand, considering how much faster I could've killed the guy on Capitol Hill with a knife like this.

The blade was thick and serrated, and I held it up, gazing into my own eyes in its reflection. I wondered if Karina ever cut herself with knives this big. Anne shrieked merrily, and Alex made some kind of an airplane noise. Then their voices were drowned out by the music of a passing ice cream truck.

I like my own eyes because they're a light brown that you can almost see into like a stained glass marble. I always just assumed the girls who liked me, liked them too.

The ice cream truck must've stopped in front of our yard for a while, because it took a minute for the music to fade out, but when it did, Anne and Alex were silent. I imagined them staring after it as it drove away, wishing they had one of its frozen treats. Then the dog barked, Anne laughed, and they were all back to running and playing happily.

The knife wasn't very sharp. It was the design that allowed it to slice so easily through slabs of meat. You could press down on its blade pretty hard and not cut yourself. So I lowered it to my wrist and thought again about Karina, and whether or not she had cut herself lately.

Karina said she mutilated herself because it made her feel better. I wasn't sure how I felt lately, but as I dragged the blade across my skin, I didn't feel any better or any worse except that it hurt like hell. A little deeper, though, and I knew I wouldn't feel anything. Not for long, at least. So as Anne and Alex laughed just outside the back door, I stood over the sink and sawed into my wrist with a serrated kitchen knife, watching blood fall onto a plate with mold growing on it.

I didn't get to any of my veins because I'm not crazy enough to actually kill myself. Instead, my mom walked into the room, saw what I was doing and slowly took the knife from me. Then she wrapped her arms around me, held my head against her chest and before I could stop them, tears were flowing out of my skull, soaking her shirt.

She didn't speak, just rocked back and forth until I got myself under control. I heard my own voice from far off telling her how sorry I was, as I pulled away and sniffed mucus back into my nose. I didn't know what I was sorry for, or why I was even crying, but I couldn't stop the words from spilling out of me. Her expression was so cold it was more frightening than the one she made when she was pissed, and once I finally stopped rambling, she brought out her cell phone and dialed 911.

* * *

A cop showed up and put me in cuffs again, but this time I was taken to the hospital instead of juvie. I was locked in a room for hours and eventually driven to Fairfax. So I missed the first month of eighth grade and spent my fourteenth birthday in the mental hospital where I met Curtis.

He had a deck of Uno cards that he liked to shuffle near his face because he said they smelled like weed. He dressed like the rich kids at Laventure, but acted like the poor white kids. He definitely would've been one of the poor white kids.

We had this plan to break these wooden chairs and use the legs as weapons to knock out the graveyard staff and escape. This was funny because we could've just as easily jumped the fence during the day without having to hurt anyone.

We told too many people about that plan, anyway, and word got back to the counselors. The entire unit's clothes were taken and we were put in hospital gowns for a week. That's one of the ways they punished you at Fairfax. They made you walk around in hospital gowns. There was this girl named Jewel, who would always try to peek inside mine.

Something else happened while I was there. They made me start taking pills. They said I couldn't leave until they had my meds right. At first I panicked because I thought they were gonna prescribe me the little red ones I used to kill Trouble and Shay. But instead they gave me these green and white capsules that made me real drowsy for the first couple weeks, then turned me into somebody I never knew existed.

Everything was different because I was different. Colors were brighter, and I smiled and I laughed and I didn't break rules because I wanted to get out. I guess I had been depressed and I didn't even know it.

But there was more because I had a new perspective and time to reflect on everything that had happened and to really work out what it was that I wanted out of life. And all I still wanted was Karina. So I decided I would get out of Fairfax and I would have her. It didn't matter how many more people we had to kill, or how far we had to run, as long as we were together because the thing in my chest still danced every time I thought of her. I was in love and somehow I knew that even though we hadn't seen each other all summer, she felt it too.

CHAPTER TWENTY

y mother's never been to an orphanage, but she was raised in foster care because her own parents were alcoholics. She spent some time with her mom in California, but she never calls her "Mom." It's always "Mother." She spent a little time with her dad, too. She calls him "Dad."

Mostly, though, she was with whatever family would take her and her sister in. As far back as I can remember, she's told me stories about her aunts hitting her in the head with hairbrushes, and her uncles climbing into bed with her in the middle of the night. So somehow I've made myself believe she'll sympathize with me when I tell her Secret Harbor's full of S.O.s. That she didn't know that before she sent me here.

A guy named Tim should have "aged out" today. That means he turned eighteen and can't stay any longer. He would've been released to the streets, but he raped a younger boy on the island.

Tim's taller than anybody here and has a moustache. He looks older than eighteen. He talked to me a few times, but I didn't know he's a S.O. If I did, I wouldn't have been so nice to him.

They woke him up early this morning and took him to Anacortes to be arrested. They must've known about it for a while, because the boy he raped left a week ago. So I wonder why Tim didn't.

The boy he raped was his roommate. He used to be my roommate. The boy he raped was Mike, and I can't help but think that if I hadn't beat up Jesus, I would still be living with Mike and this wouldn't have happened. But what I really can't help but think is that when I tell my mom what happened, she'll let me go home. So that's what I do. I stand on the balcony looking out at a pink sunset that hovers over the island across the water, with the group home's cell phone to my ear and beg like a small child asking for a popsicle.

"Please, Mom. You don't know what it's like here."

"Tony, we only get to talk for ten minutes a week. Is this how you wanna spend our call?"

"I just wanna go home."

"So—have you been making any friends there?"

"Are you even listening?"

"Tony—"

"What?"

"I said—"

"No! Listen to me, damn it! Can't you just hear me out? Don't you even care what I have to say? Or am I just the kid you can afford to get rid of? Not Anne or Alex though. Oh no, God forbid you'd ever send them away."

"Tony, stop it."

And because I feel the floodgates trembling against my tears, I just say, "What? Stop what?"

She raises her voice, says, "Stop playing the victim all the damn time! You don't know the first thing about suffering, you hear me? You did this to your freakin' self and you know it! Now you're gonna have to deal with the consequences of your actions. You're gonna sit in there, and you're gonna think about the things and the people who matter to you. And maybe you'll figure out you didn't have it so bad at home after all."

"Home?" I yell into the receiver to keep from crying. "Ha! I don't have a home! I don't even have a family! I don't have a mom, that's for sure. Just some bitter schizo who sent me away to live on an island full of rapists because she's mad at the world for her own childhood!"

Her voice could have emasculated Hulk, as she snaps, "What the hell did you just say to me?" and I picture her eyes bulging out of her head.

"You heard me!" I hold the iPhone out in front of me like a mirror and scream at it, because I want to throw it onto the ground and smash it into a hundred pieces, then stuff them all down my mother's throat. "You think you can take your own problems out on me! Like it's my fault no one wanted you when you were a kid!"

My heart's beating so fast, I'm yelling so loud, and my body's so tense I know I couldn't get myself under control if I wanted. So I don't see a staff member, whose name is Cindy, walk through the door. I don't even know she's there until she touches my shoulder and says, "Tony, give it to me."

But I shrug away, take a step back and yell, "I wanna kill you Mom! You hear me? I wish I could tie a rope around your neck and watch the life drain out of you! You think there's something wrong with me? Look at you! If there's anything wrong with me, it's your fault! You did this to me!"

Now Cindy's yelling over me, "Tony! Tony! Give me the phone!" She has grey hair, but a nice smile. She's usually nice, and I want to be nice back, but I can't. So I cuss at her and yell at the phone some more. The screen displays a start menu, though, because the line's dead. It's been dead. My mother hung up a while ago.

Cindy glances back over her shoulder just as Mountain Bob runs out. Mountain Bob's tall and skinny with shoulder length grey hair. They call him Mountain Bob because he lived in the mountains before he worked at Secret Harbor. He says, "Everything okay?"

I tell him everything's cool, and hand the phone to Cindy. So I didn't get my full ten-minute call this week.

* * *

Kyle's only thirteen and likes to wear black clothes. He arrived at Secret Harbor yesterday. Sergio moved out a few days ago, and they put Kyle in my room. I think I'll like him, because he was probably one of the poor white kids at his school. He's short, has brown hair, and plays rock music on an electric guitar with no amplifier. Kyle's cool so far, only he used to run away to Capitol Hill, so he talks a lot about his boy Turtle, who's locked up for a murder that happened in an alley last year. I told him I haven't been to Seattle since I was real young.

My digital alarm clock picks up a few radio stations out here, and at night we listen to music quietly and lay in our beds talking with the light out. I don't think he's a S.O., but I've found myself hoping he doesn't make a move on me like Sergio did. He hasn't though. Instead, he asks questions like, "Have you ever killed someone?" and of course, I lie, tell him I haven't.

He says, "Don't ever do it, bro. It'll haunt you the rest of your life. I know cause I did it once, and there isn't a night I go to sleep where I don't see the guy's face. Wanna know how?"

"How what?" I ask.

"How I did it."

"How you killed him?"

"Yeah."

"Uh, okay. Sure. How'd you do it?"

"Mercury. You know what that is?"

"The planet?"

"No, not the planet. Mercury. It's liquid metal, and it's highly poisonous. They used to put it in those glass thermometers that they stick up babies' asses. I don't know if they still use them in babies' asses actually, but they definitely used to. My mom had a few in the house, so I broke them open and poured the mercury into a gel capsule. I told this guy it was E."

"E?" I ask.

"Yeah, ecstasy. It was this guy named Trip, who turned out to be a rat. He took E all the time, so it was easy to get him to take the mercury pill. That's what addiction does to people, know what I mean?"

Kyle says he understands addiction because before coming to Secret Harbor, he lived on the streets and stuck needles into his arms every day. Of all his stories, this one I believe because he has the markings to prove it. Not just that, but he might be a little brain damaged from the drugs. When he speaks, he usually makes this weird duckface, that looks like he's chewing on the inside of his cheek.

Kyle's smart though, at least that's what he says.

"I'm borderline genius. That means my IQ's just under genius level. They tested me in juvie."

So we get to talking and I tell him about Karina and for some reason I end up telling him how much I love her, and when he hears her name, he sings, "Karina— Karina—" then laughs and says, "But that's not love, dude. That sounds like infatuation to me."

"What's that?"

"What you're describing. You're infatuated with this chick. You don't love her."

"What the hell does infatuated mean?"

"You know when all you think about is another person, and you just wanna be with them all the time, and they drive you freaking crazy? That's not love. It means you're obsessed with her. And maybe she's obsessed with you too. Who knows? Either way it isn't healthy."

So I tell him about the feeling I get in my chest whenever I touch her, and how it dances inside me like a flame in the wind. I tell him I'd do anything just to be with her. I ask how that's not love.

He says, "Because, man, love's a verb."

"A what?"

"It's an action. It's something you do, not a feeling you get. You'll get it someday, man. Who knows? Maybe someday you two'll fall in love for real." So I guess Kyle might actually be smart. Or maybe not. Maybe he's a presumptuous moron who needs to mind his own business. Either way, I still kinda like him. I tell him it's getting late, and I'm gonna get some sleep.

Then I roll over and lay awake for another hour.

* * *

Dear Karina,

I miss you too. I don't really know what to say, because you're there, and I'm here and our lives are so much different right now. I'd tell you about this place, but I guess you can just go to the website and learn all about it. I'm sure it's all lies, though, because if they told the truth this place would probably be shut down.

Yeah, I remember Jaime. He's a douche. If you see him again, tell him I said he's a douche-waffle. You think life sux out there? lol. I'll trade you for a day, bro. Actually, this place might not be so bad if you were here with me. They're making me take pills again, and I hate it, so I don't actually take them. I just hide them in my cheek and spit them back out when they're not looking. My roommate likes to crush up the Adderall and snort it. I did it a few times with him, and it kept us up almost all night.

They give us this snack here at night, kinda like juvie, but better. It's usually a small pack of Graham-Crackers, and a paper cup with water in it. Last night, I was walking to my room, and for some reason I had the urge to throw the water in my own face, so I did and my roommate was laughing his ass off. Crazy, huh?

I guess you're right. It would have been stupid to kill my mom. I just want to be with you I guess. I promise I'm gonna get out of here as soon as I can, but will you wait for me until then? I love you too.
Tony.

* * *

Sam Kitchen speaks with a little bit of a lisp. It's not very prominent, and you can only hear it if you listen closely. He has a raspy voice, dishwater hair and zits you could play connect-the-dots with all over his face. He's tall, and smiles a lot, even though his teeth are yellow.

Donny talks trash about him whenever he's not around (and sometimes when he is), because he's awkward and even though Donny seems young and sweet, he can be a bit of a bully. It's mid-afternoon, and a few of us are sitting around a table in the common area, playing a card game called O.G. This has been the most popular game in every facility I've been to, but the rules are always different for some reason.

Sometimes we play for wormy-dogs. Wormy-dogs are when a guy sits down and drags his butt across the floor like a dog with worms. For instance, if we bet six wormy-dogs, the losers would have to drag their butts across the floor six times, while the whole room laughed at them.

Sometimes we play for dead-bugs. Dead bugs means that every time the winner sprays you with an imaginary can of bug spray, you have to fall over and play dead.
Sometimes we play for push-ups.

Today, we're just playing to kill time, because time's all we have at Secret Harbor. I've been told that once the summer's over, school will start again, and the gym teacher's a twenty-three-year-old girl who looks fine in yoga-pants. So I guess that's something to look forward to.

Sam Kitchen's won just about every game, which doesn't say much about him, because O.G.'s all about luck. Donny's wearing what I've come to recognize as his mischievous look.

A heavy-set black kid named Jason sits next to me, and for some reason he slams his knuckles against the wood every time he sets a card on the table. Jason's from Texas, and I'm guessing he's a S.O., because all the guys from out-of-state have turned out to be S.O.s so far. I'm guessing they're sent here specifically for Secret Harbor's sex offender program.

Jason slams a card down on the table, and it echoes through the common area. He says, "What's up now, fool?"

Sam Kitchen grins, puts a card on top of his, then exhales a cloud of hot air into his face.

Jason exclaims, "What the hell, man? Get your stinkin' breath out my face!"

Sam says, "Whatever. I'm not the one whose breath smells like his ass," as Donny lays a card on top of his.

"Then what's that smell like? Damn, fool. At least you could brush your teeth once in a while."

"Maybe you should brush your ass."

"That don't even make no sense."

I lay a card on top of Donny's.

Donny twitches, smiles, says, "Hey Sam, why'd you kill the baby rabbits out on the farm?"

"Whatever, Donny." Sam struggles to contain a smile that stretches almost instantly from ear to ear. "Play your card."

"I already did."

"Then whose turn is it?"

"Yours. So why'd you kill the rabbits?"

"I didn't!"

"Yeah, you did. You even told me you did, so don't start lying now."

Donny looks at me, and seeing the question in my eyes, says, "Tyrrell's mom donated five baby rabbits to the farm, and Sam killed them all, one-by-one."

"No I didn't!" Sam snaps, begs me with his eyes to believe him. "It wasn't one-by-one. I accidentally unplugged the heater and they all froze to death."

"Yeah," Donny makes bunny-ears with his fingers. "Accidentally. Just like the sheep he killed a few months ago."

"That wasn't me."

"We gonna play, or what?" Jason asks.

"Yeah." Sam places a card on top of mine. Jason instantly slams one over it. Sam tells Donny, "Just because you're a freaking psycho doesn't mean I am. Keep your sick fantasies to yourself. You probably killed that sheep."

"I'm not even in the farm class. How would I of killed it? Everyone in that class knows you did it. It wasn't an accident because the sheep was strangled." Donny's eyes shine like flashlights as he speaks. He's clearly having fun.

"Whatever, Donny. Play your card."

But Donny doesn't have a card to play, so he has to draw from the deck until a usable one appears. He curses as card after card comes up duds, and I just sit quietly, wondering why the hell someone would want to strangle a sheep.

CHAPTER TWENTY-ONE

A boy was slammed this morning for refusing to take his meds. They held him down and pushed the pill down his throat. I'm not sure it was legal, but who's there to tell?

I was just headed to my room to pull my own meds from my cheek, when and I heard the screaming behind me. I turned back to see Anthony and Jesus on top of the smallest kid here, but I didn't stay to watch. Kyle told me later that they force fed him, as he crushed up my Adderall and cut two lines with a Starbucks gift card.
He asked if I wanted one.

I thought about Karina. I've been here a month now, and she hasn't written again. I wondered if she still loves me.

Then I told him sure, I'd do one.

* * *

It's my first time going to the activities building and we have to walk along a long gravel trail and endure the aroma of manure to get there. There are six of us and one staff member. She's the blond girl who helped slam Donny my first day at Secret Harbor, and she's wearing leggings and walking ahead of the group, so we're staring like we have an infection and the antibiotics are in her pants. Her name's Jen, and the only guys who don't like her, don't like girls. Her jacket's some tan color and her hair's pulled into a tight ponytail.

It's past sunset, but not quite dark. Creepy, but not terrible. Jen's hips seem to be engaged in a dance off, because they take turns jumping with every step she takes. They move to the rhythm of the waves crashing against the shore in the distance.

As I watch her walk, I wonder why the night's never troublesome in the city where people are murdered every day. Sam Kitchen nudges me, whispers, "You see that?" He looks from me to Jen's backside. She turns around, locking eyes with me and I feel my ears burn as I ignore Sam and look toward the sound of crickets singing in the woods.

We've never talked before, and I've made a point not to get caught staring at her. The longer I'm here, though, the harder it gets to not look. She says something to one of the other guys about some new movie she saw last week, and he responds in a tone that suggests Santa Claus will visit Secret Harbor this year.

Guys joke as we pass the Macdonald cottage, where a small handful of boys get to live unstaffed. They've all been on the island over a year and earned the privilege through good behavior. Like Jerry Warden told my mom the day he talked her into giving me away, everything at Secret Harbor is incentive-based.

Once we're past the Mac cottage, we walk by the farm and the smell of manure intensifies. On our right is the field where sheep and emus live. To the left, llamas. I know because Donny's pointed the entire landscape out to me from the balcony. I don't see any animals tonight, though, so I assume they're tucked away in the barn.

The activities building is a shack at the end of the trail. It's nothing impressive because it was probably built by boys at Secret Harbor a long time ago. A few years back, John built a playhouse in our backyard that was nicer than this. The activities building looks like it might blow over in a windstorm. There's a tool shed next to it that isn't any better.

Jen unlatches a padlock, opens the door, and disappears into the dark. A second later the inside illuminates and she reappears in the doorway. The way she's standing— leaning against the wall with her hip thrust out—it looks like she's striking a pose. She offers her hand like she wants someone to set something in her palm and says, "Thou art worthy to enter the mighty cave of wonders."

I get the impression Jen's not difficult to get along with and I catch the scent of some flowery perfume as I walk past her, but it's quickly overpowered by the fragrance of wood chips and skunk. So that's what it smells like inside the activities building.

The first thing you see is an old sofa, like the one Trouble and Shay were sitting on when I left them to die under the bridge. There's a door to the right, and one on the far wall next to the sofa. Most of the guys pile through that door. Only Sam and I hang back. He watches Jen as she shuts the door, then Jen glances at us and smiles bashfully. She puts her head down and trots past, into the room with everyone else.

Once she's gone, and the door's closed behind her, Sam smiles, says, "I saw that. Don't be looking at my girl, Tony."

I can understand why Donny doesn't like this kid. Something about him isn't quite right in a way that leaves you feeling dirty after he talks to you. Like you just touched a spider or something. I force a laugh and ask what there is to do here.

He waves to the door on the right. "That's the movie room. They got DVDs in there. Everyone usually goes to the game room, though. Especially when Jen's here, cause she likes video games."

"They have video games here?"

"They're all old and outdated. Like really old. Like the original PlayStations. You'll see if you go in there. I'm about to watch a movie though, so chow." He salutes me and disappears into the room on the right, which I see when the door opens, is pitch-dark.

So I step into the game room as rap music comes to life from one of four TVs, positioned in front of two couches that sit back to back. A black kid plops down with a PlayStation controller in his hands and changes the song. Three guys sit together on the other couch. One of them is Casey. Jen sits on the armrest, smiling at me as I shut the door.

There's a small table with a chessboard and two metal chairs, so I sit down in one and set up the pieces, thinking of how my mom taught me to play when I was real young, and how she would smile deviously as she beat me as fast as she could. Then a pair of black leggings appear across from me as Jen takes a seat. She smiles and says, "Wanna play?"

Up close I see that her eyes are light brown—almost golden—and I notice how pink her lips are. Jen's so pretty that my heart starts racing, so instead of speaking, I just nod.

She says, "I'm Jen, by the way," extends her hand.

I accept it, and her fingertips brush my palm lightly when she pulls it back.

I take a deep breath and try not to flush, try to keep my voice from cracking as I say, "Nice to meet you." But my ears are burning.

Carly Sims's best friend in the fourth grade was a fat black girl named Amy. Amy told me one day at recess that Carly liked me, and even though Carly wasn't popular because she wasn't rich, she was real pretty. Amy said Carly wanted to go out with me, so I told her to tell Carly that sounded fine. And even though plenty of girls had kissed me already, Carly made me so nervous that Amy had to dare me before I'd kiss her. For some reason, that's how I feel with Jen sitting across from me in the activities building.

She says, "Yeah. Likewise. White or black?"

"What?"

"You wanna be white or black?" She giggles. "I mean in the game." Behind her, Casey drills into a PlayStation controller with both thumbs.

He moves the controller like a steering wheel, and the other two guys keep looking over like something that belonged to them just walked away to play chess with me. I tell Jen I don't care, so she chooses black and I get to go first.

"Your name's Tony, right?"

"Yeah. Tony Carpenter, or whatever." I push a pawn, and without thinking about her move, she mimics mine.

"Well, good to finally meet you, Tony Carpenter or whatever. You like playing chess?"

"I don't know. I guess."

"You guess? Well have you been playing long?"

"Yeah. I used to play with my mom when I was a kid. I haven't really played much since then, but she taught me how the pieces move."

I advance another pawn, and like there's a mirror in the middle of the board, so does she. She asks me if I'm any good.

"Not really. My mom just liked to beat me all the time instead of teaching me how to win."

Jen covers her mouth as she chuckles, and I can't help but laugh too. Even though she looks so much like the spoiled kids at Laventure, I can't help but think she's probably real nice, and like magic, I don't feel nervous anymore. Not even a little, and it's the strangest thing, so I say, "Yeah, she had a way of teaching that might not've worked all the time. She taught me how to fight that way too. She'd just slap the hell out of me and tell me to fight back, but I couldn't because she was just hitting me over and over before I could even throw a punch."

At this, Jen stops laughing and looks at me like I've just told her about the baby bird I drowned in the kitchen sink. She says, "Seriously?"

"No. I mean, yeah, but not like that. I'm not saying she abused me or anything. I was having some problems at school and she thought I should learn to fight, so you know—"

"Oh! Gotcha. Still, though—she didn't like punch you or whatever, did she?"

"No. No. Nothing like that. She didn't even slap me hard. It was just like, well, you know, teaching me to move fast, and uh—"

"Hey Jen!" One of the guys calls from the couch. "You ready, girl? You're up."

"I'm good," she says in a sing-song voice without looking back. "I'm gonna go ahead and play chess. Thanks though." She says my mom's lessons must've worked, because she heard what I did to Jesus. I just look down, and she says, "No. I'm not saying you did anything wrong. Or, well, you know what I mean. I'm just saying clearly you can move fast, right? Speaking of moves—" She motions with her eyes to the board.

"Oh yeah." I bring out one of my knights.

Jen copies my play, then asks where I'm from. So I tell her.

She asks how old I am. So I tell her.

She asks if I have a girlfriend. So I stutter, but I tell her. And she laughs again.

And the sound of her laugh travels from my ears, down my torso, and reverberates in my stomach. It feels real good, but it also makes me want to either cry or vomit. I think if I'm not careful I'll develop a crush on her, which wouldn't be right considering I love Karina. So I take the opportunity to tell her about Karina as we play. Stories start flowing out of me like my mouth is some kind of a faucet, or a word-waterfall, and she listens seemingly entranced by everything I have to say.

I don't mean to ramble, but the way her eyes shine, and the way she nods at just the right times are like a throttle revving the sentences out of me. Eventually, she stops mimicking my moves, but it's obvious she's throwing the game. Trying to lose on purpose. So I think I must've bored her, and she wants the game to end.

There are only a few pieces remaining anyway, and all but one are mine, so I stop talking about Karina and our adventures, and start chasing her king from black squares, to red squares.

Jen says Karina must be a special girl, because she can tell I love her a lot.

I say, "Yeah. Yeah, I do," and checkmate her in the corner of the board. This is the first game of chess I've ever won, and now Jen can get up and leave if she wants.

But instead of leaving, she begins rearranging the pieces and says, "Again?"

And again, I beat her. Not because I'm good at chess or smart—I'm neither of those things—but because she's letting me win. Jen's smart though. I figure this out pretty quick. She's twenty-two, and she tells me she's studying to become a child psychologist.

"Just one more year and I'll have my B.A."

I'm not sure what a B.A. is, except it must be whatever degree comes after an A.A. I tell her, "Good for you," and feel really stupid the second the words have left me. Like one of the douchy kids at Laventure who wear expensive clothes and tell girls whatever they think they wanna hear.

Jen just smiles and says, "Yeah. Thanks. I'm pretty excited, actually. What about you?"

"What do you mean?"

"Well what do you wanna be?"

I tell her I don't know, maybe an assassin or something, and we both laugh.

Jen and I talk the rest of the evening, until it's time to head back, and I end up telling Kyle all about it. I say, "I wonder why she let me win."

He just grins and tells me chicks are weird and there's no point trying to understand them.

I say, "I think I like her, bro."

"Yeah? What about Karina?"

"I don't know. I mean, I do, but—I don't know. It's different. Like with Jen it's not sexual. That's not what I mean. I just think she's a really cool person, and I like talking to her. Like we could be really tight friends or whatever."

Kyle's grin morphs into a full-blown smile, and he says, "See? I told you you'd get it someday. Now you know what real love is."

CHAPTER TWENTY-TWO

I loved Karina, and that was just that. So my first day back at school, during lunch, I pulled her into the same hallway we stood in when we decided to return to Seattle to kill Trouble and Shay, and I told her I didn't want to live without her.

She stood with her back to the door so I could see the grey sky over her shoulders as she looked down at her feet like she had done something terribly wrong. But her eyes were big and doe-like. She said, "That's not why you did it, is it?"

"Did what?"

"You tried to kill yourself."

"I wasn't trying to kill myself. I was just cutting."

"Well, I hope you weren't doing it because I told you I did it. I felt hella bad when I heard. Look, I haven't even been doing it lately. I mean, it's been like a month, you know?"

I said, "Yeah." Then I lied and told her I didn't do it because of her, but I thought about her a lot while I was away, and I missed her like crazy, and she needed to break up with Mathias because I was in love with her.

"Tony—"

"I'm serious. I know you know. And I know you feel it too. I'm so in love with you it hurts, Karina. I think we're meant for each other."

"Tony, look what happens when we're together."

"I don't care! I don't care about anything but you, and I'll do anything to be with you. I'll do everything we already did over and over again as long as you're with me, because I know I'll never feel this way about anyone again.

"And neither will you, Karina. Don't you feel it in your stomach when we're together? It's like something dancing inside you, isn't it? You know what that something is? It's the part of your soul that needs mine to be complete. Know how I know? Because I have it too."

But she just kept staring down at her shoes until my heart almost exploded inside my ribcage. Then, when I thought I would never breathe again, her eyes scaled my body and locked with mine, and a single tear ran down the side of her nose. She blinked a few times, and said, "What are you saying, Tony?"

"I'm saying I wanna be with you. I wanna be with you, and I'll do whatever it takes to make that happen."

"But are you sure?"

"Of course I'm sure. I've never been surer of anything in my life. I love you, Karina Vasquez."

And somehow, none of this sounded cheesy to me. It must not have sounded stupid to her either because she sniffed, blinked back more tears, and told me we needed to do it right this time. She needed to break up with Mathias.

Her words were like electricity that shot from my ears, through my whole body and caused every hair sticking out of every inch of my skin to stand straight up. I lost control and threw my arms around her waist, but she pressed her hands against my chest, turned her head like I had garlic on my breath, and shoved me away.

"No. Stop. Not yet. Not till I do it."

"Do what?"

"Not till I break up with Mathias. I told you it has to be done right this time."

"Okay. Yeah. Whatever. When are you gonna do that, though?"

"I don't know, bro. Today."

"Let's run away again."

"What?"

"Let's leave. We can get further this time. We can go all the way to California or something. Don't you have family down there?"

She said, "Yeah. I have a lot of family in L.A. Like my grandma and my cousins."

"Then let's go. After school. Like as soon as you break up with Mathias. We don't even have to go home. We can hit the freeway and start hitchhiking, and just keep going till we're in Cali. You down, or what?"

It was a stupid question, though, because even though she'd just made me beg her to be with me, Karina was always down. So after a brief pause for dramatic effect, she pursed her lips and nodded. Then we went to the cafeteria and she pulled Mathias outside while I sat and listened to all my poor white friends talk about how much they hated the rich kids and the cholos and the nerds. But the whole time, I watched out the window, as Mathias's hair blew in the wind. He kept looking in at me like he wanted to cut me open and eat my insides—to eat the part of me that burned for his girlfriend.

Finally, he laughed, shook his head, and just walked back into the cafeteria, mad-dogging me as he approached. He slammed both fists down on the table, sat down, and our whole crew fell silent. I got ready to fight, because I'd seen Mathias pissed before and I knew he liked to fight. He just laughed, though, and said, "Go on dawg, she's out there waiting for you. Go enjoy my sloppy seconds. She's freaky, too. But just remember: all those tricks she knows—I taught her all that."

So I stood up and went outside to enjoy Mathias's sloppy seconds.

* * *

I'd thought about sex every day for as long as I could remember, but I was nervous as hell when I finally lost my virginity to Karina on her mom's bed.

We didn't wait until after school. I met her outside the cafeteria, she said, "Come on, bro," and we left just like that. We didn't hit the freeway either. Her stepdad was in jail and her mom was at work, so we went to her house first and smoked some weed she found behind a chrome picture frame hanging in her mom's room.

The doctors at Fairfax told me not to smoke, drink, or do any drugs or it would react with my meds, and I think they were right because after just one hit I was more loaded than I had ever been. I sprawled out on Karina's mom's bed, with my arms spread wide and just stared up at the ceiling. Then she crawled on top of me like a spider and stared down into my eyes as if there were a coded message in them.

Karina's house was dark. I mean the walls were white, and the doors were brown or whatever, but even with the lights on it always seemed dim inside. That's what I was thinking about as her lips curved upward so subtly that you wouldn't have noticed unless you were watching real close. Then she kissed me, and I felt myself sinking into the mattress.

The sheets were white, but like the walls and the popcorn ceiling, they were faded and smoke-stained. They smelled like musk. Karina smelled like Karina and tasted like cigarettes and spearmint gum. Her body pressed against mine in a way it hadn't before and the next thing I knew her shirt was coming off. Then mine. Then we did it and it didn't last long, but when we were done I lay on my back with her head resting over my chest and she asked if I was hungry.

I told her I was good.

She rubbed my stomach and said, "I wanted to give you my virginity so bad. Did you know that?"

I said I hadn't known.

She said, "That night in Damien's tent. I wanted you to just take it, and you would've been my first. I know I told you I wasn't a virgin, but I was. I mean besides what my dad did to me, but that doesn't count. I said I wasn't so you wouldn't be afraid to make a move. You didn't, though, and I was just like, What's wrong with me? You know?"

I told her there was nothing wrong with her, and she was beautiful, and I kissed the top of her head. But I was thinking, If she was a virgin then, then Mathias must've been her first, and in my head, I heard him say, I taught her all that.

* * *

Karina left her bedroom window unlocked and we went down to the river to sit on the same log we'd sat on the last time I told her how I felt about her. She leaned her head on my shoulder and we watched the sun set. Then, when it grew cold, she put my hand between her legs to keep it warm.

Fortunately, it didn't end up raining until one in the morning, when I waited in her driveway as she crawled in her window and came out the front door with a set of keys.

We drove off in her mom's old, beat-up car. So Karina really could drive.

We went to her gay friend Marvin's house because Marvin's mom worked nights waitressing at some strip club. Marvin was sixteen and dressed like a raver, with these weird, rainbow covered gloves that went all the way up his arms. He lived a couple towns over in Sedro Woolley, and I guess he just stayed up all night playing video games.

When he answered the door he looked at Karina, then me, and said, "Hey bitch. Who's the bobblehead?"

Karina said, "This is my boyfriend, Tony."

Marvin blinked a few times, then said, "I hate you."

"Hate you too, boo."

"Well don't just stand out in the rain like a couple of disabled lawn gnomes. Either come in, or piss off."

So we stepped into this tiny two-bedroom house and watched him play Xbox, while he talked about all the guys he'd hooked up with lately. Karina told him we were headed to California and he said, "Sounds like fun. Can I come?"

She looked at me. I just shrugged. She said, "Sure."

And the three of us drove back to Mount Vernon just before sunrise to drop the car off in Karina's driveway. Then we went to the truck stop for coffee. Marvin paid.

* * *

We caught a ride with a trucker who couldn't take us any further than Seattle, and I started panicking because that's the last place I wanted to be. But Marvin still had a little money, so he paid for us to take public transit buses all the way to Tacoma. It was more expensive than I would've expected since we had to transfer so many times and the Tacoma buses were a different company, so they wouldn't take our Seattle Metro transfers. By the time we arrived, it was almost dark, and Marvin was broke.

We walked around outside the city for a few hours, and Marvin kept slowing down and saying, "Oow Tony! Nice ass!" It really annoyed me. Not because I had a problem with gay people, or I thought he was coming on to me, but because I knew he was just trying to make me uncomfortable.

Sometime well past midnight, we walked by a twenty-four-hour grocery store and Marvin smiled deviously at Karina. He said, "We could Triple C."

Karina said, "We could Triple C., couldn't we?" I asked what the hell Triple C. was.

Marvin said. "Wait. Don't tell me you don't know what Triple C. is? Karina, you haven't popped his cherry yet?"

She said she hadn't had a chance because my mom was a dick and I wasn't allowed out of the house.

He said, "That settles it, then. We're doing it."

So we went inside the store and Karina and Marvin boosted three boxes of cold medication and a Pepsi. Then we all ate an entire box, because Triple C. was supposed to make you hallucinate or whatever.

After I swallowed all sixteen pills, I asked if we could overdose and die. Marvin said, "Oh yeah. You're gonna die tonight, Tony. You're gonna die and be reborn a new person. Just enjoy the process and try not to panic." So we walked into downtown Tacoma and roamed the city streets waiting for the drugs to kick in and I wondered what kind of effect they might have combined with my meds.

* * *

"I'm dying! Karina, I'm gonna die! Do something."

Marvin lay on his back in the middle of the street, his arms and legs reaching for the sky, waving like seaweed under water. He had warned me for the last hour not to freak out once I started feeling the effects of the Triple C., and in the end, he's the one who couldn't handle it.

I just stared down at him, and because I felt the cold air against so much of my eyes, I knew they were open wider than they should've been. Karina crouched next to Marvin, attempting to pull him to his feet, but he started crying, said, "Just leave me, bitch! Leave me to die. I deserve it after everything I've done! I'm a bad person!"

"Marvin, come on, bro. Get up."

"I hate you!"

"I hate you too, boo. Now get outta the road before someone calls the cops."

"I don't wanna go to jail, Karina! Don't let them take me to jail, please! Just let me die. Just go already and let me die in peace, bitch!"

It all happened so randomly it almost hadn't seemed real. I'm not sure what came first, but the world began dancing around me, colors became brighter, I saw tracers, Karina spewed up red vomit, she kissed me, it started sprinkling, and Marvin was in the road crying. I'd never experienced anything like the high from the Triple C. It probably should have scared the hell out of me how intense it was, but I couldn't feel anything, let alone fear. All I could do was stare, and breathe, and walk, and speak every now and then.

Karina said, "Marvin, please. You're gonna get us caught."

Marvin cried, "Go! Go! Go! Go! Just go, damn it! I don't wanna go to California! I just wanna go home!

Leave me alone, Karina! Leave me here and let me die, bitch! Please!"

So finally Karina stood up, took my hand and said, "Come on, bro. Let's get the hell outta here," and then we ran away as Marvin continued to cry in the middle of the road.

CHAPTER TWENTY-THREE

I woke up shivering under a bridge with Karina in my arms. We were huddled together into a ball like a potato-bug on a slab of cement. It was still dark, but the sound of traffic passing on the freeway announced the morning. Everything after we left Marvin felt like nothing more than a foggy dream. The memories were vague and played in short clips that couldn't have been real.

In them, I was a ghost, wandering back roads with Karina by my side. I kept saying things like, "Karina, I think we're dead. I don't think we survived the night. I think we overdosed." And "This is it. We're just walking. Maybe we'll be walking for all eternity."

Karina stirred in my arms. She groaned softly, and tears built up inside my skull because I loved her so much. Her eyes popped open and immediately locked with mine. She had never been so perfect.

Above us, cars continued to buzz past, one after another. Every one of them made my brain tingle like it were being tickled by a spider. Karina asked if I was okay.

I said, "I don't know if I should've took those pills with my medication."

"That's right! They put you on meds, didn't they?"

"Yeah."

"Did you bring them with you?"

I told her no.

"Then they'll wear off, eventually. All the drugs you've already done'll probably speed up the process. It might be rough coming down off whatever they got you on though. Did you sleep?"

"Yeah. I think."

"You think?"

"I mean, I just woke up."

"It's freakin' cold out here, bro. Let's get up and get moving."

So that's what we did. Since we were already at the freeway, we slid onto the ramp, stuck our thumbs out, and hitched a ride before the sun came up.

* * *

There's a bridge that runs over a river from Vancouver, Washington, to Portland, Oregon. Crossing that bridge was like leaping over a mountain for us, because it meant we'd made it out of Washington. We were one step closer to freedom. We caught three separate rides and landed in downtown Portland late afternoon.

A homeless kid named Deuce showed us where the soup kitchen was, and everyone in line for dinner seemed to be staring at us. Deuce had a star tattooed under his left eye, and he was dating a real pretty dark-haired girl named Bunny. She wore all black, and a lot of eye makeup. After we ate, we stood outside the soup kitchen, and Bunny said, "People are gonna try and tax you because you're newbies. That just means no one knows you yet. I'll sponsor you, though. So if anyone tries to tax you, just tell em you're

Bunny's newbies and they'll leave you alone. You'll see I got a lot a respect out here. What's your names anyway?"

Because we couldn't use Hollow and Pixie ever again, Karina said, "I'm Kitty, and this is—"

"Trouble," I said.

Karina looked at me like my face was made of maggots.

Bunny said, "Well there's already a Trouble out here, so we're gonna have to think a something different."

I asked what it meant to get taxed.

"It happens to everyone. It doesn't mean people don't like you, though. It just means they don't know you yet. You gotta earn your respect out here. I got taxed when I was a newbie. So did Deuce. Right Deuce?"

Deuce smiled and told her she was right.

Bunny said, "They'll try to take something of yours. I mean it's not like they're robbing you. They won't take everything. Just something you have that they want. Once you've been taxed once, you're off limits. So just tell em I taxed you already. That's what it means when you say you're my newbies."

I told Bunny I could just fight if someone tried to rob me.

She said, "You're not getting it little man. They're not robbing you. They're taxing you cause you're new. And it wouldn't be a good idea to try and fight. Some ah these people out here are crazy. They're killers. And even if you manage to win, no one'll respect you after that. It's a wrap. You'll just get eighty-sixed. That means—"

"We know what eighty-sixed means," Karina said. "So we just say we're Bunny's newbies? Does that mean we belong to you?"

Bunny's eyes scanned Karina's body from head to toe, then did a double take. She said, "You two are cute. I guess I could make you mine."

We all laughed, and they told us where a shelter was where we could sleep tonight. Then we parted ways because Bunny and Deuce said they needed to go somewhere to pick up clean needles. About a half hour later, it started snowing.

* * *

There's this train that runs through Portland called, "the max." You're supposed to pay to ride, but nobody watches the doors, so it's easy to just get on. That's what the street-kids in Portland do when it snows. So Karina and I followed a group of them onto the train and ended up at a mall called, "The Lloyd Center."

There was a blond girl who must've been in her early twenties, but she was my height and had no teeth. She probably would've been pretty if she weren't toothless. She kept staring at me and smiling, and I could see her tongue between her gums.

Karina kept taking my hand, and leaning against me, until we went our separate ways, then she said she didn't like that other girl. I was pretty happy she was jealous, because it meant maybe she did love me.

We stashed our backpacks outside in some bushes, then went into these stores in the Lloyd Center and stole pockets full of jewelry with labels that said, "sterling silver," and "cubik zirconia." Some of the rings and necklaces were worth over a hundred dollars, so we kept the price tags on them so we'd be able to sell them somewhere.

At one point, we were sitting in the food court and some guy wearing a red hat walked up, set a ten dollar kill down on the table and walked off.

* * *

It snowed all day, and into the evening, but the snow didn't stick, so it was as cold as hell. But it wasn't pretty. Before we left the Lloyd Center, Karina filled a plastic bag with half-smoked cigarettes from the ashtray and put it in her hoody pocket. Then we caught the max back downtown.

Bunny and Deuce weren't at the shelter they told us about, but they were right. The place let us in. They didn't even ask our names like the Thomas House had. They just gave us two blankets and said we could sleep wherever we wanted.

It was a big room—the size of the cafeteria at Laventure—and people were strewn about everywhere on the floor. Some were against walls with cell phone chargers plugged into outlets, others were in the middle of the room. Karina and I chose a spot in the corner. We put one blanket down on the wood floor and laid together on it with the other over us.

Some old person who might've been a woman, or might've been a fat guy with long hair lay a few feet from us next to a walker and snored real loud all night.

* * *

They served breakfast at the shelter. During breakfast Karina asked a girl with a Mohawk and a ring through her septum if she knew where we could sell the jewelry.

The girl said, "I should tax you for that jewelry. But I'm not gonna cause you're cute. Come with me after breakfast and I'll see if I can help you out." So after breakfast, we followed her downtown, and met some guy who said he could sell it all and meet back up with us later. It wasn't snowing anymore, but it finally stuck last night, and it was a few inches thick, so being outside was like being in a freezer. Karina gave him all the jewelry and he left with the Mohawk girl and we never saw either of them again.

* * *

A car spun out of control and smashed into a mailbox, but first I asked Karina what she wanted to do with her life.

It was dark, cold, and gloomy. We sat in this gazebo in Portland's town center, smoking cigarette-butts from her baggie and talking about our poor white friends back home, and what they must've been doing right now, and I just asked.

She didn't look at me, just nodded like she'd been expecting the question and said, "I dunno. You?"

"You wanna do me?"

"No." She laughed. "I mean, yeah. Yeah, I do. But that's not what I meant. I don't really know what I wanna do. I guess I just wanna be with you. What about you, though?"

"Same."

"Same?"

"Yeah. I mean, with you though, you know?"

"Yeah. I get it."

Then it happened. Brakes squealed, a horn screamed out and echoed into the night, and we both looked in time to see a red sedan spinning in the road right before it slammed into the mailbox, so we stood up and got out of there before the cops showed up.

* * *

Portland wasn't right for us. Or maybe it was. It didn't matter, because we'd never planned on staying there. So we didn't go back to the shelter that night. Instead we went to the Greyhound station and Karina told people that she and her brother needed money to get to some family function. It only took a couple of hours before we had enough for two tickets into the next town down, but the bus didn't leave until two in the morning.

So we cuddled up on a bench in the station where it was warm and I fell asleep and had a dream about Trouble and Shay choking on their own vomit under a freeway bridge in Seattle.

CHAPTER TWENTY-FOUR

There's a card next to my pillow—a small one—and it stands upright like one of those sandwich board signs. Like a triangular log cabin. Like two playing cards resting against each other.

In baby blue writing, it says, "To Tony."

I sit up, take it, and look inside. All I see are colors, though, because it's too dark to read the writing. Kyle's still asleep, but my curiosity trumps my desire to be courteous, so I crawl to the foot of my bed and flip the light on. Kyle groans, says, "Ugh. Bro, what the hell," but, ignoring him, I read the writing in the card:

Tony,
I had a great time playing chess and talking to you last night. Maybe next time you'll let me win! lol. Hopefully we can do it again soon?
Jen.

It's written in the same baby blue my name is. All but her name. Her name's written in pink. The same color as the hearts that are drawn all over it. She drew blue balloons to go with them.

Kyle stretches and calls me a dickwad as he asks what the hell I'm doing, so I read him the card, and it sounds crazier coming out of my mouth than it did in my head. He just lays propped up on his elbow, shirtless, smiling. I ask him what he thinks it means.

"What do you mean?" he asks.

"I don't know. I mean, what do think she's trying to say?"

"Sounds to me like she's saying she had a good time playing chess and getting to know you."

"She drew hearts on the card."

"I see that. And balloons. Maybe she thinks you're gay."

"Really? You think so?"

"Of course not. You talked to her about your girlfriend for two hours." He yawns, stretches out. "Look man, you're reading too much into it. Chicks draw hearts. They make pretty cards. Jen's a nice girl. Plus, you love Karina, remember?"

"Yeah but—"

"Look Tony, if she likes you, she likes you. Don't stress on it. Let it unfold organically. Take it slow. It'll mean more that way. And if she doesn't like you like that, at least you made a new friend. You can never have too many friends, right? What time does that clock say, anyway?"

I glance at my digital alarm clock and tell him it's 6:03.

"Good God, bud. We don't have to wake up for another two hours. Think we could go ahead and kill the light for a while?"

"Yeah," I say, "sure," and stare down at the card for a while longer before turning the light back off.

* * *

Farmer Dave found a dead emu today. Farmer Dave doesn't look like a farmer, but they call him that because he manages the farm which is also a class for guys who want to learn to be farmers. I'm not one of those guys, but I'm headed with Todd and a group of boys to the activities building this morning and I see Farmer Dave carrying the dead bird like a new bride. It looks like a much bigger version of Boomerang laying limp in my palm.

I keep thinking about the card from Jen. What I don't get is how she snuck into my room and left it by my face without me waking up. I've always been a light sleeper, but I became even more restless after the killing started. Not just that, but as far as I know, Jen wasn't even working graveyard shift. Every time I stepped out to use the restroom, it was the old lady with the knitted hat, reading a book.

Donny's finally a level two, and able to go to the activities building with me, so we go into the movie room and put in some DVD with a really old version of Spiderman. It's pitch dark in the movie room. There's a huge TV mounted to one wall, and couches lining the other three. It feels like a tiny theater.

Donny tells me Sam Kitchen comes in here to play with himself. He says someone walked in and caught him once. At one point, the door opens and Jason joins us. Donny gets Jason to tell me the same story about Sam Kitchen, and we all laugh so loud that Todd pokes his head in and smiles. Everything's cool, though, so he retreats.

Donny says, "Sam killed another animal."

Jason just shakes his head.

I ask Donny if he really thinks Sam did it.

"Of course he did it. That freak kills animals every chance he gets. He probably screws em first, then kills em so they can't tell."

Jason says, "That's sick."

Donny twitches, smiles mischievously, says, "Actually, he probably kills em, then screws em." He stands up and begins to act out the scenario. He's Sam Kitchen and the armrest on the couch is some poor dead animal. "Oh yeah! Oh yeah! You like that you dirty-birdie? Yeah you do, don't you? Whistle my name! Say pretty-bird!"

Jason stands up, says, "Something wrong with y'all," and exits the movie room.

* * *

My mind is a messy place, like a trailer-park that's been hit by a tornado, or a stack of papers in a gust of wind, and Karina stomps among the mess most of the time in nothing but her black Nikes and ankle-high socks. I wonder what she's doing. Why she still hasn't written again. If she's decided to let her hair grow. Her mom tells her all the time that nice Mexican girls don't wear their hair like boys. Karina looks good with short hair though. I can't picture her with a ponytail, because her head's a little big for her body, so her pixie cut balances that.

The Sea Wolf arrives mid-afternoon, and Mountain Bob approaches in the common area and hands me a plastic grocery bag, and a case of grape soda. He says, "This was in the office waiting for you today. From your folks, I guess. Go ahead and drop it off in your room and come on back."

I glance into the bag, and see chocolate bars, cupcakes, and other sweets. I've never seen anyone get a food package, and I'm guessing neither has anybody else, because every eye in the vicinity is trained hungrily on me as I make my way toward the dorms.

Chris, who dresses like a cowboy and plays the bass guitar, meets me in the hall, says, "Hey Tony, you think I could get one of those sodas?" He wrinkles his forehead and opens his eyes wide as he speaks, and I'm reminded of a toddler asking for a new toy.

I say, "Uh, sure," tear open the purple box, and hand Chris one of the warm cans.

He says, "Cool. Thanks, bro," and heads back into the common area.

I don't see Sam Kitchen jogging over until I'm almost to the door. Until he sneaks up behind me and pulls a soda from the box. I turn around and he's already backing up, smiling, waving the can in the air. "Hey, look at me! I got a grape soda! It's mine now! What-what?"

"Come on, Sam. Stop playing, fool."

"What you gonna do about it, Tony? You want it? Come get it."

So I set my food package down and run at Sam Kitchen, shoving him into the wall as hard as I can, because he's just challenged me and I'm not a bitch. He grunts, drops the can, and it explodes. It hisses as it sprays carbonated corn syrup all over the floor. I punch Sam in his mouth. Then his head. Then his back, because he's bent over, trying to turn away from me. He cries, "Please don't beat me!"

But it's too late and I can't stop. I'm angry. I'm crazy. I'm pissed. Not at Sam, but at the world and he's just made the same mistake as the guy in the alley, because he's given me a reason to take it out on him.

Now Curtis is next to me, watching wide-eyed. He says, "Light him up, dawg! Light him up!"

"Hey!" Mountain Bob yells. "Hey! What the hell? Stop that! Cut it out! Come on, man! What do you think you're doing?"

Then I'm falling, because Mountain Bob is throwing me at the floor. The tiles come at me so fast, I don't have time to consider how bad it will hurt when I collide with it. It doesn't hurt, though. I see red, and my ears ring, but there's no pain. Just a puddle of sticky soda between my face and the floor.

Cindy appears over me, and both staff members wrench my arms back so it looks like I'm doing a swan dive and it occurs to me why I've never seen any of my neighbors receive a food package. It's because nobody loves them enough to send one.

So I don't try to fight. Bob's telling me to relax, and Cindy's saying my name in a soothing voice, but now I'm yelling to Sam Kitchen. Telling him he can have a soda.

* * *

At Secret Harbor School, you choose a staff to be your "special." That means that this person is your friend. Your mentor. Your big brother or big sister. Your special is supposed to be somebody you can trust. Somebody you can talk to when you're feeling down. Somebody to take you off the island once in a while when you've earned that privilege through good behavior. Your special is a load of B.S. because the staff at Secret Harbor School don't care about anything but their pay checks.

It's your job to choose a staff, and ask this person to be your special, so most guys just select whatever girl they have a crush on. Casey's special is Todd, and today they're in the room next to the couches together, probably playing "squash the chili."

I know, because Sam Kitchen and I have been sentenced to a week on the couches. He's on one, I'm on the other. Though he still makes me uncomfortable, he seems to have forgiven me for what I did to him, and it's lonely on the couches so we talk to each other when we can get away with it. At night, I drink soda and eat candy with Kyle. I gave some to Sam after I beat him up.

I thought about asking Jen to be my special, but I don't want to develop a crush on her because I still love Karina. The problem is, I'm not sure if Karina still loves me. There was no way I was asking Todd to be my special. There's no staff at Secret Harbor who I care to spend quality time with, so I asked Mountain Bob because he doesn't seem like he'll want to talk too much.

He acted pretty weird about it. Like I was asking for money or something. He said he needed to think about it, then later, he was like, "Sure." So Bob's my special and Cindy told me he's afraid of the responsibility because he's so messed up himself.

It's evening, and the common area's pretty quiet tonight. Jen took a group of guys to the activities building, and just about everyone else is in the TV room because there's some movie on. Curtis hovers over, and positions himself against a wall where Mountain Bob can't see him. He says, "You crazy-ass fool," and smiles.

Even though I feel bad for what I did to Sam, I smile back. Even chuckle.

Curtis says, "You ever get back in touch with that girl? The one you kept talking about when we were in Fairfax?"

"Karina? Yeah. We been together a while now."

"Right on, dawg. She been writing, or what?"

I tell him I got a letter from her not too long ago. It's a lie, because it feels like a lifetime ago, but the truth is embarrassing.

Curtis asks if I remember that Uno deck he had that smelled like bud. I say, "Yeah," even though it hadn't smelled like bud at all, and we both laugh. Sam Kitchen doesn't try to join our conversation, but I can tell he's listening.

Curtis says, "So check it out. You wanna get outta here, or what?"

"What do you mean?" I ask.

"What do you think? You wanna run?"

"What? You mean like steal a boat?"

"Naw dawg. That's just corny. Ain't no way to steal no damn boat. Even if there was, we wouldn't get far. They got cops out here with boats. They'd arrest us before we even made it to town."

"Then I don't get it."

"Store runs, dawg."

I ask what that means, and he says, "They make runs to the store every week for food and supplies, and they take guys with them to help carry crap. We just gotta go on a store run. We get into Anacortes and we just walk off. Easy as that."

"Won't they chase us?"

"Naw. I mean, maybe. But they won't touch us. They can't slam us in public. The worst they could do is follow us around with a cell phone and tell the cops where we are."

I ask, "Do they usually do that?"

"Naw. There's like five or six other guys with them. They ain't gonna leave them alone to chase us. The problem is you gotta be a level two to go on a store run, and they gotta trust you. That means you gotta stay outta trouble for a while. Like a month. Or if you can make it a few weeks, I can probably talk Jesus into taking us. Think you can make a few weeks? Like three at least?"

I ask if that means three after my sentence to the couch ends, or three from tonight. But before he can answer, the door to the room opens and Casey walks out, followed by a smiling Todd. Todd's eyes land on Curtis. They grow wide, and he says, "Hey, you're not supposed to be here."

Curtis says, "Oh. My bad. I was just telling Tony about the Mac Cottage. So you gotta be good, Tony, and you'll be able to move up there."

Todd waves a hand. "Shoo. Go on before you get yourself in trouble." Casey's already scampered over to the TV room. All the chairs are occupied, so he plops down by my special's feet, but Bob doesn't seem to notice him. Casey sits cross-legged looking up at the TV, and I can't help but think of a small child on the living room floor.

CHAPTER TWENTY-FIVE

It was warm on the Greyhound. Not only was it heated, but all the seats were packed so we were all sharing body heat. The bus smelled like that air freshener that gives off the scent of a new car, though, and not B.O., so it was okay. I sat by the aisle. Karina lay asleep in the seat by the window with her head in my lap. I ran my hand through her short hair, for a while until it occurred to me I was petting my girlfriend like a dog.

The overhead lights were off, and just about everyone was asleep. It was still dark when we stopped in the town where we were supposed to depart. Karina woke up and told me to act like I was sleeping, so I did, and nobody kicked us off. The back seat cleared out in the next town, and we went there and fooled around since it offered more privacy.

Around ten in the morning, we pulled into Salem, Oregon and everybody had to get off the bus. That meant we wouldn't be getting back on, so Karina started telling people we were headed to a family function in California, and needed money for a ticket. People in Salem weren't as friendly, though. Or maybe they just weren't as gullible.

So we made our way to the closest freeway entrance and stuck our thumbs out for an hour before it started raining.

Karina said, "This isn't working. Wait here." Then she went under the bridge and changed into a tan skirt that was so high you could almost see her underwear. She wore her black sweater, with the hood over her head, and matching tennis shoes. It didn't take long after that for a blue semi-truck to come to a stop on the shoulder. It growled hungrily as we jogged up to the passenger door and climbed in.

A small Hispanic man behind the wheel smiled and said something to Karina in Spanish.

Returning the smile, she said, "Sorry. I don't speak Spanish."

"All good mija. Where you two headed?"

"Me and my brother are headed to L.A. to see our grandma before she passes away. We haven't seen her since we were young, and this is the last time we'll get to spend with her."

He said, "This your brother?"

"Yeah."

The trucker smiled, said, "Órale guerro. Come on in. I'm headed to L.A. You both gotta ride in the bed, though, so no one sees you. And when I stop at a checkpoint, you gotta get out and meet me up the street, cause they weigh my truck. Cool?"

Karina said that was cool and climbed in before me. I looked up her skirt as she did and saw that her panties were the same color as the truck's paint.

* * *

So we hooked up in the bed of the semi. The driver shut some curtain so nobody could see us in the truck with him, and we cuddled up in his mess of blankets, until one thing led to another.

He heard us doing it, turned in his seat and pulled the curtain open. He exclaimed, "Espara te mija! Es tu hermano!" then burst out laughing. He flashed me a thumbs up and said, "Good job, man. Good job! No more though, okay?"

I said, "Sure," and pulled my pants up.

* * *

Then we came to a rest stop and pulled into a parking space. It was pouring out, and the rain was beating against the roof like a snare drum, and rolling down the windshield so we couldn't see out. The driver turned around and said, "Listen, I give you two-hundred bucks, and take you all the way to L.A. How's that sound?"

Before Karina could respond, I said it sounded great. But she put her feet up on the bed and hugged her legs. The driver's eyes dropped and glazed over and I figured out what was happening. So even though I already knew the answer, I asked what he wanted in return.

He pointed at me, said, "Tonight, you sleep up front. She sleeping with me. Sex with me."

I said, "Sex with you?"

"Yeah, man. Sex with me."

I looked at Karina.

She just shook her head.

The driver said, "Come on, man. You tell her. Two-hundred bucks."

"What do you mean, 'I tell her'?"

"Tell her do it so you can have the money."

"I can't tell her to do anything. She's her own person. It's her choice, not mine." But my heart was pounding so hard against the inside of my ribcage that it felt like it would either explode, or bust its way out, because I hoped to God she wouldn't do it.

The driver asked, "What you say, mija? Two hundred. One time. I take you all the way to L.A. to see tu abuela."

Karina shook her head again.

I said, "If she doesn't do it, will you still take us to L.A.?"

"I don't know, man. I gotta think about that. Why you say 'no,' mija? I not gonna hurt you. I'm a nice man. What's the problem? You give it to him, but not me? And he your brother? Why you being selfish?"

Karina said, "He's not really my brother."

"I know. I'm not stupid. Listen, I gotta get out of this truck and do a couple things. You gotta get out too. You figure out what you wanna do, mija, and tell me when I get back. Two-hundred bucks. Maybe I even do two-fifty."

So we climbed out into the pouring rain, Karina in her little skirt, and I told her we needed to discuss our options.

She looked at me like I'd just canceled tomorrow, and gasped, "What?"

I said, "Our options. We could either lure this guy somewhere, kill him, and take his money, or we could just get the hell outta here before he gets back."

Karina said, "Kill him?"

"Sure. Unless you'd rather—"

"No. Of course not. Hell no. How would we kill him though?"

"I don't know. Stab him or something."

"You got a knife?"

"No. You?"

She said she didn't, so we decided to just get the hell outta there before he got back. As we made our way to the freeway, though, it occurred to me that in the future, it wouldn't be a good idea to travel without a weapon.

* * *

Karina changed out of her skirt, and we walked. And we walked. And we walked along the freeway, and nobody pulled over. Eventually, it stopped raining and the sun even smiled at us for a while. Karina watched the road signs, and she said we walked close to twenty miles that day.

Then, when it was dark and our legs didn't wanna move anymore, we passed out under another freeway bridge. It was a small one. Nothing like the one where we'd last seen Trouble and Shay. We slept on a hill, and woke up in the morning shivering, covered in snow. So at least we'd slept through the night.

* * *

There was an abandoned house in Roseberg, Oregon. We climbed in a window and sprawled out on the carpet, where Karina brought to my attention that we hadn't eaten in days. So we left the back door unlocked, found the closest store, and shoplifted some Doritos and a couple sodas. The food was already gone by the time we made it back to the house.

She still had weed from her mom's room, so we finished that and when I thought we were gonna screw around, she started crying instead. I asked what was wrong, and she said, "I don't know."

"You don't know?"

"I mean—I do, but I don't know how to explain it."

"Well, why don't you try?"

"Do you really care, Tony?"

I told her of course I cared. Why else would I be asking?

So she sniffed and told me all over again about everything her dad did, and how she still had nightmares about it, and how her sister had called her a liar. And when she was done, she told me not to tell her I understood because there was no way I could ever understand. So instead of telling her I understood, I undressed her real slow and told her I loved her.

* * *

We took a couple more buses, hitched a few more rides, and slept under some more bridges. Then, one night a week and a half after leaving Mount Vernon, we stepped off a Greyhound in downtown Sacramento, where it was cold, but not as cold as Oregon, and the streetlights were all red and flashing for some reason.

The bus station was the kind of place you'd expect to find used needles and condoms on the bathroom floor, so we didn't go into the bathrooms. The people hanging around were different from the homeless kids in Seattle. They looked like they slept in mud puddles and hadn't eaten in days. They were reminiscent of creatures from a zombie movie, and not many of them were kids.

We didn't stick around for Karina to tell people we needed money to get to a family function. As we stepped out into the night, a toothless woman in cut-off shorts, with veins running up her legs like lightning bolts looked Karina up and down and said, "You ain't gotta be scared, cutie. There's money in these streets."

She stood leaning against the wall, with a group of people I instantly knew we wanted nothing to do with. I took Karina's hand and pulled her along, hearing the toothless woman laughing and coughing behind us.

* * *

Over the past year, I'd gotten used to the smell of cigarette smoke, yet even though I smoked when I was with Karina or the poor white kids, I still didn't like it much. Sacramento smelled like cigarettes, but for some reason Karina couldn't even find half smoked ones in the ashtrays, and it was making her crazy.

The streets were pretty much devoid of vehicles, aside from police cars that drove around real slow. One of them even had a cameraman in the passenger seat, which must've meant they were filming one of those reality cop shows.

The sidewalks were strewn with people sleeping on top of flattened cardboard boxes. Some even had other flattened boxes on top of them like blankets. It was so crowded you had to weave between sleeping bums just to get by. A tall, old black guy popped up like the crypt keeper as we passed, looked right at me, and yelled, "Hey!"

I almost jumped out of my shoes, as I said, "Yeah?"

"You got any spare change? Man?"

"No. No, sorry, man. I don't got any money."

He cursed, threatened me, and told me to keep walking, so that's what we did. Eventually, the sidewalks cleared out, which meant we must've made it to a nicer part of town.

Karina was being bitchy because she was having some kind of a nicotine fit and I was hungry, so I told her I didn't like the way she was talking to me. She said she didn't care what I did or didn't like, and the next thing I knew we were standing at some intersection screaming at each other.

My tongue was like a hurricane that I couldn't seem to get a leash on, and I called her a bitch because she was being a bitch, and she punched me in the mouth for calling her a bitch. It didn't hurt because she's so tiny, but it kinda hurt because I loved her. After that, neither of us were screaming. We stared into each other's eyes, and hers went wide. She opened her mouth like she wanted to apologize, but instead of doing it, she just stood there, her jaw hanging, her lips quivering.

I said, "Screw this. Good luck on your own," turned around and stomped up the darkest street I could find. But I hoped she would call me back, or beg me not to go. She didn't though, so I just kept walking.

* * *

It only took a few minutes for the panic to set in. Not a childish fear—I felt like I could've strangled the Hulk, I was so mad—but a calculated misgiving. It wasn't just because I knew I couldn't survive on my own. It was because without Karina, what was I even doing? This whole thing had been about us being together, and I'd just left her alone on the streets two states away from home.

So I turned around, jogged back the way I'd came, and found the intersection empty. I looked frantically down every road, then cupped my hands around my mouth and called her name, but Karina was gone. She was gone, and Sacramento was huge and even though there were people all over the city, I was alone. Not just that, but Karina was alone, and for some reason Karina seemed to have a sign on her back that said, "Victim."

I needed to find her. I needed to protect her from predators and I needed her to help me survive because she was street-smart and I wasn't. I needed her to love me, and I needed to tell her I was sorry. So I ran back toward the station and found her halfway there, sitting alone at a bus stop, staring out at a patch of trees.

In the end, neither of us said we were sorry. We just held each other until there was nothing left to do but get up and keep moving.

* * *

There's an outdoor mall in downtown Sacramento. That's where we were arrested a few hours after we climbed off the Greyhound. That's where Karina cried in the back of the cop car.

The mall's walkway lights up at night, but the stores are all closed. So we moseyed into the middle and sat on the edge of a fountain conspiring on how we could get money to get the hell out of this city. I looked into the water and said, "There's quarters in there."

Karina said those were people's wishes. I said, "And?"

"Bro, you can't take people's wishes."

"Why not?"

"I don't know. It's like immoral or whatever."

"Immoral? We're broke and hungry. That money's not doing anyone any good sitting in the bottom of a fountain."

She said, "Tony, leave it. Please."

But I had already made up my mind, so I took off my jacket, reached into the water and scooped up as many coins as I could. Before I even brought them out of the pool, a female security guard appeared and said, "Hello? Uh, hi? You guys know the mall's closed, right? Can you do me a favor? Go ahead and drop those coins and come with me."

We probably could've run. I was ready to run. We probably would've gotten away, because she probably wouldn't have even chased us. But Karina said, "Uh, yeah.

Sure," and we followed her into a small room with a control panel and multiple screens displaying the various surveillance footage around the mall.

She was pretty. She wore her security uniform in a way that made you think it might've been painted on. She was real friendly, too, and made small talk, asking our names almost randomly amidst other seemingly pointless banter. Neither of us were stupid, though, and Karina and I both knew what was happening.

I would've lied. I would've given a fake name, and I probably would've gotten away with it, but Karina still hadn't had a cigarette and I think deep down she was ready to go home. So she told the girl, whose dark ponytail was so tight it looked like it was stretching her face, who we were. And since I loved Karina and there was no point in lying now, I nodded in agreement.

A few minutes later, a tattooed cop who looked like he had steroids for breakfast showed up and the security guard gave him our names. This time there was a runaway report on Karina as well, so he cuffed us both, put us in the back of his car and stood outside smiling and talking to the pretty guard. Even though Karina was getting what she wanted, she cried in the car. And even though it was her fault, I wasn't mad at her. I told her I loved her and everything was gonna be cool. I even scooted close to her and touched her face with my face. But she just kept trying to read something in my eyes.

Like she couldn't believe I wouldn't be mad at her for outing us. I told her, "Seriously. Everything's cool. It's gonna be okay."

She sniffed and said, "But we didn't get long enough together this time."

CHAPTER TWENTY-SIX

Karina sits across the room, and she says she's never loved anyone as much as she loves me. She says she's sorry, so sorry she hasn't written in so long, and she promises there's a letter on its way.

"I wrote it in blood, Tony, because I don't want you to forget the promise we made."

I tell her I've never forgotten, and I blink back tears because I know she's not really here. Kyle and I ate a bottle of allergy pills between the two of us, and we're tripping nuts. It's past midnight, and the old woman's outside reading, as usual. Only tonight, she's surrounded by cats. The cats, it appears, have abandoned their posts by our doors to lay at her feet.

I've tripped nuts before. Mushrooms grow in the football field behind Laventure in the fall, because of some fertilizer they used to make the grass grow. A few of us picked them and ate them on Halloween last year. The Triple C. made me see tracers and gave me crazy thoughts about being dead. But I've never had a conversation with someone who wasn't really here until tonight, so the allergy pills are pretty legit. The problem is, I can't stop twitching like Donny Bravo.

It hit Kyle first, and his eyes went wide, staring out the window because the cats were walking on the hill in perfect line formation like soldiers marching off to battle.

He said, "Bro, what the hell are they doing?"

So I closed the window, and he started talking to somebody, but that somebody wasn't me. Then I started tripping and Kyle just kinda faded out.

Sitting on the edge of his bed now, is Karina. She tells me again that she's sorry.

"Tony please don't hate me. I wanted to love you so bad. I really did. I wanted you to be my first, bro. If you'd of just made a move that night in Damien's tent, I think everything would've been different. Girls are weird— you know? We're so screwed up, we don't even understand ourselves.

"And me? I'm extra screwed up. I think you always knew that. My dad made sure of it. I never meant to hurt you though because it's not your fault he hurt me. You were just the unlucky boy who fell for me."

Even though I know it's not really her, I tell her she's wrong. I feel the need to convince her because I hate it when she starts tearing herself down. I say, "Karina, you never deserved what your dad did to you, and it's not your fault. You're the most amazing person I've ever known. Don't say those things about yourself."

Karina smiles, but it's not a happy smile. She feels sorry for me because I'm the unlucky boy who fell for her. She shakes her head, says, "You were always so sweet to me, no matter what I did, or what I said to you."

"Karina—"

"Tony, you gotta let go. This isn't healthy. I mean whatever this is—your obsession with me. I'm not healthy, bro. Let me go and move on."

"You said you wrote me a letter though. In blood."

"Because I can't be the one to let go! Can't you see that? You have to be the one to do it! It has to be you, Tony. You're the strong one, anyway. You've always been."

I tell her I don't believe her. She's not even real. She's a hallucination, and the real Karina still loves me.

"Then why do you believe there's a letter on its way?" she asks. "If I'm not real, then why would there really be a letter written in blood on its way to you?"

"I don't know!"

"Tony, if you're just trippin' nuts, then all this is coming out of your own head. That means this is how you feel—what you think—not me. So why don't you just let go? What's keeping you from falling for that other girl?"

I tell Karina I'm done talking. But she isn't, so for the next hour she tells me how good of a guy I am, and how I need to find a way to bury my feelings for her and move on. When I finally start to come out of it, Kyle's having an uncontrollable fit of giggling. He says he's never tripped that hard in his life, and I guess I haven't either.

* * *

I feel like I'm connected to hoses that've been pumping something dark into me for a long time now. How long? I don't really know. It's been happening as far back as I can remember, I just never thought about defining it before. It's like my soul's strapped down to an operating table with tubes protruding in different places. Sometimes I think I'm someone's science experiment. That some being—call it what you will—is just creating a species out of me that looks human, because I've killed before and contrary to what Kyle says, I don't see their faces before I fall asleep at night. I just see Karina's.

I don't feel much. I can't remember a time in my life (except for the time I've spent with her) when I was happy, but I don't think I've spent much of it unhappy either. I've always just kinda glided through space, doing little more than existing.

So that's what the darkness inside me is. It's not evil, and it doesn't have any ill intent. It's just there and it doesn't really care about much. It's getting bigger though, and I think it's finally pushed out just about every trace of humanity that was once there. My love for Karina seems to be all that's left, and I'm scared that soon that'll be gone too. That's why I can't let go.

* * *

When nobody's sentenced to the couches, we're allowed on the carpeted area, so I usually hang out on them even when I'm not in trouble. Maybe I've just grown accustomed to places of punishment.

Today I'm alone, thinking of my conversation with Hallucination-Karina last night, and Donny Bravo floats over and says, "What'cha doin', Tony?"

"Just chillin'. What's up, Donny?"

"Same."

Even though he's only a year younger than me, he reminds me of someone much younger. Like a small child. He and Kyle have become my closest friends at Secret Harbor. Donny's mischievous, but bashful. You get the impression he's always plotting to take over the world, and maybe he is, only he's probably not smart enough.

He takes a seat next to me, twitches, and looks away as he says, "Anthony farted and I had to get outta the TV room. Those freaks in there must like it, cause none of em even moved an inch."

I shake my head and call Anthony some obscene name because I don't like him at all.

Donny says, "Jen's taking a bunch of guys on a hike after lunch."

I ask him what that means.

He says, "You don't know what a hike is?"

"I mean, yeah. Of course I know what a hike is. But are they going into Anacortes or something?"

"Yeah right. They're not about to take the prisoners outta Alcatraz for something fun. They got trails around here though. There's a bunch ah bikes too. Sometimes they take em and they'll be gone all day. There's this lake a few miles away, and I heard Jen goes in, in a swimsuit. Like a two-piece, or a g-string or something."

I look at him unbelievingly and say, "A g-string?"

Donny laughs. "I mean probably not a g-string, but you know what I'm saying. She's the only staff who likes to go on hikes, so they only happen when she's working and it's a nice enough day. They took fishing poles once."

"Really?"

"Yeah. There's a pond on the side of the lake, and I guess they got catfish in there or something. I don't really know. Sam Kitchen tries to go every time cause he's a perv and he's obsessed with Jen. He creeps her out too. This one time, she didn't take him and he just paced back and forth in the common area till she got back."

I don't have trouble imagining this, so I'm guessing it's probably a true story. I ask Donny if he's ever been on one of Jen's hikes.

"No. You gotta be a level two to go. Whenever I manage to stay outta trouble long enough to get a level two, they never have hikes. Then, as soon as I screw up and I'm a level one again, they do one."

I tell him, "Then let's make a pact. We'll keep each other out of trouble long enough to get our level twos, then we'll talk Jen into taking a hike and letting us go with. Sound cool?"

Donny says that sounded cool and we shake on it. Then he asks, "Could you tell me another story? You know like the other ones?"

And because I'm a bad person, and Donny's my friend, I spend the next ten minutes spinning a tale in which Donny Bravo has a blond-haired girl— who bears a striking resemblance to Jen—chained up in a dark, dark basement where he uses scissors to cut off her clothes, and mutilates her body with power tools. Donny loves these stories. Halfway through this one, his pants begin to swell and his eyes glaze over. When I'm done, he excuses himself and walks quickly into the bathroom.

* * *

It's mid-afternoon on a Friday and I'm alone on the balcony, thinking of how Kyle smoked my Adderall off tinfoil last night, when Sam Kitchen comes out and stands next to me. I don't acknowledge him, just stare out at the water. Kyle said the Adderall tasted like marshmallows and asked if I wanted a hit. I'd passed on that.

Sam asks if I want to be alone, and I tell him I do, but he doesn't leave. He says, "You know Tam's gay, right?"

"Yeah."

"Just checking. I saw you talking to him the other day, and when you turned around, he was checking out your butt."

I'm sure this isn't true, but I just nod, hoping he'll go away. He doesn't though. Instead, he tells me he's the one who killed the emu. I already knew this.

He says, "I was out on the farm with a rope, and it was running by so I made a noose and lassoed its neck. Then, when it was a few feet away, I jerked the rope and its neck just snapped. It fell down twitching and making these choking sounds for like ten minutes, dude. You should a seen it."

I tell him, "Cool," even though this isn't cool.

He says, "I heard you got a card from Jen."

"What? Who said that?"

"Whoa, bud! Relax. I'm not gonna snitch her out. She'd probably get fired if they knew she was giving love notes to kids. Just don't get too excited. She's given them to hella guys here. I got one once too. Back when she first started working. What a whore, right?"

Instead of answering, I just chuckle, but Sam Kitchen isn't laughing. He stares at the side of my face for too long, and in my peripheral I can see he's smirking. He stares so long my heart starts thumping against the inside of my ribcage because he's creepy and weird. He stares so long I don't know if I can keep myself from turning and punching him in his acne ridden face again. Then, finally, he pats me on the back and walks away.

* * *

There was a letter on my bed today. This is what it said:

Dear Tony,

Sorry it's been so long since I wrote. I know what you must be thinking. Don't stress, though, bro. Everything's cool. Well, that's kind of a lie I guess. Nothing's really cool out here. Especially without you. My stepdad's a dick. My mom doesn't care. Same as always.

How's life in there? Made any boyfriends yet? lol.

Can you get visits? I mean, is there a way I can come see you? Or maybe you could get like a weekend pass or something? If you can't tell, I have my little red friend this week, and unless you forgot what that means, it means I'm on my period, and you know how I get when my friend shows up.

Marvin says hi, and nice ass. He says you gotta hurry up and get out so we can go on another road trip. He totally wants to dose you out on Triple C. again. Every time we talk about how you thought we were all ghosts that night, we almost die laughing.

Anyway, bro. I'm gonna cut this off here, because I don't wanna bore you to death, but I really miss having you around to be crazy with, so come back to me soon.
Karina.

P.S. I still love you so much it hurts.

I read the letter twice before I folded it up and put it on my shelf. Then I picked it back up and read it again. Not because of what it said, but because it was written in bright red blood.

CHAPTER TWENTY-SEVEN

The Sacramento Juvenile Detention was different from Skagit, because instead of steel bunk beds, there were two large, wooden boxes sitting across from each other with mattresses on them. I was so tired; I think I was out before my face touched the pillow. When I woke up, the sun was beating through a rectangular window, and I discovered I had a black cellie, who'd spent time in the California juvenile prisons already. I sat on my bunk, he sat on his and I told him about Karina.

He said, "See? That's the difference between you and me. You got a girlfriend. I got a baby-momma!"

So that was interesting.

Every time we left the cell, we were led by two guards into a shower where we had to strip down, lift our private parts, bend over, spread and cough. Then, before we were allowed back into the cell, it was the same drill. Sometimes it was even a female guard who'd strip search us, and some of them were really pretty.

We walked in single file lines, with our thumbs hooked into our pants, and our heads down, while big, angry guards stood on our sides with their hands on cans of pepper spray. It was against the rules to make eye contact because people liked to find reasons to fight and stab each other.

The Sacramento juvie was nothing like the one in Mount Vernon. It wasn't co-ed, so I didn't see Karina anywhere. We sat on plastic chairs and ate pancakes with the trays in our laps, then, somebody read us the Cat in the Hat, and that was school for the day.

* * *

Some caseworker said I'd be leaving, then I was cuffed, driven in a van to the airport. They didn't take the handcuffs off until right before I stepped onto the plane, so I'm sure the passengers were all staring at me like I was Hannibal Lecter, but who knows, because I slept the entire flight.

* * *

My parents paid for my ticket. I was ready to fight if they wanted a fight, but I guess they didn't. John picked me up at the airport in Seattle, and the drive back to Mount Vernon might've been the most awkward hour of my life.

The only time he talked to me was when we stopped for burgers and he asked me what I wanted. Then, when I got home, my mom didn't say a word to me either. Alex and Anne were happy to see me. Anne ran circles around me as soon as I was in the door, and Alex told me it was cool if I wanted to play in his room.

I might have, too, but the cops showed up a few minutes later and took me to juvie for another youth at risk violation.

* * *

I only spent a week, and when I was released, my mom said, "Your little girlfriend made it back okay. Just thought you'd wanna know."

She picked me up by herself, and as we pulled out of the lot in her white SUV, she stared at the road, her eyes bulging from her skull, and asked how long I planned on staying this time.

I told her I wasn't gonna run again.

"Shut up, Tony. Just shut your freaking mouth, okay? Can you do that? For once in your life can you just not lie?"

"I'm not lying."

"You're always lying, Tony. That's the problem, isn't it? You're so caught up in your own lies that you actually believe 'em, too, and it's sad, you know that? It's freakin' sad, and I almost wanna feel sorry for you. But I can't. You know why, Tony? Because you're selfish. All you are is a selfish, little, spoiled brat, and you wouldn't know the truth if it bit you right in the ass."

I said, "Whatever."

"Yeah?" We came to a stop at an intersection. "Whatever? That's what the hell you have to say? I flew you home from two states away, and it's just whatever, huh? Well that's just great, Tony. Just freakin' great. I'm real proud ah you, you know that? You've really grown into a big man. I mean, running away? Living on your own? Hitchhiking? Real smart, Tony. So tell me, how long can we expect to be graced with your company this time?"

"Where's Anne?" I asked.

"I left her with Sharon. I don't know what you're gonna do, or how you're gonna act, and I'm not putting my daughter in danger by having her in the car with you."

"With me?" I said. "I'm calm. You're the one who's freaking out." Behind us, a car horn went off and my mom and I both looked up at a green light. She hit the gas, took a right into the nearest parking lot and killed the engine. In front of us, a couple who looked to be in their early twenties sat across from each other at a table outside of a restaurant that was also a brewery. They glanced over at us briefly, then returned their attention to their meals and one another.

My mom glared at me and said, "I'm done playing games with you, Tony. I can't do this anymore. You drink. You do drugs. You bring drugs into my house—I know you do. And you won't listen. Do you know what would've happened to me at your age if I acted the way you're acting? I would've been bleeding from the bottom of my neck to the back of my legs. My dad would've strapped me down to my bed and whipped me until the neighbors heard me screaming."

"And he's a great example of how to raise your children?" I asked. "Because he did such a good job raising you?"

"No! He sure as hell didn't! He sent me away! And you know what? I didn't have it any better when he did! Between my uncles and their evil wives, they might as well've just stuck me in an orphanage so I wouldn't have had to deal with what they did to me. I've tried to give you a better life than what I was given, Tony! I've done everything I could to make sure you didn't go through what I went through. And all you've done is spit in my face.

"You know sometimes I wish your father were alive to kick your ass. You think he'd be proud of you, with the way you treat me? He'd beat the hell outta you, just like he used to beat the hell outta me! And you know what? You'd deserve it.

"You know, I thought about leaving you down there. I swear to Christ I almost didn't send a ticket."

I told her she shouldn't have wasted her money on me. I told her I went to California because that's where I wanted to be. I told my mom that if I'd wanted to live at home, I would've stayed at home.

She said, "All you care about is that stupid girl. You really think she cares about you, Tony? You're gonna throw your whole freakin' life away for some little tramp, then someday you're gonna be wishing the people who really cared were still there.

"Do you know what we do whenever you run, Tony? Have you even thought about it? I have John driving all over freakin' town looking for you, while I'm on the phone calling everybody who might know where you are. Last week, John went all the way to Seattle to search the streets for you. Have you even considered the effects your actions have on your family?

"But like always, you don't care, do you? I'll tell you what Tony Carpenter. You really don't wanna live in a nice home, with a nice family, and have nice things? Keep running away. Keep doing what you're doing, and I'll grant you your wish. I'll send you away and you'll get a taste of what it's like to not be wanted. How's that sound?"

I told her that sounded fine. I told her do what she needed to do, and I'd do likewise. Then my mom took a deep breath and let it out real slow before starting the SUV and driving us home.

* * *

I didn't stay 24 hours. I messaged Karina on social media, then, that night, I climbed out my bedroom window and met her halfway between her house and mine.

California had clearly been too much for her, so we stayed in Tent-City, where we shared a small tent with another couple. They were older than us, but we smoked and drank and hooked up in front of them, and they did the same.

There were shovels, and axes and other tools in the makeshift shed, so I would help dig toilets and cut down trees and whatever. One night we did Triple C. and ended up running naked on the beach. I thought we were dead again, so I guess that's just what Triple C. does to me.

We made it a week before I was picked and taken to juvie with calluses on my hands.

* * *

My mom made good on her promise and I was released into a foster home. It was only supposed to be temporary, anyway, but the woman took me with her to the store my first day in her house and I jumped out at an intersection and ran to Karina's.

That night we sat on her bed and she cut my arm with a razorblade. Then she cut her own, mixed our blood together and used it to write the word "forever" on a sheet of lined paper. I asked if that was a promise, and she answered by taking all her clothes off and climbing on top of me.

* * *

That's how things went for most of eighth grade, so Karina and I didn't spend much time in school. We just ran, and ran, and we'd get caught, and run again. I told her often that I loved her, and she never said it back but she wrote it on the walls in juvie and I'd see it whenever I was there.

We boosted some bottles of liquor and sold them until we had enough money for a prepaid cell phone. That way whenever we were caught, I could call her and we could meet back up later.

Then, they put a youth at risk case on her, too, and the next time we were caught, she found out they were sending her to treatment for three months. So I lay with my face against the cold concrete, yelling under the blood red door that I'd be waiting for her when she made it back.

Then, for the first time, she said, "I love you, Tony. Please don't leave me," and her voice echoed through the day room, so everyone could hear.

Girls cooed and guys whistled. Somebody yelled, "Oh! Isn't that cute?" But I didn't care, because her voice, combined with those three words were like chocolate.

CHAPTER TWENTY-EIGHT

Jerry Warden's on the island today. A group of guys have been causing problems, and all four of them are stuck on the couches. Jerry made it his business to show up and threaten them personally. Donny and I kept to our pact, and we both got our level twos the same week.

Unfortunately for Donny, however, there won't be any hike because this morning Curtis talked Jen into taking him and me on a store run. So today I'll be getting the hell out of here. Donny's not coming on the store run which is good, because he'd probably want to run with us. As much as I like Donny, he'd only slow us down, and I suspect he needs his meds.

I told Kyle this morning I wouldn't be coming back, and he just said, "Good luck man," and kept playing his guitar. I didn't tell Donny, and I feel a little bad about that.

When I was young, my class took a field trip to this zoo in Seattle, and we looked down at an alligator who sat as still as a statue, staring at us. I asked my teacher if it was dead, and she said, "No. It's just holding real still, hoping someone'll get close so it can eat them."

Jen's looking good today. She's looking better than I've ever seen her look, and Sam Kitchen's been sitting at a table in the common area playing cards. But in his peripheral, he hasn't stopped eyeing her like that alligator at the zoo. You get the impression that if she got close enough, he'd bite her and do a death roll.

Jerry's having fun, and you can tell his favorite part of running a boy's home is being a dick to boys. He wears the sourest face I've ever seen a person wear, like somebody smeared sewage on his upper lip. Hi expressions are terrifying because they all seem to convey some strange combination of distaste, and indifference. Like he could skin you alive without losing any sleep. His expressions are terrifying because firstly they're all so opposite to the one he wore the day he talked my mom into giving me away and secondly because he has ultimate power over so many lives.

Sam pouted when he found out he wasn't on the list for the store run. Maybe because Jen's wearing leggings and a baby blue tank top that shows cleavage I didn't even know she had. There's a tattoo on her left shoulder of a flower with a tiny fairy that appears to be pollinating it like a bee. I didn't know she had that either.

The joke here, lately, has been to say, "Get me a beer," in a deep East Coast accent. This is because we watched a movie on the Lifetime Network, where some guy slapped his wife across the face and said that to her. So when Mountain Bob told Donny he needed to keep his voice down yesterday, Donny's response was, "Get me a bee-ah."

Bob shook his head and walked off muttering that he'd like to kill that kid.

When Curtis asked Jen to take us on the store run, her face lit up and she smiled from ear to ear. She beamed at me, bit her bottom lip, and said, "That's a great idea! But—wait. Is it cool? I mean, Jesus'll be there too."

Curtis said, "What? Come on. Tony and Jesus are cool now. They squashed that ages ago."

Jen didn't look at him, just stared into my eyes like she'd lost something in them. She asked, "You sure?"

I told her I was sure. Jesus and I had a misunderstanding, but everything's cool now. So I'll be going on the store run today and I won't be returning, and the only regret that I have is that I won't see Donny or Kyle again. Kyle's preoccupied, and though he's thirteen, he's very much his own man. But I feel vaguely responsible for Donny, so I spend some time with him out on the balcony before the boat leaves.

We both stare in through the huge windows and he says, "Look at Jerry Warden. He looks like he's missing his gay lover right now. That's why he's so pissed. He's like, 'Look what you did! You made me have to come out here and do my job, and now I'm missing out on some serious gay sex!' Look at him. Look how he walks."

And even though there's nothing funny about the way Jerry Warden walks, I hate him and I like Donny, so I agree.

Donny says, "You know how he lost his teeth?"

And I don't, so I ask, "How?"

"Someone knocked 'em out with a mop-wringer."

"A mop-wringer?"

"You know the thing on the mop bucket where you put the mop in to wring it out? A guy grabbed one of those by the handle and whacked him in the face and knocked out three of his teeth right there in the common area. And the crazy thing is, he still acts like a punk."

I can't help that I feel a mild sense of satisfaction just picturing this scenario, and that I hope the story's true. I ask Donny if he saw it happen.

He twitches and says, "Naw. I wish I did. It happened before I got here. We heard it from staff, though, so it's gotta be true."

And even if it isn't true, I choose to believe it is, because I still haven't forgotten that I planned to kill Jerry Warden the first chance I got. I think I would, too, if I thought I could get away with it. I tell Donny it was probably some kid Jerry was buggering who knocked his teeth out.

Donny laughs, says, "Hey Tony, when you go to the store today, can you do me a favor?"

I say, "Yeah. Sure. What do you need, man?"

He says, "Get me a bee-ah."

* * *

Every seat on the Sea Wolf's occupied, and Jen's sitting next to me. We've both been staring over the side of the boat—watching the water pass—for most of the ride, but every so often she'll nudge me and say something like, "Is that an orca?"

Her cleavage is concealed behind her lifejacket, but she's still in the blue tank top. I think, She must be cold, because taking a ride on the Sea Wolf's akin to sitting outside in a windstorm.

Curtis is wearing his red hat, which matches his shoes, and it's turned backward as usual.

I tell Jen, "Uh, I don't know. Maybe," even though we both know there's no orca there.

Jerry's on the boat. He sits up front, just behind the driver, and I'm glad because the last thing I want to behold right now is one of his rancid faces. His salt-and-pepper hair bounces in the wind, and it gives the impression he's under water. I imagine him in the bottom of the sound, blue in the face because someone's hit him with a mop ringer and dumped him over the side of the boat.

Curtis hasn't said one word, hasn't even looked at me since we stepped aboard. I wonder if he's having second thoughts. I wonder if I'm having second thoughts. I have no problem with running because for so long now, running is just what I've done. But something about the thought of running on Jen doesn't sit well with me. Maybe it's because she's been so nice to me. Or maybe it's because I've managed to develop a crush on her after all. Or maybe it's just because her leg is touching mine.

Casey sits across the aisle from us, and the way he's smiling, you'd think he's on his way to Disneyland. Casey always smiles like that, though, and for some reason it makes it difficult to like him—unless you're Todd, I guess.

The Sea Wolf pulls into the marina, parks next to the dock where I first boarded it, and the first one off is Jerry Warden. He doesn't say goodbye to anyone—not even his staff—just peels off his lifejacket, tosses it onto the floor of the boat, and walks off. It's still early in the afternoon and the Anacortes marina's active with people climbing on and off boats of various sizes. An old man holds hands with a girl in a bright-green lifejacket, who can't be older than five, and walks her along the pier. Jesus stands and climbs onto the dock.

Jen's up next, and I watch as she removes her own life vest. She catches me looking, and smiles. I quickly avert my gaze as she follows the line of guys departing the Sea Wolf. When I look back, Curtis is standing, staring out at the water, watching me in his peripheral stone faced. His lips barely move as he whispers, "You ready for this. No backing out now, dawg."

So I guess he hasn't changed his mind.

* * *

One group of guys leaves in the van with a staff member named Matt. Seven of us, including Casey, go with Jen and Jesus. We walk through the parking lot. The store's just across the street from the marina. It's some big supermarket. Curtis walks so close to me that we're touching. When we make it to the sidewalk, and our group's turned toward the intersection, he says, "Ready?"

"Now?" I ask.

"Come on, dawg. Now." He steps off the sidewalk into the four-lane street, and I mean to follow, but instead I freeze, because it feels like time's somehow slowed down, and I hadn't expected this to happen already. He says, "Come on, Tony. What are you waiting for? Let's go, dawg."

Then my feet are in motion. Then we're jogging side-by-side across the street. Then cars are slowing down to keep from hitting us—they're honking at us. Then Jesus's voice is calling behind me, "Hey! Hey man! Where you guys going? What are you doing?"

Then I hear Jen's voice. "Tony."

And I consider stopping. Turning around. Telling her I was only kidding. But instead, I think about Karina and I keep running.

* * *

We run and we run, but like Curtis said, they don't chase us. Maybe if we'd just walked they would've. Maybe one of them would've stayed with the group, while the other followed us around with a cell phone and told the cops where we were. But that's not what happens and it feels like we're just running from our shadows.

It's hot as hell out today, and my face is already covered in salty sweat. We come into a heavily wooded residential neighborhood, and finally we stop running.

Curtis says, "I got a homie that lives around here. I gotta remember the way to his pad."

I say, "Cool. Will he let us hide out for a while?"

"Yeah. He probably got some bud we can smoke on, too."

So we walk up this steep hill, and the trees grow thicker and thicker, but the houses grow nicer and nicer, and Curtis looks intently at each one of them before moving on. Once we make it to the top of the hill, the trees clear a bit and the ground levels out.

Curtis says, "This is it."

Looking around, I ask, "Which house?"

"I don't know. Hold on dawg, lemme try and remember."

Then a small, red convertible pulls up next to us, and Curtis cusses.

"You cool," I ask.

"That's Jerry."

"What?"

"That's Jerry Warden."

And my heart drops into my leg, because I look at the face behind the wheel and it is him. He has a cell phone to his ear, and the only reason I hadn't recognized him before is because he's smiling. He says, "What's up, guys?"

Curtis tells him to piss off.

"Well that's not very nice. Tell you guys what, jump in the car, and we'll pretend this never happened. How's that sound?"

Curtis nudges me, whispers, "What do we do, dawg?"

I look around. "Which house is your friend's?"

"I don't know. I'm trying to remember."

Jerry says into his phone, "Yeah. Yeah, I got 'em right here. They're not gonna run. Was just a little mistake. No big deal. They're hopping in my car right now. Hold up on the dogs, okay?"

Curtis says, "Dogs?"

"Yeah. They got police dogs at the bottom of the hill. Listen guys, I told 'em you're gonna be cool about this, but I got the cops on the phone right now, and they can hear everything we're saying. They say they won't send the dogs up if you go ahead and get in the car with me. If you don't, though, well I can't make any promises, but have you seen what those dogs do to people?"

I say, "B.S. They wouldn't send cop dogs to get a couple of runaways."

"You're not runaways, Tony. You're escapees. Now I already told you, if you get in the car right now, I'll be willing to overlook this incident. We'll get you back on the island and pretend this never happened. But if not, I'm gonna tell the cops to go ahead and send the dogs up this hill, and it's gonna get real ugly. Then, when we take you back to the home in handcuffs, I promise you, you'll be spending the rest of your summer on the couches. Time's running out guys. Gotta make up your minds now, cause I'm done being nice."

So I make up my mind, and so does Curtis. He moves first, walking around the front of Jerry's car and pulling the passenger door open, as I sprint around the closest house. Behind me, Jerry says, "Tony's running." But I don't stop or look back.

I make it into a backyard with a swing set, hop over a wooden fence and run into a semi-clear patch of forest, weaving around trees. I run until my legs burn and my lungs are ready to explode. I run until the forest grows thick with blackberry bushes, then I slow down, but not much.

Using my hands, I maneuver through thorns, feeling them dig into me and rip flesh from my face, my arms, different parts of my body. I still can't stop, though. I'm moving downhill, and soon I hear the water. Then I see it. That's when I finally stop at the edge of the forest and double over, placing my hands on my thighs and trying to breathe. My arms are covered in blood. I wipe my face and see more on my palm.

Slowly lowering myself, I lay in a thick patch of grass, and listen to the sound of the crashing waves. A nearby ferry. Hungry seagulls.

There are no cop dogs, because Jerry's a liar, but for some reason I find myself considering going back and seeing if his offer of immunity's still on the table. Then I think of the invisible leash they've somehow put on my subconscious, and I hate Jerry more than ever. More than I hated him the day he talked my mom into giving me away, or the morning he delivered me to the cop to be taken to juvie.

I hate Jerry because he's programmed me to be a prisoner which means I'm a prisoner in my own mind now. But I know my love for Karina can set me free, so I choose to focus on her, and to daydream about the last time we were free together.

CHAPTER TWENTY-NINE

Droopy had a gun. He lifted his T-shirt, and showed us the wooden handle sticking out of his waistband, pressed against a wall of belly fat. He told me it was mine if I could get him a case of Corona from the Green Apple grocery store within the next half-hour. I looked at Karina and asked what she thought?

In the past three months, I'd only been in trouble once. I wrote to the treatment center she was in, and the letter was returned with a note, saying I wasn't on her list of approved contacts. My mom found it in the mailbox and read that I planned to run again as soon as she was free, and it had caused a huge blow-up.

I told her I'd changed my mind though, and because I was back on my meds, and because I was taking kick boxing lessons, and because my grades were improving, and because I was able to move dishes from one place to another in a reasonable amount of time, she believed me. Now Karina was free, and as soon as I saw her post online, I ran and called our number to tell her how much I missed her. She said she'd meet me at Edgewater Park.

She was dressed different, in jeans instead of leggings and a bright orange T-shirt. Her face was a little fuller, like she'd been eating better, and her hair had grown about an inch. But what stood out was that there was something new in her eyes. It was a kind of sparkle that I'd never seen there before. It was an awareness that made you wonder what she was thinking about you. It was spring and though it wasn't warm yet, the sun was bright and accentuated them and it made her more attractive than ever.

So I did Triple C. with her and we went to a different park in downtown Mount Vernon, where a group of bums were scattered about in the grass, drinking and smoking like it were some kind of a picnic.

That's where Droopy showed us his gun. He was probably in his late twenties, with a bald head and dirty clothes. He was chubby, and drunk out of his mind. He said it was a twenty-two revolver, and it held seven shots. He said the Coronas had to be in bottles, not cans.

"She takes longs and shorts, kid. That means you can shoot rounds made for a rifle with this baby. What do ya say? Wanna make a deal?"

Karina just shrugged, but she seemed to deflate and I could tell she didn't think it was a good idea, so I told Droopy we were good, and lay back on the grass with her head on my chest.

She didn't talk much. In fact, she hardly talked at all since we'd met up, and it was as awkward as hell. Then the Triple C. kicked in, and the next thing I knew we were in the Green Apple, and I had a case of Coronas hanging at my side. Then we were in the parking lot and an employee was yelling at us.

Then I was at the park explaining to Droopy that I'd had to throw a bottle at the cashier when he tried to chase me and that's why a bottle was missing. Then Droopy was wiping the revolver with his shirt, handing it to me and telling me to get the hell out of here.

* * *

The chrome was old and dirty, and it had a long barrel and no hammer or safety switch that I could find. I didn't know much about guns, aside from what I'd seen on TV, but the thing was pretty easy to figure out. It cracked open, and the barrel folded down so you could see all seven bullets in the cylinder. The only thing I didn't know was whether or not it would actually work if I pulled the trigger.

So we went to where Damien's tent used to be and I fired it three times into a tree. It twitched in my hand, and sparks skipped from the barrel, but it worked just fine, and for some reason this thrilled me. We spread our clothes on the ground and fooled around on top of them, with the revolver sitting next to us. When we were done, we laid on our backs, looking up at the trees that moved in the wind, leaving tracers and blending with one another. The birds sang and their song echoed inside my skull. Finally Karina had something to say.

She said, "Bro, I'm frying so much nuts right now."

"Yeah. Me too."

"You hear those birds?"

"Yeah."

"Bro, they sound pissed."

And now that I listened closely, they did sound pissed. Karina said, "You know it's cool if you couldn't wait."

"What? Wait for what?"

"You know—for me."

I told her of course I waited. I was here, wasn't I?

"I know. I know. That's not what I mean, though. I was gone for like three months, Tony. So if you were with anyone else—"

"What? No! Hell no. I wouldn't—"

"I'm just saying—"

"Karina, I wasn't with anyone else."

She took a deep breath, held it in, then said, "Kay."

I tried to think of a way to convince her that I was telling the truth, but the trees kept moving and the birds kept singing and the right words just wouldn't come. So I told her I loved her, my heart sped up because she'd said it, too, before she left for treatment and I wanted to hear it again.

"I know you do, Tony. I love you too. I thought about you, you know that? Every day, I imagined what you must be doing and sometimes it drove me crazy because I couldn't help but wonder who you were doing it with. I tried to write you, but they had this list of people I was allowed to contact and you weren't on it.

"There was this one bitch there, this girl named Jess. She was cool, so I asked her to get a hold of you when she got out and tell you why I couldn't write. She said she'd look you up online. Did she ever get in touch?"

I told her I hadn't gotten any messages from anyone named Jess, and she said, "I guess it's good, cause as soon as she left, I started tripping. Thinking she'd start talking to you, and you two would hit it off or whatever. Isn't that the craziest thing you ever heard? I'm locked away somewhere and I'm sending other bitches to talk to my boyfriend? Then I'm gonna stress about it, like I'm not the one who did it in the first place?"

She laughed, and I felt a sensation like fingers massaging my brain. A girl named Monica went to treatment a few months ago, and when she came back, she told us that she learned the chemical in Triple C. that got you high, also ate microscopic holes in your brain. The birds sang and I imagined that's what was happening to me as Karina went on.

"There were guys there, too—I mean the place was co-ed, or whatever— and most of the other girls were hooking up with them. Even the ones with boyfriends. I guess the only ones who didn't were like the ones who the guys didn't wanna hook up with. These bitches would sneak into the guys' rooms, or sneak guys into their rooms and screw around every chance they got. They were like thirsty as hell, and there was this one guy named Derrick who really liked me, and Jess was always trying to get me to sneak into his room.

"But I told her I had a boyfriend, and she was like, 'You think your boyfriend's not screwing someone else right now?'"

I laid there and waited for her to tell me she hadn't hooked up with Derrick, but she didn't say that. Instead, she said, "I don't think this was a good idea, Tony."

And the birds kept singing. And my brain tingled some more. And I asked her what she meant.

"This. Tony, you have a gun."

I said, "We have a gun."

"Bro, I don't want a freaking gun." She sat up and looked out at the forest. "I don't want this. Not anymore."

I sat up and asked her what she was saying.

"I'm tired of running, Tony. I don't wanna run away or hitchhike around the country anymore. And I really didn't wanna get a gun."

"Then why—?"

"I don't know. I mean, I guess I just always wanted to make you happy. But not like this. Not anymore, bro. I had a lot of time to think in treatment, and I think I wanna stay home for a while. Like, maybe we could just see each other at school and be a normal teenage couple. Doesn't that sound nice?"

In the distance, a boat motor growled somewhere on the river.

Karina said, "I mean I know your mom hates me and all, but maybe we could change that."

As she spoke, she hugged herself, started to shiver, and the next thing I knew she was getting dressed. She asked me to get rid of the gun, and because I loved Karina and wanted to make her happy, we walked to a secluded beach so no one could see as I threw it into the middle of the river. Then I told her the plan sounded fine—we could live at home, see each other at school, be a normal teenage couple—and we held hands and tripped nuts, staring out at the passing water.

* * *

Karina tossed the phone on the sand and walked into the river with her shoes and her clothes on. She just waded out until it came up to her waist and she opened her mouth and gasped because the water was cold.

I said, "What are you doing?" and she told me she was being free.

"Tony, come be free with me. Kiss me."

The river moved all around her and her body split it down the middle like a string cheese. I said, "With my clothes on?"

"Just come here, bro. Please."

And because I'd never told her no before, I didn't think about it, just stepped into the freezing cold Skagit River, wrapped my arms around her waist, and pressed my lips against hers.

* * *

The Triple C. had mostly worn off, and it was almost dark when we finally emerged from the woods and made our way toward the road shivering, wet, and dirty. She said she had something I could change into at her house.

I thought about the future, and what it would be like to stay out of trouble and just see each other at school. To be a normal teenage couple and not use drugs or run away or kill people. I thought about staying on my medication and working on my relationships with my mom, Alex, Anne— even John. I thought about never going to juvie again, and then red and blue lights lit up the night as a cop car stopped next to us.

* * *

We were both arrested for shoplifting the Coronas, and as I was being handcuffed, I kept thinking, I'm so glad she talked me into throwing the gun in the river.

Our clothes soaked the back of the car, but it was cool, because the seats were plastic. Karina smiled and laughed as we were driven to juvie. She said, "Tomorrow's a new day, bro. It's gonna be okay. Everything's good. You know I love you, right?"

I told her I knew. I told her I loved her too.

Three weeks later my mom stood in front of a judge and pled with him to order me to Secret Harbor. A week after that, I was released from juvie and driven to Anacortes to catch my first ride on the Sea Wolf.

CHAPTER THIRTY

I lay in the grass just beyond the edge of the forest for hours listening to the sound of the water and thinking, I'll be with her soon. I just need to get into Mount Vernon and I'll find her and we'll run and hide somewhere.

The last time we were free together, Karina said she was done running. But I know things have changed since then, because I called her from juvie. Within days of being released, Karina was Karina again—smoking, drinking, doing whatever. So I know she'll run away with me, because we love each other and that's the only way we can be together.

The dogs never show, and it's late afternoon when I finally get up, clean my wounds with stinging saltwater from the sound, and head into Anacortes. The buses are still running, so I tell a driver I need to get to a family function in Mount Vernon and he looks at me funny, then lets me board for free. I take a seat near the middle, across from a lady reading a book, and as we pull onto the highway, the first traces of doubt begin to surface in my thoughts.

What if she doesn't want to run? What if I don't even find her? What if she's in juvie?

What if she doesn't want to be with me anymore? Why hasn't she written more?

So I scoot to the edge of my seat and ask the lady with the book if I could possibly use her phone to call my parents to pick me up in Mount Vernon. She's a nice lady, because her eyes scan my cuts and I can tell she's considering asking how they got there. Then she smiles, reaches into her purse and hands me a white iPhone. I tell her thanks, and dial mine and Karina's number.

There's no ringing, though, just a message telling me that the person I've called has a voicemail box that has not been set up.

So I call again because she might've just been getting another call the first time.

And I get the same result.

So I consider throwing this woman's phone on the floor and stomping on it, even though it's not her fault. Even though it's not the phone's fault. I hand the phone back to her and tell her thanks. It feels like everyone's eyes are on me, and she makes it worse by saying, "What happened? Couldn't get through? Well you just let me know if you need to try again, okay?"

I tell her I'll let her know.

* * *

Officer Whittaker's tall, black, and muscular. He has braided hair that he ties into a ponytail. Even though he's just the security guard at the Mount Vernon bus station, they call him Officer Whitaker because the rumor is that he used to be a cop in New York.

He chased me once for being a runaway and tackled me in front of everyone at the station. I had a butterfly knife, which is illegal to carry, but when the cop showed up, he didn't press charges.

It's early evening and the sun's beginning to set when I step off the bus at the Mount Vernon station. I feel Officer Whittaker's eyes burning into me, but there's no way he knows already that I'm a runaway, is there?

"Tony!"

I jump, and spin around to see Amber prancing over, her arms outstretched, her eyes wide and shiny. I almost don't recognize her, because she has short hair now like Karina, and it's dyed blonde. She jumps into the air and embraces me around the neck, and for a second I think she's gonna kiss me. For a second, I think I'm gonna kiss her back because she smells like fruity shampoo and I haven't been with a girl in months.

Then she pulls her face away, but her lower body's still pressed against mine and for some reason I hold her there as Kenny approaches from the direction she's just come. She examines my cuts, then my eyes and says, "What the hell happened to you?"

"Sticker bushes."

"Jeez. I heard they sent you to some prison on an island in New York or something."

In all the time I've known her, even when we were together, Amber's never been this outgoing or confident, so it must be her new hairdo that's causing it. Now Officer Whitaker's definitely watching. He stands facing away, but his head's turned my way and his hand's resting on his hip where a gun would be if he were still a cop.

I say, "A group home, actually. In Anacortes, though. Not quite New York."

Kenny makes it to us, stops and says, "What up, bro? Long-time no see. What happened to your face?"

Amber says, "He got in a fight with some sticker bushes, apparently." Kenny asks when I got out of Secret Harbor, and she dislodges from me, turns to face him, says, "Wait, you knew where he was?"

"Yeah. He was out on Little Alcatraz. When they set you free, bud?" I tell him they didn't. I ran.

Amber gasps, says, "Are they looking for you?"

"No. Probably not. Probably got a runaway report though."

Officer Whitaker looks away, goes about his business as Kenny asks when I left Secret Harbor.

I say, "Today. Look, I gotta get outta here."

Amber looks toward Officer Whitaker, who's talking to a woman with a baby, then back at me and says, "Do you have somewhere to go?"

"Uh, yeah."

"Where?"

"I gotta go to Karina's."

The silence that commences is so awkward that it almost seems loud. I can pretty much predict that I don't like what I'll hear if I ask what the problem is. So I ask what the problem is.

Kenny says, "Look, bro—"

Before he can finish, however, Amber says, "She's gone," and at first my heart starts skipping beats, and the ground sinks under my feet. Then she says, "She left with Mathias. Didn't you—"

"What do you mean 'she left with Mathias'?"

"I mean they left. They posted a picture online and said something about leaving together and nobody's seen either of them since."

And my heart keeps skipping beats. And the ground keeps sinking under my feet. And I ask, "When," in the weakest voice that's ever spoken a word.

Amber looks at Kenny, and they both appear to go into deep thought. Buses make beeping noises as they raise up and their doors shut.

Kenny says, "I don't know. Like a month ago, maybe?"

Amber says, "No. Longer. It was a while ago. I thought you were out when it happened."

Buses start pulling out of the station in a single file line. They'll be back in an hour. Then they'll stop running for the night. I tell Amber no, Karina was with me the last time I was out. I tell her there's no way she left with Mathias because I've gotten letters from her on the island.

"She's been writing you?" she asks.

"Yeah."

"Maybe Mathias doesn't know."

"She's not with Mathias!" I raise my voice. "Why the hell would she be with him?"

The buses are all gone now, and the station's pretty much empty. Officer Whitaker starts walking toward us, and Kenny says, "Bro, chill. Please. I got weed on me. In fact, I'm gone. Come on, babe." He takes Amber's hand. Amber looks at me a moment too long, her mouth open, her eyes sad and doe-like, then Kenny pulls her along and they make their way out of the parking lot.

Officer Whitaker asks me if everything's cool, but I ignore him and start walking toward Karina's house.

* * *

After I kissed Carly Sims in the fourth grade, we held hands a couple times, but the kiss never happened again. It was an awkward kiss, anyway. It went down at the swing set, while Amy stood by directing me on what to do.

"There you go. Yeah, like that. Wait. What are you doing, Tony? Don't pull away. Keep kissing her. Close your eyes!"

We walked the playground every recess, and even though Carly was pretty, she was super shy so Amy would always prompt me to make a move. Then, after a couple weeks, Amy told me Carly wanted to break up, and it was like there was a hand inside my chest crushing my heart.

I didn't love Carly, but rejection hurt. On the last day of school, Amy sat with me on the bus ride home and asked me to be her boyfriend. She was fat and it grossed me out, but I didn't tell her that. I just said, "No."

She blinked back her tears, but she smiled and told me it was okay. We could just be friends, and maybe someday I'd like her.

I don't know why I'm thinking about the fourth grade as I speed walk toward Karina's house. She's with Mathias. I know it's true, because I'm not stupid, but I have to confirm it.

It's dark already when I make it to her porch, but there's light behind the living room curtain. I knock a little too hard, and someone inside coughs. A moment later, the door opens and I hear a television. Karina's mom appears with a cigarette in her hand. Behind her it's cozy, warm, safe. For a second, I wonder why Karina would ever trade the inside of her house, even to be with me, let alone Mathias. Then I see her crack head stepdad sitting on the couch.

Karina's mom's a small, stumpy Hispanic woman, with premature wrinkles in her skin and a raspy voice. She speaks perfect English, and I've always just assumed that like her daughter, she doesn't know Spanish.

"Jesus. What do you want?" She says.

"Who is it?" Karina's stepdad calls from behind her.

"It's Karina's little boyfriend."

"Who?"

"That kid."

"She with him?"

"Not that one. The one they sent to that—place. The white one."

"The runaway?"

"Yeah. That one."

"Well tell him to get the hell outta here, before he brings the police to the damn house."

She asks me again what I want, and I tell her I need to talk to Karina.

"Well she ain't here."

"Well, do you know where I can find her?"

"I don't—" She squints into the cherry as she sucks on the end of her cigarette, then blows a stream of smoke over my shoulder. "Look, Karina's gone. She left with that other kid—the one with the pony-tail—and they went God knows where. Sorry to break it to you, but you might've dodged a bullet with that one. Might as well forget about her and get over it."

"Listen, I just—"

"Go away, Tony. Go home, or back to that—" She waves her cigarette. "That place or whatever. Go anywhere but here."

I want to protest. To argue because if I can convince her she's wrong, maybe it'll make it true. But before I can, the door shuts and the sound of the TV disappears along with Karina's mom.

* * *

So what do I do? I go out to the woods in Edgewater Park and I walk the trails in the dead of the night. But I hear her voice, even though she isn't there. I hear her laughing in the bushes, in the trees, all around me. I hear her because her love has been the last thread holding onto my sanity, and now that thread's snapped.

The forest is scary as hell at night, so I make my way into tent city where a fire's burning and a combination of the bums I know, and some I don't are sitting around drinking and smoking. They let me join them and give me a tent to sleep in.

Then, the next morning, I walk into a grocery store and boost four boxes of Triple C. Then I catch a bus back to Anacortes and walk into Secret Harbor's mainland office to turn myself in.

CHAPTER THIRTY-ONE

Jason was slammed today, and I'm not sure why. I was at a table playing chess with Donny, who's not very good at chess, and I heard the commotion. When I looked over, Anthony had him face down on the tiles, and Mountain Bob was just running over. Bob put his knee on Jason's face, and Jason started calling him all kinds of names.

Bob smashed Jason's face into the ground because he must not have liked the names Jason was calling him. He just removed his knee, wrapped his long fingers around the back of Jason's head like he was palming a basketball, and turned it so his nose was pressed against the floor.

He said, "You wanna run your mouth? Go ahead, talk now. Go on. Say something, you little punk. Yeah, that's what I thought."

Jason stopped calling him names and just begged him to stop.

Now Jason's on the couch and I'm still at the table in the common area, but I'm not playing chess anymore. A bunch of us are sitting around listening to Curtis talk about our adventure off the island.

"For real, we went to my homie's house and we were smoking weed the whole time. Tony even hooked up with my boy's sister."

Everybody looks to me for confirmation, and I don't see any point in lying, but I don't see any point in telling the truth either, so I corroborate Curtis's story just to be nice. We've been back over a week, and I've done this countless times already.

We were only sentenced to a week on the couch, which is a week longer than Jerry Warden promised Curtis for coming quietly. They went easy on us because we both turned ourselves in, and I'm guessing it's just a leash tightening tactic that they used to train other boys to do the same if they ever run. They even told us we can have our level twos back after we've been off the couch and stayed out of trouble for a week.

Jen visited me my last day on the couch. Curtis had already finished his time, and she just strolled over, sat down next to me and made sad eyes and a duck face. Then this happened:

JEN: You're not gonna get up and run from me, are you?

TONY: Look, I'm really—

JEN: What? Sorry?

TONY: I mean—yeah.

JEN: Well don't be. I'm just messing with you.

TONY: Yeah?

JEN: Yeah.

TONY: Well, I probably owe you an apology anyway.

JEN: You think so?

TONY: Kind of. I didn't mean to run on you. I mean, I did mean to run, obviously. But you've been real cool to me, and I didn't wanna do it when you were working.

JEN: Right—

TONY: I'm serious.

JEN: Oh I believe you.

TONY: Okay—?

JEN: So why'd you do it?

TONY: I don't—well it was just—I mean it was the first opportunity I got, so I guess I just took it.

JEN: That's not what I meant, knucklehead. I mean why'd you run in the first place if you were just gonna come back? Don't tell me you missed me that much.

TONY: Yeah, you wish. I mean I didn't plan on coming back. I was gonna go—

JEN: Find your girlfriend?

TONY: Yeah.

JEN: And?

TONY: And what?

JEN: Okay, you wanna dance? I can dance.

TONY: Excuse me?

JEN: You know exactly what I meant, but you're dancing around the topic. So you wanna dance, or you wanna talk to me? I'm a pretty good listener—at least that's what I've been told. But if you don't feel like discussing it—

TONY: Yeah. I mean, no, I didn't find her. Well not technically. I found out she disappeared with some guy—God knows how long ago.

JEN: Well, are you sure it's true?

TONY: Pretty sure. First, I heard it from some of our friends. Then I went to her house and heard it from her mom, so, yeah. It's probably true. They said she posted a picture online and said they were leaving together and nobody's seen them since.

JEN: Wow, Tony. I'm sorry.

TONY: Well, it is what it is, I guess.

JEN: No. No, it isn't. It's a terrible thing to have to go through, and it hurts. But it isn't just what it is. It's what you make it, and you're strong, and you're smart, and you're handsome and there's someone else for you. I promise. You know someday—maybe even someday soon— you'll be glad you came to a place like this, because now you know who's really gonna be there for you, and who isn't.

And you know if you ever need to talk, or just wanna hang out, I'm here.

TONY: Yeah. Yeah, I know. Thanks.

JEN: When can you get your level two back? Do you have to wait another—

TONY: No. I'll get it back in a week.

JEN: Then let's make a deal. Donny said you two've been talking about wanting to go on a hike out to Blackberry Lake. The summer's almost over, but we still have a few nice weeks left. Get your level, and we'll take a hike before it starts getting cold. Sound good?

TONY: Yeah. Sure. That sounds cool.

JEN: That means no more trouble. Not till I can get you out on those trails at least once. Pinky swear?

TONY: Yeah. Pinky swear.

JEN: Good. Then it's a plan.

* * *

Tam was released today. I didn't say goodbye to him because we've barely spoken since the day we met. He was sent to a foster home, and it made me think of the movies where the kids sit in orphanages, waiting to be adopted. Tam wasn't beaming with joy like the kids in the movies. Most of the kids in Secret Harbor have been in foster care and group homes since they were very young.

One evening Kyle's special, a dark haired staff member who plays guitar, was in our room and I learned why Tam's being raised by the State. Kyle's special's name is John, and it's obvious he doesn't like me. There's no reason, our personalities just don't seem to mesh. I don't remember why he and Kyle were talking about Tam, but John said, "His whole village was slaughtered in Africa. His parents, siblings, neighbors. He was just a baby, and he was one of the only survivors. Now is that lucky, or what?"

Then he played Stairway to Heaven on Kyle's guitar.

* * *

I keep seeing Karina's face just before I fall asleep at night. I'll start to doze off, then she'll be lying next to me, her almond eyes gazing into mine. Or I'll hear her voice and jerk awake. It's a problem, because I've obviously drifted further away from reality than I thought, but I'm not sure how far. It's a problem because Karina doesn't love me and I don't want to think about her all the time. It's a problem because I need to sleep.

After I boosted the Triple C., I popped all the tiny, round tablets out of their cards and wrapped them tightly in a plastic bag. I taped the bag to the inside of my leg right before I turned myself in. Kyle's excited, because he says he used to do Triple C. all the time. Only he doesn't call it Triple C. He calls it Darland. It's late night and we're sitting up in our beds with the light off and rock music humming quietly from the radio. I ask him why he calls it Darland.

"Cause, bro, that's where you go when you take it. You know how it always feels like you've entered another world? Well that world's called Darland. Only it's not actually a world. It's an amusement park."

I ask if he came up with this concept, and he says, "I look like a chemist to you? I'd had to of created the chemical Darland. You know what the chemical is, right?"

"No."

"Dextromethorphan."

"Dexter what?"

"Dextromethorphan Hydrobromide. That's the stuff in the cough and cold medicine that gets you loaded. It's in Robitussin too. That's why people drink Robitussin to fry nuts. They call that robo-frying."

I asks him how he knows about the Dexter chemical, and he says, "Cause it's written on the labels. But to answer your question, no. I definitely didn't come up with the name Darland. Everyone where I'm from calls it that. We been calling it that for years."

"You mean everyone in Seattle?"

"Well, everyone on the Hill does. I think they call it that over on the Ave too, though."

"The U-district?" I ask.

"Yeah."

Kyle tells me that he and his friends usually take a half a box of Darland when they wanna fry nuts. I tell him I've always taken a whole box, and he says, "Jesus. Both tickets?"

"What do you mean, 'tickets'?"

"You know how the box has two punch cards inside?"

"Yeah."

"Well, each one of those is one ticket to Darland. Eight pills. It's all you need. You mean to tell me you've been taking sixteen at a time?"

"Yeah," I say. "I mean, two tickets—I guess?"

"Bro, even I'm not that crazy. You're lucky you're still alive—or that you don't have brain damage. Do you know how dangerous that is? First of all, Darland can cause you to overheat and go into a coma. Know what that means? It's literally frying your brain. Second, you know that stuff eats microscopic holes in your brain, right? Like little, tiny worms—crawling around in your head."

I don't respond, because something he's said is crawling around inside my head now. Because maybe I do have brain damage.

Kyle says, "So what do you say we just take one ticket a piece? I mean, not now, but when we do it. We can fry out more than once that way."

I tell him, "Sure. Yeah. Sounds legit."

Kyle says he knows I've been down about my girl. Maybe we should do it soon to take my mind off her. I say that's a good idea and we both decide it's bedtime.

But sometime in the night, I wake up to the sound of his deep breathing and a sense of self-loathing I never knew possible, because it's just occurred to me that I've missed something that should have been obvious. I've been lied to. And maybe I do have brain damage, because there's no way I should've missed this.

Karina didn't run away with Mathias. She couldn't have. The letters I wrote her were sent to her house. And she responded, which means she was there to receive them. So why did Amber, Kyle, and Karin's mom lie to me? And where the hell is Karina?

* * *

It's a Friday, and Jerry Warden's on the island. He's made himself invisible for the most part, doing whatever downstairs with the counselors. Jen's looking somehow finer than usual, in leggings so thin they might rip if she sits down, and a pink tank top. She's standing with Todd, talking about who-knows-what, while we all eat lunch.

At the table next to mine, a native kid knocks on the wood, creating a hip-hop beat which Lil Poet's rapping over.

Today's the day we'll be going on a hike, only the plan's somehow evolved, and it'll be a bike ride instead. Donny can't stop talking trash about Sam Kitchen, because Sam's spent all morning trying to get on the list to come with. The list's full, though, so Sam's pouting at a table on the other side of the common area.

Donny says, "Look at him. He looks like he's gonna cry. I'll bet he doesn't even talk to anyone the whole time we're gone." Then he twitches.

Anthony tells Lil Poet to keep it down.

Donny says, "He won't even be able to go whack off in the activities building because there'll be no one to open it. He'll just have to get a mirror and a pen and play dot-to-dot on his own face. Or find a sheep to strangle or something."

Lunch today isn't good, but it's not bad either. Something that's supposed to resemble Mexican food. Some kind of enchilada, I think.

Donny says, "Maybe he'll just strangle himself before we get back and do the whole world a favor. I can't wait for that weirdo to move out to the Mac cottage."

I ask if that's supposed to happen anytime soon.

Donny says, "It would've happened already if you hadn't beat him up. Getting in a fight put him back on the list."

"Oh," I say. "Sorry."

"Don't be. It was the best day of my life." He grabs my arm with both hands and looks into my eyes. "You completed me, Tony!"

"Okay. Okay." I shrug him off. "You're welcome then."

Donny says the enchiladas taste like ass, and he eats his faster than anyone at the table. After lunch, I go to my room, and start thinking of what I might want to bring to the lake, because we're leaving in less than a half hour.

CHAPTER THIRTY-TWO

It might be the hottest day we've had all summer, and it's already late August. I'm in a pair of dark blue shorts with Hawaiian looking flower designs all over them, and a white T-shirt. Jen's riding up front, and her hips sway as she pedals. They straddle the seat of her bike like they were made just to be there.

Todd's in the very back and we're going uphill. Kyle, Donny, and I ride just in front of him, and I imagine he's disappointed Casey's not closer. Casey's just behind Sam Kitchen, and Sam Kitchen's just behind Jen.

In the end, Sam got to come because one of the guys on the list got in trouble at the last minute, and he ran to Todd before Jen could invite someone different. It's become pretty clear at this point that Sam makes Jen uncomfortable. Sam makes everybody uncomfortable, I think, except maybe Todd.

So the line looks like this, in order: Jen. Sam. Casey. Curtis. Donny. Me. Kyle. Todd.

We're all wearing backpacks with our lunches and water bottles in them, and we're riding matching orange mountain bikes on a thin trail with a cliff to our right. I'm out of breath because I've spent the last two years smoking and drinking. If my bike tips over, or hits a rock, I might fall off the cliff and die. I think I'm having a good time, and I'm trying not to stare too much at Jen, but Todd says, "Beautiful view, isn't it, Tony?" So I guess I need to try a little harder.

* * *

After about a half-hour, we come to an opening with a fire pit surrounded by rocks arranged in a perfect circle, and we stop and rest for a while. There's no shade where we are, but there's a cliff that looks a little like the rock on The Lion King, where the monkey held the baby lion up and all the gazelles and other prey animals bowed down to it.

I climb off my bike, set it on its side, and peer over the edge. But I don't see any gazelles or zebras, don't see anything but trees and bushes growing out of a really steep hill. If somebody fell off this cliff, they'd just disappear into a void of different shades of green.

Behind me, people begin to sit down in a circle around the fire pit. In nature, I can't help but notice that Donny's different. He smiles and looks like a kid someone might actually want to adopt, instead of the creepy, twitchy boy I know who wants to grow up and become a serial killer. He squints into the sun and drinks from a bottle of water, but he isn't talking much.

Sam Kitchen waits to sit until Jen's taken a seat, then plops down next to her. So Jen brings out her phone and starts fidgeting with the touchscreen, as Todd lowers himself next to Casey, and I'm wondering if Secret Harbor makes people messed up, or just attracts messed up people. Then Curtis asks if I brought another pair of shorts.

I say, "No. Why?"

"Don't you wanna put on something dry after you're done swimming?"

"Oh, I'm not gonna swim."

Jen shoots me a look like I've just said I plan to drown a litter of puppies. She says, "What? No. You gotta get in the water, Tony."

"Why?"

"Because that's the whole point in riding to the lake, knuckle-head. That's why we brought the bikes. So we'd have more time to swim."

"I'm not really much of a swimmer."

Todd says, "Well how will you ever learn if you don't get in the water?"

Jen says, "Come on, man. Don't be boring."

"I don't know—"

"Booooo!"

"I just—"

"Booooo!"

"I didn't bring a change of clothes."

"Just swim in your boxers."

Todd says, "Yeah. Swim in your boxers."

This makes my skin crawl, but Donny thinks it's funny, so he repeats it. Then Curtis, and soon everyone's chanting, "Boxers! Boxers! Boxers! Boxers!"

"Okay," I say. "Okay. Okay. Okay. We'll see."

Jen laughs, which causes everybody else to laugh. Then Sam says, "Hey Jen, remember when we made Smores here?"

Jen says, "Uh, yeah. Just a couple months ago, right?"

"Yeah, at the beginning of the summer. Think we could do that again sometime?"

"Well, I'm thinking this'll probably be the last trip this year."

"Oh, come on." He leans toward her as he speaks, smiling like they both know some secret that the rest of us are unaware of.

Ignoring him, she says, "Okay, if anyone needs to go into the woods, go now. We'll pick back up in about—" she looks at her watch, "five minutes."

Casey asks why we'd need to go into the woods, and Sam says, "To shake your little snake."

Todd snaps, "Sam! That's inappropriate!"

"Whatever," Sam says. "It was a joke. Jeez, lighten up."

"Well, why don't you try having some class? How about that?"

Donny smiles, twitches, says, "Yeah, Sam. Have some class."

Since I don't know how much longer it'll be before we make it to Blackberry Lake, relieving myself doesn't sound like the worst idea in the world. So I find a relatively clear path and make my way into the woods. Kyle follows with his water bottle hanging at his side. Once we're out of hearing distance from the rest, he reaches into his pocket and holds his hand open, keeping it low. He says, "What do you say?"

In the middle of his palm is the bag of Triple C., still exactly how I packaged it.

"You think it's a good idea?" I ask, even though I'm sure it's the worst idea anybody's ever had.

He says, "Why not?"

"I don't know, I mean—out here?"

"What makes one place any better than another?" I'm not sure there's a right response, so I just shrug.

Then I think of the conversation I had with Jen on the couch. The thought of having to apologize to her again sits in my stomach about as well as a cyclone. But so does the idea of looking like I'm afraid of getting in trouble, so I say, "Think we can get away with it?"

"What? Sure. Why wouldn't we? Look around, man. It's beautiful out here. We're in nature. There's nowhere better to fry nuts. Know what I read about Dex?"

"Dex?"

"Dextromethorphan. You know the stuff I told you about in Darland that gets you loaded? Well, I read the Native Americans used to use it in the forest to enter the realm of the dead. And it's been reported that a lot of people who take tickets, or robo-fry've had similar experiences."

I tell him when I take Triple C., I usually think I'm dead.

He says, "See? Let's peep out the realm of the dead, my guy." "You know they're gonna know."

"What? How? Unless you tell them."

"How can we hide it?"

"Look, man, I told you. You been taking too much. You gotta just punch one ticket. It's a nice, mellow trip. Trust me. You'll be cool."

So I say, "Okay. Why not?" and Kyle smiles as he tears the bag open and starts counting out tablets.

But before he's done, a deep voice calls from behind us, "Hey! What the hell do you guys think you're doing?" and Kyle jumps, spilling red pills all over the ground, stuffing what he doesn't spill into his pocket. I watch most of them disappear beneath a layer of twigs, red leaves, and flattened bushes, then turn around to see Sam Kitchen smiling from ear to ear.

Kyle says, "What's your problem, man?"

Sam isn't fazed by attitude. I suspect it's because nobody likes him and he knows it. He reaches for Kyle's wrist. "What'cha got there?"

Kyle pulls his hand out of his pocket and out of Sam's reach. "Don't touch me, man. What the hell?"

Then, like they could sense they were being excluded from something great, the other guys start showing up. Soon everybody but the staff are here, and they all want to take Triple C. Kyle's not happy, but if we don't share, someone might tell. So we split what we're able to salvage from the earth six ways, and somehow, everyone ends up with exactly one ticket to Darland.

* * *

When the ground levels out so we're not going uphill anymore, when we take a right onto a side trail that we're only on for a couple minutes, when the trees clear out—then the lake appears. I'm relieved because I haven't started to feel the effects of the Triple C. yet. Or maybe I have and I don't know it, because it's the first time I've only taken half a box.

Blackberry Lake isn't really a lake. It's a big pond surrounded by grass that's mowed like somebody maintains it regularly. Probably whoever lives in the three-story house on the other side with cracking white paint, a huge lumpy yard, and a small dock with a rowboat next to it. The water's surprisingly clear, though.

The house looks like something you'd expect to see in some movie from the nineteen-sixties. Like it should have a tire swing hanging from a tree in its gigantic lawn. It's huge, yet cute, and as I take it all in, Jen drops her bike, takes the bottom of her shirt in both hands and peels it off right in front of me.

She's wearing a blue bikini top, and I know before her leggings come off that the bottoms match. She pulls her hair out of its ponytail, slips the hair tie around her wrist, and prances into the lake gyrating a little too much as she moves. As soon as her feet touch the water, she gasps, but doesn't lose a bit of momentum.

"Come on, Tony! Don't be a girl!"

"I don't have a change of clothes."

"Boxers! Boxers! Boxers! Boxers!"

And soon everyone's chanting again, so I strip down to my blue boxer shorts that are barely a shade darker than Jen's bikini and make my way into the water, bracing myself for how cold it's gonna be. But it's not too bad, so I wade out until I'm standing next to Jen and it comes up just past my waist.

She smiles, splashes water on me, says, "See, you big baby? It's not bad."

"Naw. It's cool."

"Easier than killing someone, at least."

I'm not sure I've heard her correctly, so I ask, "What?"

"I said it's not bad."

"Hey Tony!" Donny calls as he walks slowly and cautiously into the lake. "Get me a bee-ah!"

Soon, everyone's in—laughing, splashing, wrestling—and Sam Kitchen's standing off to the side, water up to his bellybutton, staring up at the house. Jen's treading, talking with Donny and Kyle about some guy she dated in high school, and I notice that the birds, chirping in the trees, have grown obnoxiously loud.

I hear a gust of wind and the water begins to swirl around me. I know this is impossible, that I'm beginning to feel the effects of the Triple C. But it's okay, because this isn't so bad. As long as it doesn't get too much worse, I'll be able to function without giving myself away and getting in trouble. Without disappointing Jen again.

But then Jen floats over on her back and smiles up at me, and I know instantly that it's not really her, because she's still talking to Kyle and Donny somewhere else. So now I'm tripping pretty hard. I smile back anyway, and she sinks into the lake and swims around me like a mermaid.

And the birds continue to chirp. And the wind continues to blow. And now the water's really picking up, swirling around me like a tornado. I'm caught in the center of a whirlwind. Colors are coming to life and I hear my mom's voice inside my head.

You're always lying, Tony. That's the problem, isn't it? You're so caught up in your own lies that you actually believe 'em.

Jen emerges from the lake right in front of me so we're caught in the middle together. She looks so deep into my eyes that I can feel her gaze inside my body. A lock of her soaking blond hair's pasted to her face. It runs diagonally between her eyebrows and over her nose, just missing her lips. The water continues to swirl around us. She opens her mouth and speaks, but the only voice I hear is still my mom's.

I almost wanna feel sorry for you. But I can't. You know why, Tony? Because you're selfish. All you are is a selfish, little, spoiled brat, and you wouldn't know the truth if it bit you right in the ass.

Then she sinks beneath the surface again, and there are only birds, and the wind, and Jen, and Donny, and Kyle, and the other guys laughing and splashing and having a good time.

I've heard of having a bad trip, and I always just assumed that that's what happened when I thought I was dead whenever I took Triple C. But I know now that it wasn't. This is a bad trip, and maybe Kyle was right. Maybe I did give myself brain damage. Maybe this is the last straw and I'll never come back down this time.

All you care about is that stupid girl. You really think she cares about you, Tony? You're gonna throw your whole freakin' life away for some little tramp, then someday you're gonna be wishing the people who really cared were still there.

Fingers massage my brain like they did that day in the woods, and I imagine tiny worms crawling around inside my skull. Little maggots eating away at my decaying mind. Somewhere in the distance, Jen calls my name, but I don't listen because all I can focus on is my mom's voice.

Do you know what we do whenever you run, Tony? Have you even thought about it? I have John driving all over freakin' town looking for you, while I'm on the phone calling everybody who might know where you are.

And even though I promised myself the day I was dropped off at Secret Harbor that I would never cry again, I can't stop the dirty sensation building up in the crevices of my eyes. Now tears are streaming down my face, and I'm sniffing. And I'm sniffing. And I'm sniffing. And the water's spinning all around.

And my mom says, *I'll tell you what Tony Carpenter. You really don't wanna live in a nice home, with a nice family, and have nice things? Keep running away. Keep doing what you're doing, and I'll grant you your wish. I'll send you away and you'll get a taste of what it's like to not be wanted. How's that sound?*

Then Jen's right beside me.

"Tony? Tony? Are you okay? What the hell's going on with you guys? Are you all high on something?"

Her hand's on my back, leading me toward the shore. Telling me it's gonna be okay. But she's pissed. She's yelling at the other guys.

"Get out of the water and get dressed! Todd? Damn it! Where's Todd?" And I'm almost to the shore, but I stop walking because Karina's there, standing at the water's edge in the blue jeans and orange T-shirt she wore the last time I saw her. She's staring at me like I've done something to hurt her.

CHAPTER THIRTY-THREE

"**C**ome on, Tony. Come on. Keep walking. Almost there. Everybody! Let's go! I said out of the water!"

Jen nudges me and then I'm in motion, edging closer and closer to Karina. And the closer I get, the more real she becomes. She's so real there's no way I'm hallucinating. She's so real, my heart's skipping beats. So I step out of the water and stop inches from her face, and then she's gone and all I see is the darkness beyond the tree line.

Jen says, "Tony? Tony, listen to my voice. Come over here and sit down. Todd! Todd! Somebody get me my radio. Curtis, can you find Todd for me?"

Curtis says, "Yeah," slips on his shoes, then disappears into the woods.

Donny laughs, and says, "Boobely-boobely-boo!"

Jen yells, "Sam! Come on! Outta the water! Now!"

I look toward the last place I saw Sam Kitchen, where he still stands waist-deep in Blackberry Lake, staring at the house. The water's swirling around him, more violently than it did me. Sam Kitchen stands still as a statue and I think, He's in the realm of the dead. He's seeing all the animals he's killed. The sheep he's strangled. The baby rabbits he froze. The emu whose neck he snapped.

Jen's hands gently touch my face. She turns my head so I'm looking in her eyes and I see fireworks exploding in them. I feel her breath on my lips as she says, "Tony, stay here, okay? Please be cool. Kyle? Kyle, watch him please."

From somewhere far off, Kyle says he's got me, and his voice echoes like he's in a tunnel as Jen runs into the water.

Donny says, "Boobely-boobely-boo!" and lets out a high-pitched laugh. "Boobely-boobely-boobely-boobely!"

Kyle steps up next to me, says, "Handle your drugs, man. You can do this. You said you usually take way more. You're cool, bro. You're cool. You're just having a bad trip. So is Donny. We shouldn't of gave him Darland with all the meds he's on. Listen, I'm gonna get into Jen's backpack and find her radio. You cool if I leave you for a second?"

Jen makes it to Sam Kitchen and though the water barely comes up to his waist, it's halfway up her ribcage. It's not swirling anymore and I'm not hearing any voices, so I think Kyle's doing a good job talking me down. I think, I'm gonna be okay. I tell him I'll be okay.

He says, "Cool. I'll be right back."

I watch as he starts looking around for Jen's backpack.

Donny says, "Hey Tony! Get me a bee-ah!"

Then Jen shrieks and I look just in time to see Sam Kitchen with one hand tangled in her hair, the other around her neck. He thrusts her below the surface of the water, and it's so clear you can see her down there clutching at his wrists. Then the Lake's bubbling and splashing but it's not a hallucination this time.

Sam cries, "You see what you're making me do? Do you see this? You think I wanna do this to you, Jen? You think I wanna hurt you? I like you! I like you a lot and you know that! But you're driving me freaking crazy!"

Donny points and laughs like an orangutan as Jen kicks, flails, struggles to break free.

Kyle flies to his feet, screams, "Sam! What the hell, man?" and runs into the water. I tell my feet to move, to help him neutralize what's happening. And my feet are ready to obey, but then Karina's there again. She's standing next to me, staring out at the scene that's unfolding in Blackberry Lake.

Jen keeps trying to come up for air, but Sam Kitchen doesn't care. His face is contorted and miserable. I can't tell if he's crying, because it's covered in water. He screams, "Is this what you want, Jen? Is this what you want? You think you're real cute, don't you? You see what happens when you play games with people's heads?"

Karina says, "Tony, Tony, Tony. You like her, don't you?"

"Karina—"

"Bro, shut up. Can you do that, Tony? Can you shut up for once and stop trying to impress everyone? Just answer the question without saying what you think I wanna hear. Do you like the chick, or not?"

"Yeah. I think I do."

"You don't like that guy, though."

"No."

"You think he's a creep."

"Yeah."

"And it probably doesn't help that he's basically you."

"What? He's not me."

"Sure he is, bro. Everything you hate about him— the animals, the people—it's gotta be like looking in a mirror."

Donny's laughing so hard now, he's lost control. He's doubled over, clutching at his stomach, trying to breathe.

Kyle makes it to Sam and grasps at his shoulders, but his body's so slippery he can't get a grip. Sam doesn't even acknowledge him, just keeps frowning, screaming at Jen, telling her it's her own fault he's trying to kill her.

Karina says, "Come on, bro. Are you really gonna tell me this whole thing doesn't look familiar to you?" She opens her hand in a welcoming gesture toward what's happening in the Lake, and I think of Boomerang. She says, "I'm not talking about your stupid bird, and you know it, Tony."

Kyle punches Sam Kitchen in the side of his head, and finally Sam releases his grip, turns and scowls at Kyle. Jen emerges, gasping, coughing, spitting up water as Sam jumps on Kyle, putting him in a headlock and twisting him into the water.

Karina says, "Think, Tony. Think real hard. We both know it's not a coincidence I'm here. And it sure as hell isn't just because you're on drugs. I told you to let me go. I told you to bury your feelings. You didn't listen, though, and now you're gonna have to deal with the consequences. You're gonna have to remember what you did. So think, bro. Think long and hard because I'm not going anywhere until you remember."

Kyle and Sam Kitchen are fighting to secure headlocks on each other— scratching, punching, cursing—and Jen's trying to break them up now. Donny just keeps laughing as Curtis flies out of the woods, followed by a shirtless Todd and Casey.

Todd says, "Jesus Christ! What the hell's going on?" He raises his walkie talkie, and opens his mouth, but his eyes go wide and he doubles over, dropping the radio and clutching the back of his head. Donny stands over him with a rock as big as four of his fists. He's not laughing anymore. He holds it with both hands, raises it high, then brings it down hard on Todd's head. You can hear a 'thud' as Todd crumbles into a pile of pale white limbs. All the commotion stops. The splashing, the fighting, the screaming—

Blackberry Lake falls silent. Donny raises the rock again. Jen cries, "Donny! No!"

But Donny doesn't stop. He smashes Todd's head with the rock and Todd's body straightens out like a two-by-four, then starts convulsing. A high pitch squeal comes from his mouth, then noise like static from a radio, but nothing tangible. His eyes are open, but they're crossed, staring at the tip of his own nose. Donny kneels before him, hits him again. And again. And one more time. And finally Todd stops moving. His head doesn't look right. It's misshapen and there's blood everywhere.

Casey heaves and vomits. Sam Kitchen just stares. Curtis stands frozen. Jen's crying so loud you'd think she didn't know Todd was a pedophile. Karina steps between me and the now-dead staff member. She's so close, my first thought is that she's gonna kiss me and put my hand on her chest. But instead, she asks if I remember yet what really happened the last day we were free together.

And suddenly, I do. But I wish I didn't.

CHAPTER THIRTY-FOUR

I guess it's crazy I thought it would be a good idea to do Triple C. the day I found out Karina had gotten out of treatment. My mom had boxes in the house, though, because she didn't know you could fry nuts on it. So I got two boxes out of the medicine cabinet and left out my bedroom window.

Droopy had a small flip phone. I asked if I could use it to make a call, and he was cool about it, but you could tell he didn't really want to be. It was small and outdated, and looked like phones I'd seen in older movies, like Training Day, or whatever. It was so light, it seemed like you could squeeze it in the palm of your hand and break it.

He called it an "Obama Phone." When I asked why, he said, "Look, kid. You get Obama phones from the welfare office, cause when Barrack Obama was president, he said they gotta give ya one. You know, for people like me and you, who can't afford ta buy a fancy one. You can use mine, but you should probably go down to the welfare office an get your own, so you don't have ta keep borrowing mine. Try not to use up all my minutes, 'kay?"

So I dialed the number Karina and I used to share and tried not to use up all of Droopy's minutes. She picked up right away, and even though it was her voice, it sounded like someone else because you could hear the smile in it.

"Hello?"

I'd never met Droopy before today, and I hadn't had a plan of action when I left home. All I knew was that I needed to get to a phone. The park was full of homeless people, and he's the only one I'd spotted holding one, so I just asked.

The spunk in her voice caught me so off guard, that at first I couldn't even respond. My body grew light and that flame in my chest started dancing again, and I couldn't even breathe. Then my jaw was in motion, but the only word that came out was, "Hello?"

"Tony?"

"Uh, yeah. Hi."

"Hi."

I asked her where she was. She said, "At home."

I asked when I could see her. She said, "I don't know."

I told her I'd run again, so we could be together. She said, "Tony—" and that was it.

"What? What do you mean, Tony? 'Tony' what?"

"Tony—"

"Stop saying my name! What's the problem?"

Karina took a deep breath and let it out slow like she were trying to blow out the flame in my chest. The problem was, that flame had been dancing in the wind for a so long now that it was immune, so I said, "Listen. Just meet up and talk to me. Whatever it is, we can talk about it. I don't care what you did while you were in that place, or who you were with. People make mistakes."

"What? What are you talking about? I wasn't with anyone."

"Then I don't—"

"I mean the place was co-ed. The other girls were hooking up with guys. But I'm not a thirsty bitch. You know that."

"So you didn't—"

"No. There was this guy named Derrick who was always trying to get me into his room, and everyone else liked this guy. This girl Jess—she was my roommate—kept telling me I was hella stupid for not doing it, but I think you know me better than that, Tony."

"I do," I said. "I know I do. But you just said—I mean what's the problem?"

Droopy waved a hand in front of my face, pointed at his wrist like there was a watch there. There wasn't a watch there. I nodded and said, "Listen, Karina, I ran away. I can't go back now. Just meet me. Can you at least just meet me somewhere and talk?"

She said, "I can talk now."

"No! Listen to me! You're not listening! I need to get off this phone! I can't keep talking right now. Just meet me, please."

She paused again and I wanted to go through the phone and shake the words out of her. Then, finally, she said, "Where are you?"

"Just up the street from your house. At the park downtown."

"Which one?"

"The one by the Casa Grande apartments."

"I don't wanna go there. Can you go somewhere else?"

"Of course. Anywhere. Just say where and I'll be there. I love you."

"Fine. Edgewater Park."

"Okay. I'll be there now."

"No. Gimme like an hour, okay?"

"What? Why?"

"Tony, I'll be there. Just gimme an hour."

"Okay. Fine. What part of the park?"

But she had already hung up, so I handed Droopy back his phone. He shook his head, annoyed, and stuffed it into his pocket. Then he looked around and showed me his gun.

* * *

I did it all on my own. I boosted the Coronas. I threw the bottle at the cashier when he tried to chase me. I bought the revolver from Droopy. And why? Because I needed Karina, and that meant I needed to talk her into running again. I needed to show her I was prepared. That I could take care of her.

But first I took a box of Triple C. because I was a pussy and I was terrified to boost anything sober. I took the pills, then I waited and when they started to work their magic on my mind, I went into the Green Apple grocery store and did what I had to do.

I made it to Edgewater Park first, and the birds were chirping so loud in the trees that they sounded pissed, and the trees were swaying like they were under water, and I had a twenty-two revolver stuffed into the front of my pants, concealed by my shirt.

Drugs are a funny thing, because even though they make you act like an idiot, sometimes they can make you smarter, or open your eyes to things you wouldn't have seen sober. Maybe that's what it's like being mentally disabled. Maybe disabled people have smart thoughts, but no control over their actions.

When I hung up Droopy's Obama phone at the park, I already suspected I wasn't going to like what I found out when I met Karina at the park. But then, when the Triple C. kicked in, I knew like I knew my own name that something was terribly wrong, I just couldn't figure out what.

So when she showed up with Mathias, it was almost a relief to at least know. She wore her blue jeans and orange shirt, and that new sparkle in her eyes, and he looked exactly the same as every other time I'd ever seen him, only now he left tracers as he walked because I was frying nuts.

He smirked, said, "Sup dawg?"

She smirked too, but even though her eyes were shiny, she was nervous as hell.

My whole body just went stiff. We were standing near a jungle gym where kids played and laughed, and mothers sat by watching, and I didn't care. I wanted to scream, even opened my mouth to do it, but my jaw just shook, and no words came out. Then I was hyperventilating, grinding my teeth so hard it's a wonder they didn't fall out of my skull.

The ground started doing this thing like a flag, waving in the wind. It was rolling under my feet, and Karina said, "Hi," and that's what it finally took to break my trance.

"Hi?" I asked. "That's what the hell you have to say? Hi?"

"Tony—"

"No! Don't say my name! Don't even think about saying my name, ever again!"

Mathias took a step toward me, but Karina put her arm out and stopped him.

I yelled, "Don't stop him! You don't have to do that! What's up, bro? You got a problem, you wanna talk about?"

Mathias bared his teeth, said, "Cut it out, dawg. What's your problem? People are looking. I'm gonna a give you a break, cause I know you're in your feelings right now, and you're obviously faded off a something, but get it together before you get the cops called, fool."

Karina said, "Both of you, chill. Please. Tony, you wanna talk? Let's go talk. All three of us. Let's get the hell outta sight before someone does call the cops. You do deserve an answer anyway."

And I did deserve an answer because since I met Karina I hadn't done much more than love her, and before she left for treatment, she said she loved me back. I did deserve an answer because Karina and I not being together had just never been an option. I did deserve an answer, because now she was here with Mathias. So we made our way into the woods, and I walked carefully so the gun wouldn't fall out of my pants.

CHAPTER THIRTY-FIVE

Jen's still crying. She's moving as fast as she can toward the shore, swinging her arms as she tries to run, but the water's slowing her down. Karina moves so she's once again standing beside me and we watch this scene unfold together.

Kyle yells, "I'll go get that boat so we can get him inside and call an ambulance!" But nobody pays him any mind as he dives in the water and begins swimming across Blackberry Lake.

Curtis has one hand cupped over his mouth, and his eyes are as big as quarters as he stares down at Todd's motionless body. Donny stands up and lets his arms fall to his sides. The rock's still cradled in one hand, half of it covered in dark red blood.

Now Sam Kitchen's running for the shore, racing Jen, passing her. He reaches land first and dives for her black backpack, ripping it open and finding her phone, then her walkie talkie. He tosses them both into the middle of the lake, then snatches up Todd's walkie talkie as Jen cries, "Sam! Sam! Please."

But Sam sends the radio hurling into the water and she turns, watching it sink like she can bring it back with her eyes.

He says, "Donny! Help me find his phone!" and Donny seems to snap out of a daydream. He drops the rock and both of them start rummaging through Todd's pockets as Jen resumes running toward them. She makes it just as Donny finds the phone, and she dives for it, landing on top of Todd and squirming around like a snake before getting up. There's blood all over her stomach and breasts. All over her blue bikini. Donny stands, tosses the phone like a Frisbee into Blackberry Lake.

Karina says, "Aren't you gonna help?"

I ask, "Who?"

"I don't know, bro. Who do you think you should help?"

Jen falls to her knees and touches Todd's face. She's crying so hard she has to gasp for breath. She feels his neck for a pulse, then slaps him across the face.

I tell Karina I'm sorry. She says, "No you're not."

"Karina—"

"Bro."

"I just, I tried to—"

"No you didn't, Tony. You did what you did, and it is what it is."

"No it's not."

"Then what is it, bro? Why don't you tell me?"

I take a deep breath, say, "Are you a—"

"Come on, Tony. You're better than that."

Jen's mumbling now. She's pacing, talking to herself, looking around like there's something somewhere that can unkill Todd. Casey's still heaving but he must've emptied his stomach, because nothing's coming up.

Sam yells, "Kyle! Hurry! Paddle faster!" Then he tells Jen to get dressed. She stops pacing, looks at him, and sniffs, her lips trembling. He raises his voice, repeats himself. She jumps, startled, then looks around for her clothes as Sam starts barking orders. "Donny, put your shoes on! Curtis, you too! Tony? Tony, snap out of it, man! We gotta move fast now, or we're screwed. You guys wanna get outta here? This is our chance. It's either that, now, or we go to prison. So make up your minds and do it fast. Casey! You too!"

Karina says, "See? He's you."

"No he's not," I respond.

She laughs. "So you still don't remember?"

"Yeah."

"What do you mean, 'yeah'?"

"I mean, yeah, I remember."

And I'm thinking I might know why I remember now too. And why I forgot in the first place.

It's the Triple C.

And my own mind, not wanting to remember. Or just not wanting it to be true.

Or just the Triple C.

CHAPTER THIRTY-SIX

The birds were pissed and that was a fact. They weren't just chirping. They weren't just singing in the trees. They were screaming. I'd heard birds scream like that once before, on a snowy day when I had just assumed they were pissed because they were freezing to death. Today, they were pissed for no apparent reason. Unless they were reflecting what I was feeling. Or maybe I was just tripping harder than I realized.

The trail was wide enough that you could've driven a truck on it. In fact, tire marks indicated that people had done just that many times. But the tree lines ahead of me kept moving, coming together and touching each other.

Nobody spoke as we stomped through the forest. Karina led the way, and after a while, we took a right onto a much smaller, concealed trail. We went to the place where Damien's tent used to be. The place she had first told me about her dad, and where we first kissed. The place where she moved my hand under her shirt and stuck her tongue in my mouth.

It was just a cleared out pit the size of two or three of the cells in juvie. It was the kind of place I would've played in if I found it when I was nine or ten. It was the kind of place you'd expect someone to take a body in the movies. Just past the trees, there was a pile of soaking wet clothes, and garbage, and whatever else.

Karina fidgeted with the cell phone we used to share, as she spoke first. "Okay. Well, here we are."

We stood on the side of the pit in a perfect triangle, like we were gonna pass a pipe, or a joint or something. I said, "Well are we gonna talk, or what?"

"Listen Tony—"

But Mathias cut her off. "Look dawg, it's obviously over. Don't be a little bitch about it. You act like she's the only girl out there."

Karina said, "Mathias!"

"No. He gotta hear this. Tony, you're my boy. You're cool and you're hella crazy and I like that, but you gonna have let this one go."

I told him I didn't wanna hear it from him. If Karina had something to say, she could say it herself. So he looked at her and said, "Go on then. Tell him." And the birds screamed, and something moved in some bushes, and my head tingled.

Karina said, "Tony it's over. I'm with Mathias now. We're leaving soon. Like tomorrow. We both decided we wanna try and change our lives. Or like stay clean or whatever. You're not ready for that, and you know it. Mathias has family in Nebraska who're gonna help us out. Bro, you know I can't fix my life if I stay around here. My stepdad's a crack head. My mom's whatever, and all my friends are bad influences."

I asked, "What about me? Am I a bad influence?" And when she didn't respond, I said, "I can change, too, Karina. You didn't even ask me if I wanted to change. Did it ever occur to you that I just wanna make you happy?"

"Yes. And that's the problem, Tony. I don't want you to rearrange your whole life just to be what I want. That's not right. The connection needs to be real, and it needs to be based on who we already are. It has to be—what's the word? Organic."

Even though we weren't close enough to the river for me to hear the water moving I did. I could hear it flowing and it was so loud that it almost drowned out the angry birds. It echoed inside my skull. It bothered me on a level that it shouldn't have and it only took me a second to realize that it was because it wasn't really the river I was hearing.

It was the sound of the bathroom sink, filling with water as my baby cockatiel stood on the counter smiling up at me, chirping happily because he knew I loved him. But the birds in the trees at Edgewater Park weren't happy because they knew something Boomerang hadn't. They knew I was dangerous. They knew what I had done to Boomerang, and they knew what I wanted to do to Karina right now.

I didn't want to want it. I couldn't help it. So I told her I hated her and I wished she were dead, and not two seconds later tears were pouring out of her eyes and Mathias took a step toward me. I shoved him as hard as I could. He flew back into a tree, then his eyes narrowed and he shoved me back.

Only there wasn't a tree behind me, so I fell onto the ground and the gun landed next to me.

Karina's eyes registered what they were seeing first and expanded like balloons. Then Mathias saw it.

He said, "What dawg? You gonna shoot me? Go ahead! Shoot me! What's up? You think I'm scared ah that—"

But before he could finish I snatched the revolver by its handle, stood up and pointed it at his face.

Karina cried, "Tony! Tony, don't!"

And I squeezed as hard as I could. And the gun exploded in my hand. And a spark flew from the barrel.

And the sound echoed like thunder in the woods. And the trees rustled because the pissed off birds all took flight and got the hell out of there.

Mathias's mouth opened wide and he fell to the ground, curled into a ball, groaning and crying. But I could hardly hear him because Karina was screaming so loud. Blood poured out of his skull, into his eyes, so he closed them tight and just moaned.

I turned and looked into Karina's eyes. She stopped screaming, dropped the phone, and stared back into mine. I knew she was gonna run. Mathias tried to form a word, but all that he could manage was, "Gah-gah-gah—," and I knew I had to finish the job. I leaned down and pressed the tip of the gun against the side of his head and he jumped, but remained curled into the fetal position. Then I shot him again and his body went limp.

Karina was in motion before I even straightened back up, running into the woods, so I pointed the revolver at her back and fired another shot. She cried out, fell onto her hands and knees, scrambled to her feet, and kept running.

I chased her. I chased her because I loved her. I chased her because she ran. I chased her because I knew I'd really screwed up now, and I didn't know what else to do. She ran all the way to the beach, then fell face first in the sand, gasping and trying to breathe, bleeding out the middle of her back.

I fell to my knees next to her and she looked up at me with doe-eyes. The same way she often looked at me when we were intimate, only now they were covered in a layer of tears. I took her face in one hand, because I still held the gun in the other.

She whispered, "Tony, please."

I said, "Ssshhh. Ssshhh. Chill. Relax. It's okay. I love you. It's gonna be okay."

Now I could hear the river because it was only a few feet away. It moved slowly, yet violently toward the water, and all I could think was, What am I doing?

I still loved Karina. I would always love her, and even though she brought me to the woods to tell me she was leaving me for Mathias, she had trusted me to love her and not to hurt her. So I set the gun down, and I told her I was sorry. Then I scooped her up into my arms like a new bride.

And I tried to stand up.

But it wasn't easy, because we were the same size. So I stumbled as I made it to one foot.

Then the other.

And she struggled to breathe. And stared up at me. And I walked into the river and lowered her into the water. And held her down.

Her shirt inflated, and at first she fought. Kicked. Flailed. At first I could see her, but a red cloud blew out of the hole in her back and expanded until the water was too dark to make out anything. I knew she wasn't dead yet when she stopped fighting. Then she vibrated for a few seconds and her limbs floated so carefree they seemed to move in slow motion.

* * *

I carried her body to the shore, then I fell to my knees and held her close, bracing myself for the tears that I knew would come next. But they didn't. So I prepared to vomit, or hyperventilate, or to freak out. But nothing happened because I was on Triple C., so feelings didn't exist.

* * *

I took Karina back to the place where Damien's tent used to be and set her next to Mathias. Then I picked up our phone, looked at pictures of her lying in bed with him. Of her in her underwear and bra in her bathroom mirror. Pictures of her and Mathias together by the water. The phone was connected to her accounts, so I posted that one online with the caption, "Leaving town together. Bye everyone." Then I broke the phone.

I wasn't tripping nuts anymore. I was still high though when I sprinted all the way to Tent-City. Since nobody was there, I took a shovel and ran back to where Karina and Mathias were.

Then I dug. And I dug. And I dug. I dug until my hands bled, but the hole was deep and wide enough for both of them, and I rolled them into it. Before I filled it back up, I considered burying the revolver and the phone with them, but instead I tossed the other box of Triple C. into the hole. I threw the gun and phone into the river.

I covered the grave in leaves and twigs and by the time I was done you couldn't tell there were two people buried there. I was dirty and wet, shivering. It was almost dark when I exited Edgewater Park and got arrested for shoplifting the Coronas.

CHAPTER THIRTY-SEVEN

Jen steps into her black leggings and pulls them on—first one side, then the other—as Donny slips on his shoes with no socks. Sam walks over and pulls Casey to his feet, says, "Come on, man! Pull yourself together!" Casey already has shoes on because he and Todd were out in the woods.

I remember everything. I killed Karina. I shot her, then drowned her like I drowned Boomerang, and I buried her and Mathias in the woods at Edgewater Park with a box of cold medicine. I went to juvie, and when the Triple C. wore off, I somehow forgot.

"You didn't somehow forget," Karina says. "You suppressed it. The whole day. You suppressed it and you rewrote it in your own mind. And you know exactly why you're remembering now, too, don't you?"

"The drugs," I respond.

"Yup. You buried them with me. You buried them in the same place you buried me. Not just in the earth, either, but in your own mind. And now every time you take Triple C., you have to go back to that place.

"You have to go back and dig around in the hole you put me in, just to find the high. But you can't just find that high, Tony, can you? You can't just find that high because I'm there too."

"You wrote me," I say.

"Are we gonna keep playing this game, bro?"

Jen pulls her tank top on and it sticks to her body. Todd's blood seeps through the pink fabric creating crimson splotches in various places.

When I don't respond, Karina says, "Come on, Tony. Don't start losing it on me now. We both know who wrote those letters."

Jen glances down once more at Todd, sniffs, brushes her hair behind her ear.

Casey's voice trembles as he says, "He killed him. He—he—"

"He did you a favor," Sam says. "Quit being a little bitch about it."

Curtis says, "What the hell are we gonna do now?"

"We're gonna go in that house," Sam replies.

"What? Why?"

"Do you wanna get off this island, or not? I got a plan. Just trust me, okay? Tony?"

Karina says, "Bro, try and stay with me. Who wrote the letters, Tony?"

"Stop."

"No! Answer the damn question! It's for your own good!"

"I did! I wrote the freaking letters to myself and I told myself they were from you! I even cut myself and wrote a letter in blood, because I didn't want to forget our promise. Are you happy now? Is that what you want me to say?" But Karina's true to her word, because as soon as I've finished remembering the last bit, she's gone.

* * *

They talk about me right in front of me. Curtis, Donny, Sam Kitchen. They say things like, "Is he gonna be okay?" and "He's cool. He's just trippin'."

I'm not tripping that bad anymore, though. When Karina left, she took my high with her. But I'm not right either, because she didn't take the memories of what I did.

Kyle makes it back with the rowboat so fast he looks like one of those black and white movies where they speed up the frames while circus music plays in the background.

Jen says, "Sam. Tony. Guys—we need to—we need to get to a phone." Sam tells her that's why we're taking the boat across Blackberry Lake, then we all pile in and row to the tiny little dock in front of the huge, cute house.

Once we're in the yard, Sam says, "Donny, Curt, Kyle—uh—Tony. You guys wait out here with Jen. Casey, come inside with me."

Jen says, "What?"

Ignoring her, Sam tells us not to let her run. If she runs, do whatever we have to do to stop her.

Again, she says, "What?"

"Don't let her run or she could stop us from getting off the island. Listen to me, Jen. If you just chill and don't make any drama, nothing'll happen to you. But if you try and stop us, we'll have to do whatever it takes to keep that from happening. You understand, right?"

Donny, Curtis—even Casey—all nod. I stand quietly, thinking about the way Karina looked up at me just before I set her in the river, and Kyle says, "What the hell, man? This isn't why I swam over here and got the boat."

Sam says, "You wanna go to prison, Kyle?"

"What? Why would I go to prison? I'm not the one who tried to drown a girl in the lake."

Jen says, "Sam, think about what you're doing. You don't have to—"

"Shut up!" Sam exclaims. "Stop it! You'll say anything right now to try and stop us from leaving, and you don't even care that we could end up spending the rest of our lives in prison! I'm tired of being lied to and treated like an animal by all you staff members! It doesn't matter that I'm the one who dunked you in the water! Todd's dead! And we're all accomplices! Now I'm getting the hell off this island, and the rest of you can come with, or you can stay! I don't really care. But until I'm on a boat, we're all sticking together. And if you try to stop me, then I'm gonna stop you however I have to do it!

"Who else wants off this stupid island?" He raises a hand, glances at each of us individually, urging us with his eyes to mirror him.

Curtis's hand goes up first. Then Casey's.

Donny twitches, says, "Hell yeah I want off this island," raises his hand. And because I want off Cypress Island too, I raise my own hand. The only two people without their hands in the air, are Kyle and Jen.

Sam Kitchen says, "Fine. I don't care if you come with or not, Kyle. But if you try and stop us, I swear to everything I love, I'll kill you. Tony, Donny, Casey. Watch these two. If they try to run, you know what to do."

* * *

The front door has a glass window big enough to crawl through. There's a red curtain over it, and four concrete steps leading up to the door. Sam knocks for less than a minute before making Jen and Kyle sit on the steps then throws a rock through the window. He reaches in, unlocks the door, and opens it. Then he tells Donny, Curtis, and me to stand around the prisoners. If either of them even stand up, we know what to do.

He and Casey stomp over the welcome mat and disappear into the house. Kyle watches them go, then looks up at me. He says, "We gotta do something, man."

I tell him it's gonna be cool. We just need to get off the island.

He says, "Come on, dude. Snap out of it. You're just high right now."

Jen says, "Tony—"

Curtis tells them both to please stop talking. Donny says, "Kyle, shut your mouth."

Then Karina's standing next to me again. She smiles, shakes her head. I say, "I thought you were gonna leave once I remembered."

"See? That's the problem, isn't it? You always just hear and see what you want, instead of the truth. You're so caught up in your own lies that you actually believe em. You wouldn't know the truth if it bit you right in the ass."

"Then what is the truth, Karina? Why don't you tell me? Are you a ghost? Is that it?"

Curtis asks if I'm cool.

Donny says, "He's still frying nuts."

Jen says, "Tony? Tony, you're gonna be okay. Everything's gonna be okay. What did you guys take?"

"Cough medicine," Kyle responds.

"What? Why?"

Karina says, "Oh, don't tell me you're actually buying into this 'realm of the dead' crap. You don't believe in that type of garbage, and you know it."

Kyle ignores Jen's question, says something to me about numbers. If I just do the right thing, there'll be three of us and two of them.

Karina says, "Ghosts are just memories, Tony. So I guess in a way, I am. But the truth is: I said I wouldn't leave until you remembered. I never guaranteed I would leave. That's up to you, bro. Can I ask a question? I mean without you getting offended? Did you ever love me, or were you just infatuated with me?"

And I still love her so much there aren't words for how much I love her, so I tell her that.

"Then why'd you bury me, Tony? I'm not talking about the girl you left in the woods, either. She's gone. Dead. And we both know you didn't love her; you were just obsessed. But what about me—your perception of her, and who you wanted her to be—why would you bury me in one of those tiny holes in your mind? Don't you know it's dark in there? Lonely? Bro, don't you remember what my dad did to me?"

Kyle says, "Donny, come on man. We're boys. You don't even like Sam. What the hell are you—"

But before he can finish, Donny punches him in the side of the head, yells, "Shut up! Shut up! Shut up! Shut the hell up, damn it! You're not gonna ruin this for me!"

Kyle springs to his feet, then fists are flying until Curtis joins in and Kyle hits the ground, rolls up like a potato bug as they both kick and stomp on him. He yells, "Jen! Run!"

Karina points with her eyes at Jen, as Jen stands up. Karina says, "But you're not infatuated with her, are you? You're in love."

Jen doesn't run. She grabs Donny around the waist and tries to pull him away from Kyle. But Donny breaks free and elbows her in the face. She falls to the ground, cries, "Guys! Stop it! Please!"

Karina asks if I'm gonna do something, or just stand and watch. So when Jen scrambles up again, I jump on her. Tackle her. My body becomes a cage, pinning her to the grass.

Karina claps, says, "There you go, bro! Love her like you loved me! Maybe you can take her over to the Lake and—"

"Shut up!" I scream. "Shut up! Shut up! Shut up! Shut up!"

So Karina disappears, and everyone else falls silent. Donny and Curtis stop kicking Kyle and all three of them stare at me. My face is so close to Jen's that we're almost kissing. I growl, "Stop. Jen, Kyle, just stop fighting, please. No one's gonna hurt you, I promise. We just wanna get off the island, then you can go."

And before I can make any more promises, Sam Kitchen and Casey walk out the front door and they're both carrying guns.

* * *

Two rifles and a revolver. Sam Kitchen carries the rifles like they're nothing more than broomsticks hanging at his sides. Casey clutches the huge revolver in both hands.

When Jen sees them, she writhes and manages to roll out from under me. Sam hands one rifle to Curtis. It's smaller than the other, black with a thin barrel, a lever on the side, and a short magazine sticking out the bottom. He says, "Here. It's just a lil deuce-deuce. Think you can handle it?"

Curtis examines it, pulls the lever and a small, twenty-two caliber bullet flies out the side.

"Hey!" Sam says. "Don't waste the shells. It's already chambered. I used to hunt with one of my foster parents when I was a kid."

Jen gets to her feet, cries, "Sam! You're still a kid! Don't do this! Don't throw the rest of your life away! Put the gun down!"

Sam Kitchen's rifle has a wooden stock, and a rusted barrel. He pulls a bolt on the side and points it at Jen's face.

He tells her it's a thirty-thirty, and it'll destroy her skull if he shoots her with it.

"Please, Sam. I'm sorry. I didn't mean to insult you. I didn't mean to hurt your feelings."

So Sam laughs, turns the weapon on Kyle, who's just getting to his feet. His face is covered in dirt and blood. He puts one hand out, just about covering the barrel and says, "Sam. Sam. Come on man. Don't—"

BOOM!

Sam Kitchen shoots him through the hand, in the chest, and Jen doubles over and screams and Kyle crumbles back into the grass and flops around for a while, then never moves again.

CHAPTER THIRTY-EIGHT

Nobody's home, but there's an old, three seater truck with chipping blue paint and rust on the rims on the other side of the house. Sam has the keys in his pocket and he says he knows how to drive, so everyone but him piles into the back.

Jen's not crying anymore. She's not begging either. She just keeps her head down and does what she's told, and she's told to sit against the cab so we can stop her if she tries to run.

After Sam Kitchen shot Kyle, Curtis yelled, "Dawg!" but now he sits on the wheel well clutching his rifle like it's an anchor, keeping him from floating away. You can see in Casey's eyes that he's mortified, so as the truck growls to life, Donny takes his gun from him.

Sam Kitchen called it a Dirty Harry. He also called it a forty-four, and it's the biggest revolver I've ever seen. It's made of real pretty blue steel, and looks like something you'd need two hands to operate. Like a small rifle.

Kyle didn't take long to pass away. He didn't move too much after he fell. I suspect I'll have some crap to deal with once the Triple C. wears off because he was my friend and I've just watched him be put to sleep like a rabid dog. I feel nothing now, however, aside from what I feel about what I did to Karina.

The smell of exhaust takes me back to the various cities we traveled to together. To Seattle. To Portland. To Sacramento. Then the truck's in motion and Jen's sitting with her back to the cab, her knees propped up, her forearms on them, staring down between her legs. I'm next to Donny. Casey's across from us, sitting by Curtis.

We pull onto a gravel road and pick up speed. Donny asks if anyone knows where the hell we're going.

Curtis says, "This road'll take us back to Secret Harbor."

I ask why the hell we'd wanna go back there, but Donny's smiling like a Jack-o'-lantern.

He says, "So we can take the Sea Wolf when the next shift comes on. That's smart. Who'd a thought Sam was actually smart? Hey Tony, get me a bee-ah!"

"But what about the staff?" I ask.

"What about em? We can deal with em."

"Deal with them?" I ask even though I'm not stupid and I know what he's implying.

He twitches, says, "I don't think we got a choice, fool. I mean, I guess we could tie em all up or something, but this is what we've always talked about, isn't it? Killing all the staff or whatever? Burning that place down? Well let's do it. Then let's get the hell outta here."

Jen starts hyperventilating, and Donny smiles as he says, "Except Jen. We'll let Jen live. She can come with us and be our special friend. Hey Jen? Will you be my special? Will you get me a bee-ah?"

Curtis says, "Donny, leave her alone, man."

"I'm just playing."

"Whatever, man. Let's just do whatever we gotta do and get off this damn island. We can play later."

Donny says, "Hey Tony, didn't you say you wanted to kill Jerry Warden? Lucky he's on the island today."

* * *

We pull up in front of the activities building and spill out of the truck like overflowing water. Sam Kitchen opens the toolshed, hands an axe to Casey, says, "Hold this." Then he hunches down so he can look into his eyes, but Casey won't meet his.

Sam says, "You gonna be cool?"

Casey sniffs, replies, "I don't know, man."

"Speak up! Answer me! Don't be a little bitch, Casey!"

"Leave him alone!" Jen cries. "Just stop, Sam! Stop being a bully!"

Sam tells Donny to shut her up, so Donny, using both hands, levels the giant gun at her face. She purses her lips, stares into his eyes trying to be brave, but her whole body's shaking.

"Not like that!" Sam yells. "Don't kill her, dude." Then he laughs.

Donny asks, "Then what are we doing with the staff?"

"Oh, we're gonna take care of them. All of them. Not Jen, though. That's my boo. And I'll even share. I know you want some of that, Donny. I've seen you looking before, so don't try and lie. And I know you do, Tony. You sick freak. So be cool, treat my girl good, and we'll all have a treat later."

Jen swallows and tears build up in her eyes, but she doesn't speak as Sam Kitchen once again addresses Casey. "Now are you cool, or are you gonna be a liability?"

"I'm good. I'm good, man. I swear I'm good."

But Sam raises his thirty-thirty and sticks the barrel in his face. "Open up."

"What?"

"Open your mouth."

"But—"

"Open your freaking mouth, before I blow your head off your neck bone, Casey!"

Donny's laughing like a hyena at this. Curtis doesn't say a word.

Jen watches helpless.

Casey says, "Okay! Okay!" and opens his mouth, blinking back tears as Sam Kitchen shoves the rifle so far in that he starts gagging, takes a step back, drops the axe. But Sam advances and shoves his gun deeper. So Casey falls to his knees and his eyes go wide. He takes the barrel in both hands and tries to pull it out of his throat, but Sam isn't having it.

"NOW ARE YOU COOL, OR NOT?" Choking. Gargling.

"ANSWER ME?" Croaking. Heaving.

"WHAT? I CAN'T HEAR YOU?"

Finally he pulls the rifle out and you see how deep it was in there, and you wouldn't have believed it was possible.

"I'm cool! I'm cool! I swear, Sam! I'm cool! You can trust me! I just wanna get off this island, too!"

"Then don't be a little bitch." Sam says. "Pick up that axe and give it to Tony. I know Tony's cool."

* * *

All the potential weapons are removed from the toolshed, and Jen's put inside with the sliding, wooden door left open. She's instructed by Sam, who's somehow managing to run this whole messed up show, to "sit down and don't even think about moving till I get back." Donny tells him, "If we're taking out all the staff, I want to shoot Anthony in his ugly face. And Tony wants Jerry Warden."

Sam smiles at me, "Yeah? That true, Tony? You want Jerry Warden?" And because I've wanted to kill Jerry Warden since the day I met him, and it doesn't seem like a good idea to disagree, I tell him it's true.

"Deal," Sam says. "Someone's gotta stay with Jen, though, and it's gotta be you two. I don't want her to smile and wink at one of these guys and they let her go. No offense Curt." He waves his rifle at Donny and me, asks, "That cool? I'll bring Jerry and Tone down here if I can. You got my word."

We both say that's cool, then we post up in front of the tool-shed's open door. Donny has his forty-four. I have a heavy, rusted axe with a greasy wooden handle. The guys pile back into the truck with multiple gasoline cans and fly up the hill toward the common area and the dorms, kicking up so much gravel and dust that Donny, me, and Jen all start coughing.

As the cloud expands and the air clears, Donny turns toward Jen. I watch as the blue truck comes to a stop just below the balcony of the common area. Karina steps out of the dust like a ghost and stops only feet from me. She opens her mouth, and her and Donny both say, "This is so exciting," at the same time. Donny's only mocking, though, speaking in a girlish voice.

The guys jump out of the truck and run up the wooden staircase on the side of the building.

Karina says, "So, you gonna smoke that guy?"

"Jerry Warden?" I ask.

Donny says, "Huh?" Karina nods.

Jen says, "Guys, let's get outta here."

I tell Karina I might not have a choice.

She laughs, says, "Bro, when have you ever not had a choice?"

Jen says, "Tony? Tony, come on, sweetheart. Stay with me, 'kay? What kind of cough medicine did you guys take?"

Donny tells her to shut up and get him a bee-ah.

Karina says, "Tony, you always had a choice. We always had a choice. That guy in the alley, Trouble and Shay, there were always options. You just chose whichever one protected you, even if it meant other people had to die. You know why? Because you're selfish. All you are is a selfish, little, spoiled brat."

Jen tells Donny they need to get me help. She says, "Donny, he's your friend."

Donny says, "He's just trippin'! Shut up and let him trip!"

"Donny—"

"Okay. Then I'll shut you up, how bout that?" He steps into the shed.

I tell Karina I never would've poisoned Trouble and Shay if she hadn't told me to. I wouldn't have even known how. Jen says, "Donny, please."

Karina says, "And what if you'd told me no? How about that, Tony? Did it ever cross your mind that you could've had a say in the matter, too? Or did you just want an excuse to be with me and killing people was as good of one as any? You were ready to kill your own mom, bro. I mean even I wasn't that out there, and you know what my dad did to me.

"So why don't you answer my question again and let's be honest this time. Did you ever really love me, or were you just infatuated with me, Tony?"

Donny tells Jen he's going to shoot her and she starts begging. She says she'll shut up. She'll do anything he says. She's not ready to die.

I tell Karina I don't know anymore. She says, "Then think about it."

So I think, and then I tell her I still don't know.

"Then don't you think that's your answer? You shot me, Tony. You held me under water until I was dead, and you buried me in the place where you first thought you loved me. You killed me because I didn't wanna be with you anymore. That's not love, Tony. You're obsessed with me. How many more people are gonna have to die because of it?"

Donny tells Jen to take off her shirt, and she's crying loud but she says, "Okay."

"What the hell are you talking about?" I ask Karina. "Nobody. Nobody else has to die for us."

"Then why are you out here talking to me, instead of stopping what's happening in that shed?"

Gunshots erupt in the common area and echo in the sky like thunder. I tell Karina I can't stop any of this.

"Why?"

"Because I'm a part of it."

Donny says, "Take everything off. Then get me a bee-ah."

Karina says, "There you go again, acting like you don't have a choice. Who says you have to be a part of this, bro? You can back out any time you want. You might get killed if you do, but there's always a choice. So let me ask you another question. Are you infatuated with that girl like you were with me, or do you actually love her?"

I hear the sound of shattering glass and look to see chairs flying though the huge windows overlooking the balcony in the common area.

I tell Karina, "I don't know. I think I love her."

"Didn't you listen to a word your roommate said? Love's a verb, Tony. It's an action. Something you do."

"Then I guess I don't love her."

"Then do it, stupid!"

"What?"

"Love her, bro! Make the choice! Do the right thing for once in your life and think of someone other than yourself!"

And the problem is, Karina's not even really here. The problem is, I'm tripping nuts and everything she's saying is coming from my own mind. And the problem is, she's right. I'm right. So I take her face in my hand, and I kiss her long and deep. I close my eyes and I touch her tongue with mine, and even though she's not real, the kiss is. It's so real, it ignites the dirty, dancing fire in my chest. But when I open my eyes, she's gone, so I grip my axe with both hands, turn, and step into the toolshed.

* * *

It's about the size of one of the small juvie cells— maybe six by ten feet, made of old, rotting wood. There's no floor. The floor's just gravel, the same as outside the toolshed. There's a bench on the far wall with nails, screws, small tools. Jen stands in front of it, dirty and naked. Shaking and wide eyed.

Donny's a few feet away, staring at her body, blue steel hanging at his side. He doesn't advance on her, but when I'm close, I see his eyes are glazed over and horrible. Like he's in some sort of a trance. With no shirt, it's impossible to conceal the swelling beneath the front of his shorts. He says, "Your body's not even that nice."

Jen jerks and hiccups, attempting to get her crying under control. Donny says, "I don't know why you think you're so special. I've been with lots ah girls like you. So has Tony. Right, Tony?"

There's a rope hanging from a hook on the wall next to him. It's long and coiled up, and since I don't see any other rope around, I imagine it's the same one Sam Kitchen used to send the emu to heaven. I step around

Donny, lean my axe against the wall, and take down the rope, examining it for the simplest way to uncoil it from the figure eight that it's tied into.

He twitches, says, "Good idea," out the side of his face, never taking his eyes off Jen.

She says, "Tony, please," and you can hear a defeat in her voice that only a sociopath wouldn't sympathize with. Like she knows there's nothing she can do now but beg. Like she knows even begging is a long shot. Like she knows she's gonna die soon.

The rope's pretty thick, like the one they use to tie the Sea Wolf to the docks, and as I attempt to untangle it, it only makes it worse. There's a couple feet of it I'm able to pull out in a loop, though, so I grip it as tight as I can and throw it over Donny Bravo's head—around his neck— and I pull as hard as I can.

The forty-four explodes in his hand, and sparks fly in the gravel inches from our feet. The noise echoes in my head, bounces off every wall inside my skull. My ears ring so loud, I barely hear Jen shriek, as she backs into the workbench. I wrestle Donny to the ground and wrap my legs around his waist, locking my feet together in front of him. His hands come up and he tries to dig his fingers between the rope and his neck. But my grip's too strong. It's so strong I can feel rope burns forming on my palms.

Tiny rocks dig into the exposed skin on my arms and back, as Donny kicks, flails, struggles to break free. He's groaning and choking. Spit bubbles are forming in his mouth, and his eyes are wide and panicked. I know, because I'm looking down into them, trying to comfort him with my own.

Trying to express to my friend how sorry I am that this has to happen. He scratches at my face, and I'm not sure how deep his nails dig, because I'm loaded and my adrenaline's pumping so hard I'm next to numb.

Then Jen has the gun. She's standing over us, clutching it in both hands, pointing it at my face, crying, "Tony! Tony! Stop Tony! Stop right now, or I'll shoot you!"

But I don't stop and Jen doesn't shoot. Or try to stop me. Donny's tongue emerges, swollen and short as another gunshot rings out from the direction of the common area. Then Donny kicks and he kicks and he kicks at the open air with the bottom of his feet—and falls limp. So I choke him a little longer.

* * *

Jen scoops up her leggings, her shirt, and her shoes with one hand. Points the weapon at me with the other as I climb to my feet. She says, "Don't come near me. Don't even think about it. Back up! Back up, now!"

So I put my hands up and back out of the shed, but I beg her with my eyes to understand that I'm trying to help her. Not hurt her. That I love her. She follows me, and when she's out, she glances up at the common area.

I follow her gaze and see flames reaching out the windows. She backs up, says, "Stay away from me. If you try to follow me I swear to God, I'll shoot you!" Then she turns and dashes around the building, presumably to put on her shoes before running through the woods.

Three more shots. Another broken window. If I follow Jen, she'll shoot me.

But I can still run and hide somewhere else. Or I can attempt to right my wrongs.

I can try to save two more lives.

So I drag Donny's body out behind the activities building and hide it in some bushes with the rope still around his neck. Then I retrieve my axe from the shed and wait for Sam Kitchen and the rest to return with Jerry Warden and Anthony.

CHAPTER THIRTY-NINE

The flames grow fast. They spread, and start wrapping around the roof, connected to the cloudless sky by a long stream of thick, black smoke. There must be twenty or more boys marching toward the activities building. Toward me. Jason's near the front. So is Lil Poet.

Karina's here again, standing next to me, watching them approach. She says, "What'cha gonna do?"

"I don't know yet."

"Well you better think fast." I ask if she has any ideas.

She says, "I'm in your head. If you don't have any, how would I?"

"I don't know. You seem to know more than me."

"I am you, bro."

"So I guess it would be pointless for me to say I'm sorry for what happened at the river?"

She snickers. "You mean when you murdered me?"

"Yeah."

"Well would it make you feel any better?" I tell her no.

"Then there's your answer."

The small army approaching is halfway to me now, walking between the fields of sheep, emus, and llamas. I don't see Curtis, Casey, Sam Kitchen, or any staff in the crowd.

Karina says, "You're probably gonna die. You know that right?"

"Yeah."

"Even if you don't try to stop them. They'll find that dude's body, then that creepy kid's gonna shoot you in the face."

"I know."

"You could've run. They never would've found you. You could've got away and you probably wouldn't have even gone to jail. When the blond chick calms down she'll realize you saved her, and she'll tell the cops. But she's also gonna realize she could've saved you. She could've took you with her. I wonder if she'll feel bad."

"I wouldn't have gone with her," I say.

"Ha! Look at you, hero. That's hella funny. All of a sudden you're just Mr. Nobel, trying to save lives or whatever. You really think you can help those people, though? I mean the girl—yeah. All you had to do was fight off some kid with a hard-on. But look at this, bro. You see all those guys? You really think you can stop that many people?

"And what if that blond bitch does feel bad after you're gone? What if she thinks it's her fault for not taking you with? She'll have to live with the guilt the rest of her life—all because you were too proud to run and hide. You call that love, Tony?"

The majority of the building's consumed in flames now, and I can even smell the smoke. It's been a hot summer, and it occurs to me that there's a good chance the forest will catch fire as well. Cypress Island's not big. There's no town, only what used to be Secret Harbor, and a few residents.

The crowd stops outside the Mac cottage, and I finally see Sam Kitchen. He's fully dressed now, in jeans and a grey T-shirt. He breaks away from the rear, runs inside the house, and comes back out soon after. Nobody's home, because the guys in the Mac cottage are on some outing today.

Then the crowd's marching again, and Karina says, "So have you figured it out yet? I mean how you're gonna save those poor staff members? Because I'd say you got about twenty seconds to think."

And I haven't figured it out, and she knows it because she's just a part of me anyway. But she seems to be the part of me that's better at thinking, so I ask her again if she has any ideas, but she's already gone.

* * *

Their faces are solemn—just about all of them—and it's clear instantly that they're prisoners, rather than accomplices. And why would they be our allies? There's not enough room on the Sea Wolf for all of them. The crowd parts and Jerry Warden appears with Sam Kitchen urging him forward at gunpoint.

Sam says, "These are the ones who decided to join us." So I assume they all said what they had to say to save their own lives. I assume they'd all overpower us and put a stop to this madness if we didn't have guns. And I assume Sam knows this, he just doesn't have enough bullets for all of them.

Jerry Warden looks like he might pass out any second. His face is flushed. His eyes are huge. Sam shoves the end of the rifle into his back and Jerry cries out, a combination of pain and fear.

The path between the two halves of the crowd is like a hall Sam's marching Jerry down. Curtis walks behind Sam, still wet and shirtless, clutching his black rifle with both hands. His expression isn't much different from Jerry's at the moment. He looks like he might be sick.

Jerry looks down at my axe, then into my eyes, says, "Tony. Tony, think about this. Don't throw your whole life away. This can still be fixed."

Sam Kitchen hits him in the back of the head with the butt of his rifle and he falls to his knees, clutching the point of impact, cowering like an abused dog. I step forward so I'm standing over him and the crowd expands. I think, I could do it. I could just split his head open like a piece of wood.

I don't have to be a hero, because this is the man who talked my mom into giving me away. The man who's done nothing but lie every time I've ever heard him speak. This is the man who runs this sorry excuse for a boy's home and lets his staff abuse kids. Who lets kids get raped. The man who enjoys watching kids suffer.

And for a second I think I might actually do it, because everything I'm thinking is true. And everyone's watching me like they think I might actually do it, because they know it too, and because I'm grinding my teeth and breathing like a cow and gripping the wooden handle of the axe so hard my knuckles are bone white.

But then I know I can't, because I've already done so much wrong. I've already killed so many people, and I've hurt my family, and I've done it all because I was obsessed with Karina. Then, I killed her too. So I need to redeem myself if that's even possible. I need to try to do what's right for once, even if it's not for the right person. Even if it means I'll die trying, and I still fail.

But here are the problems:

I'm outnumbered.

My only weapon is an axe.

They have guns.

Sam's a sociopath.

I might be a coward. Time's running out.

So I decide there's only one viable option, and I ask Sam Kitchen where Anthony is.

All he says is, "He didn't make it." But he's looking around like there's something on his mind as I raise the axe high, as if ready to bring it down on Jerry's head.

Jerry says, "Oh God no!" falls into the fetal position, covering his face with his forearms. But I have no intention of harming him. Sam's close enough that I can avert my swing and hit him instead. If I can get my hands on his weapon fast enough, I can shoot Curtis. Maybe— just maybe—Jerry will join the fight. Maybe he'll get Curtis's gun. Maybe he won't shoot me.

But as if he can read my mind, Sam takes several steps back and points his thirty-thirty at me. I just freeze, axe held overhead, because I know I'm screwed.

Sam says, "Where the hell are Donny and Jen?"

* * *

Jerry Warden's praying, which is odd because I don't take him to be a praying man. He's still curled into such a tight little ball that if you threw it in the sound, it would probably float, and he's crying and mumbling something about the valley of the shadow of death.

I slowly lower the axe, as Sam Kitchen bares his teeth and repeats himself. The thirty-thirty's trained right on my chest. The place he shot Kyle. Every eye in the vicinity's wide, watching like they hope he'll do it so they have a good story to tell later. But only Jerry's talking. He says he's at a table in the presence of his enemies.

I tell Sam, "Donny ran. I tried to stop him, man. He had that gun, though, and he was gonna shoot me. He said he needed to protect Jen."

"PROTECT HER?" Sam yells. "PROTECT HER FROM WHAT?"

"I don't know. He was out of his mind. He took her with him."

"Well where'd they go?"

I point my axe in the opposite direction of where Jen ran, and where I left Donny Bravo's body. "That way. They went into the woods. I would've chased them, but he had a freaking gun, man. What was I supposed to do?"

Sam seems to be considering this, but he doesn't lower the rifle, and nobody suggests he do so. His eyes become slits and he purses his lip, then, finally, he says, "Why didn't you say something?"

"I just did."

"Damn it! You know what I mean! Why didn't you tell us earlier?"

"You just got here, fool! I was gonna tell you! Would you lower that flippin' gun?"

His whole body seems to tense because he wants to shoot me, but he doesn't, and I can only guess this is because he still needs help, and at this point Curtis and I are his most likely allies. He lowers his weapon, tells Curtis to keep watch, then runs around the activities building. So he knows I'm lying. And he's about to find Donny's body. And I'm screwed.

Jerry keeps praying, and I ask Curtis where Casey is, even though I'm pretty sure I already know.

"He took him out," Curtis says in a defeated tone. "He went in and ordered everyone to the carpeted area. A bunch of guys ran out the front entrance and Casey tried to go with, but Sam shot him in the back. He's got crazy aim, dawg. Like a freaking sniper or something."

"A hunter," I correct.

"What?"

"He said he used to hunt with one of his foster parents. What about Anthony?"

"Him too. He took the twenty-two and had me hold the other gun. He shot Anthony in the face, then told these guys whoever was with us, to start trashing the place. Everyone joined, but he shot some ah them anyway. He said he didn't trust em. He shot Cowboy Chris, and he wasn't dead, but he was just lying there. We set the place on fire and he left him there to burn up."

I tell Curtis I need his rifle.

"It won't do you any good," he says. "It's empty."

"Then why the hell are you carrying it around still?"

"Cause these guys don't know it's empty."

Jerry Warden hears this, and moves one of his arms, looks up at us. He says, "You guys, let's get outta here. We need to run before that little psycho comes back."

Curtis says, "That's not the worst idea."

I say, "No. Even if we run into the woods, he'll just start hunting us like animals."

"He doesn't have enough bullets for all of us."

"What about the people he does kill?"

Jerry says, "Tony, he's right." I tell him to shut up. He does what I say.

Curtis asks, "Then what the hell are we supposed to do? He's got the only usable gun."

"We all need to overpower him."

"Where the hell are Donny and Jen?"

I tell him I killed Donny and Jen ran off with the forty-four.

Jerry asks if he has permission to get up, so I tell him to hurry. To run in to the woods and hide. He looks like he doesn't believe me, so I kick him in his ribs and he scrambles to his feet, runs off, snot and tears running down his face. Then I raise my voice and start to tell the crowd we need to work together if we're gonna get out of this alive.

But before I've spoken three words, thunder erupts and echoes off the sky like we're in a dome. It echoes so you can't tell what direction it came from, and before I even feel the bullet tear through my body, I'm clutching at my abdomen. I move my hand. Look at my palm. See blood.

Then I'm on my knees, coughing. There's a burning sensation in my back and my stomach. I fall onto my side and see Sam Kitchen approaching with the butt of the thirty-thirty, pressed against his shoulder and the tip of the barrel pointed at my face. Draped over one of his forearms is the rope I used to kill Donny.

CHAPTER FORTY

I can feel it pouring out of me. Flowing over my stomach like warm water. There's no pain yet. No panic. Only a sequence of events that might be unfolding out of order.

The sun's in my eyes so I have to squint. I cough some more, and take deep, deep breaths. Some people gasp. Others stand silent, watching, because this is what they hoped they would see. The axe is lying next to my face. A sheep says something and I remember being young. Really young. My mom and I were living together in a small two-bedroom house in the middle of a field that smelled like horse crap, but I didn't spend much time at home. She was pretty still, but she was mad a lot, and I used to eat from the saltshaker when she wasn't looking.

One day I swallowed a penny while she was vacuuming, and she snatched me up by my wrist, so I was hanging like a slab of beef in a slaughterhouse. She swatted my backside, but it didn't hurt too bad.

Now Sam Kitchen's standing over me, staring into my eyes, smiling. It's a bit of a relief, because he's blocking the sun. So I smile back and think of how my mom always left me with her dad, who never minded babysitting when she had to work or go out to bars at night. She couldn't leave me with my own dad, because my dad was dead. I always tried real hard to conjure up memories of him, but I was only two the day he got into a car with a group of friends and smashed into a telephone pole because they were all drunk and high on cocaine.

My Grandpa liked to play games with me that I wasn't supposed to talk about. They hurt and they were uncomfortable and they left bruises on my body, but I was his favorite grandson, and he was the closest thing I had to a father. Later, he asked me if I remembered the games we used to play, and I said, "sure," even though I hadn't put much thought into it and didn't know what he was referring to.

Sam kicks the axe away from me. Drops the rope next to my body. Puts a foot on my face. Says, "Where is she?" But I'm remembering the first time my mom brought John around after she met him in one of her bars. She introduced him as John-Boy and he laughed and I was only four and wasn't sure if this was funny or not, so I laughed too. I was five when they got married, and seven when we had Alex.

Sam Kitchen raises his shoe, brings it back down hard and I feel tiny rocks dig into my face as he presses me into the ground. "Answer me!" he yells. "Where the hell did Jen go!"

My mom gained a lot of weight when she was pregnant with Alex, and most of it never went away. One time she fought with John, because she said he loved Alex more. She sat on the floor in front of her closet with an open suitcase, yelling and stuffing clothes into it. She said, "I'm sorry, Tony, but I can't stay here and see your dad treat your brother better than you."

I remember being happy she was sticking up for me, but knowing she wasn't going anywhere. And even though John knew too, he still broke a jar of sugar on the kitchen floor.

Now the barrel of the thirty-thirty's pressed against the side of my head. Sam says, "Don't be a retard, Tony. You can still get outta this alive. Tell me where she is and I won't shoot you again."

It was years later when I learned my mom was caught cheating and told him she did it because he didn't treat her son good enough. That's why she fought with John that day. That's why John broke the sugar jar. Because she was packing her suitcase and threatening to go stay with her lover. It was never about me, so they never fought about me again.

Sam looks like he might cry, because he thinks he loves Jen. He thinks he loves her like I thought I loved Karina, and if she hadn't run, he would have killed her the same way I killed Karina. He says, "Tony, please."

Then Karina's standing next to him, looking down at me with the warmest, most motherly smile I've ever seen resting on her face. She tilts her head, but doesn't speak. Mathias steps up next to her. Then Trouble and Shay. David. Kyle. Casey. Even Anthony and Todd. An image of my biological father in an orange vest from a picture I looked at often growing up appears and soon they're all standing around me, forming a circle with Sam Kitchen. Somewhere in the distance, I even hear Boomerang. The dead watch me for a while, until finally David speaks.

"You're a mess, fool."

I open my mouth to laugh and tell him I know, but all I can do is cough. Even though I was shot in the back, through my abdomen, it burns in my throat.

Kyle says, "See man, the realm of the dead, is all in your head."

Sam shoves the rifle so hard into my temple, it's like he's trying to use it to drill through my skull. He says, "I'm gonna count to three, Tony!"

And I'm thinking all in all, I know my mom always loved me. She just had a rough life, and nobody ever taught her how to show it. I always suspected she didn't love John, though. I always suspected she married him out of convenience.

My biological father, Big Carter, scowls down at me, shakes his head on account of he's disappointed in me.

Sam yells, "One!"

Karina drops to one knee, runs a hand through my hair. "Tony, you did it. You saved two lives. But look around. Look at the ones you destroyed. Do you really think what you did today can atone for that?"

"Two!"

I suck in a choking breath, feel air hissing and spraying out of my stomach. I try to say I'm sorry, because it's all I can do now to obtain some semblance of absolution for what I did to her.

She says, "No Tony, I'm sorry."

Sam yells, "Three!"

BOOM!

I squeeze my eyes shut so tight that my eyeballs might fall into my throat. All I see is red. Then I hear the voice of the girl I love, and I might as well be in heaven, but all I smell is smoke.

"GET BACK! GET BACK! EVERYBODY! BACK UP, RIGHT NOW!"

I open my eyes and look into Sam Kitchen's. He's lying next to me on his side, staring right at me, his jaw hanging loose. A huge chunk of his forehead's missing and you can actually see brains spilling out.

My father, Karina, Kyle, David—all the dead are gone.

Jen hovers over me, fully dressed in her leggings and bloody pink tank top. She clutches the forty-four in both hands and spins around, pointing it at everybody, then stopping on Curtis. "DROP THE GUN, CURTIS! RIGHT NOW!"

So Curtis drops it, throws his hands in the air, and takes two steps back. She tells the crowd to sit down on their hands. They all obey, then she kneels next to me, lifts my head and sets it in her lap. For just a second, I see the burning building, then I'm caught in Jen's gaze. She brushes my cheek with one hand, tells me it's gonna be okay. The Sea Wolf should be showing up any minute.

I was infatuated with Karina. Obsessed with her. Karina hated my mom. My mom hated Karina. That's all there ever was, and now people are dead and I can't breathe too good. I need to speak, though. There's something that has to be said, and it has to be said now, because there may not be another opportunity. So I take a useless breath and struggle to make words.

Jen says, "Save your strength, Tony. Keep fighting. Please."

And I know she's right. I might still make it out of this alive, if I just save my strength. Keep fighting. But what needs to be said is more important than making it off Cypress Island alive. So I choke out three words, because if I only ever speak three words again, I want them to be these three.

"Bodies. Edgewater. Park."

Jen says, "What? Tony. Tony, just relax. It's gonna be okay. Hold on, okay? Just hold on a little longer, and we'll get you help."

But I can't hold on any longer, so I watch Jen cry and fade away as the whole world turns black.

EPILOGUE

From the Skagit County Herald.

MISSING TEENS FOUND DEAD AFTER GROUP HOME RIOT.

The remains of two missing teens were found buried in Westside Mount Vernon's Edgewater Park, after a youth provided information during a riot in a state housing facility that led police to the bodies.

Investigators are saying that fourteen-year-old Karina Vasquez, and her boyfriend Mathias Tweten planned to run away together back in May, but when Vasquez's ex-boyfriend, fourteen-year-old Tony Carpenter found out, he lured them off one of the hiking trails in the park, and shot and killed them. Carpenter then buried the two teens and was later arrested for shoplifting.

Because Vasquez posted a photo earlier that day of her and Tweten on social media, captioned, "Leaving town together," the family of the victims believed they had merely run away. Vasquez had a history of running away and had been picked up in various cities around the country.

In a bizarre twist, a riot in a group home located on Cypress Island off the coast of Anacortes, where Carpenter was being housed, led to the deaths of two staff members and six residents, including Carpenter, who suffered a punctured lung from a gunshot wound. However, Carpenter provided information to a staff member before he passed, pertaining to the locations of the bodies. Acting on the tip, police scanned Edgewater Park with cadaver dogs, and found the remains.

From the Skagit County Herald.

GROUP HOME BURNED DOWN, UNDER INVESTIGATION.

An investigation has been launched into allegations of abuse, both physical and sexual, at Secret Harbor School, a boy's home located in the San Juans, off the coast of Anacortes.

After a riot last week led to the deaths of six teenagers, two administrative staff members, and the home being burned down, Secret Harbor's residents provided police with information pertaining to conditions in the group home.

Jerry Warden, the home's administrator, was arrested on multiple charges, such as child abuse, neglect, and reckless endangerment. Warden is currently out on bail, but declined to comment when asked about the allegations.

* * *

From the Skagit County Herald.

MEMORIAL SERVICE HELD FOR THOSE LOST IN GROUP HOME RIOT.

A candlelight service was held Friday, at 9:00 PM, at the Anacortes Marina for those who lost their lives during the deadly riot at Secret Harbor School.

The turnout was small, yet emotional, as mourners lit candles for their loved ones and set them floating into the Puget Sound.

Among those present, were family members of fourteen-year-old Tony Carpenter (who was shot and killed, and is suspected of murdering and burying his girlfriend in the woods in Mount Vernon's Edgewater Park), and twenty-three-year-old Secret Harbor staff member, Jennifer Cutler, who claims Carpenter saved her life during the riot.

Katherine Carpenter, Tony's mother, told reporters "I forgive my son. He wasn't right, and he wasn't on his meds. He was just in the wrong place at the wrong time."

A memorial was erected on the beach with the names of the deceased; however, Carpenter's name was omitted.

ABOUT THE AUTHOR

Michael J Moore lives with his wife, author Cait Moore, in Seattle, Washington. His books include *Highway Twenty*, which appeared on the Preliminary Ballot for the 2019 Bram Stoker Award and the bestselling post-apocalyptic novel, After the Change, which is used as curriculum at the University of Washington.

His work has received awards, has appeared in various anthologies and magazines and has been adapted for theater. Follow him at:

twitter.com/MichaelJMoore20

facebook.com/michaeljmoorewriting

https://michaeljmoorewriti.wixsite.com/website

and

https://instagram.com/michaeljmoorewriting

NOTE FROM THE AUTHOR

Word-of-mouth is crucial for any author to succeed. If you enjoyed *Secret Harbor*, please leave a review online—anywhere you are able. Even if it's just a sentence or two. It would make all the difference and would be very much appreciated.

Thanks! Michael

Other HellBound Books Titles
Available at:
www.hellboundbookspublishing.com

Highway Twenty

An engineer from out of town disappears. Then Conor Mitchell's girlfriend. Then his parents.

The townspeople of Sedrow Woolley, Washington are vanishing at a horrifying rate.

But they come back.

They all come back days later, and they're different: Hungry. Insectile. Creatures posing as humans.

Because Conor knows the truth, and because the entire police force has already been changed, and because there's nowhere to run from an evil that only wants to spread, his sole option is to fight.

But they have no intention of letting him leave town.

Tremble

Widow and single mother, Rebecca Noland, wants nothing more than to rekindle the passion with her overworked fiancé, Detective Dan Slaviche.

Expecting to surprise him by slipping into his apartment before he comes home from work, her curiosity gets the best of her when she discovers the key to unlock his desktop. What she finds there is a nightmare that sends her, along with her seven-year-old son, running for their lives.

Terrified and broke, her only option is to flee to her family's estate in Tremble, Tennessee where memories of her mother's violent death still haunt her childhood home. But bad memories aren't the only things that await her. As Dan abandons all morals in his attempt to locate his bride-to-be, Rebecca struggles to make the house a home for her son while growing closer to her next-door neighbors. But her sanity comes into question when she realizes the entity responsible for her mother's murder is lying in wait, intent on destroying anyone who tries to come between it and the object of its deadly obsession... *her.*

Satanic Panic

An incrcdible homage to 1980's horror!

Satanic Panic, a mass hysteria created in the nineteen eighties, has returned to a small college town in the Midwest.

Ritualistic murders and the presence of the occult have bled below the surface of the town in the form of icy accidents and other coincidences.

And when three lifelong friends find themselves on the radar of a killer—and leader of a satanic cult— they must fight for what's good without being seduced by the evil that possesses their campus.

The Toilet Zone
RESTROOM READING AT ITS MOST FRIGHTENING!

Compiled and edited by the grand master of 80's schlock horror, Bret McCormick, each one of this collection of 32 terrifying tales is just the perfect length for a visit to the smallest room....

At the very boundaries of human imagination dwells one single, solitary place of solitude, of peace and quiet, a place in which your regular human being spends, on average, 10 to 15 minutes - at least once every single day of their lives.

Now, consider a typical, everyday reading speed of 200 to 250 words per minute - that means your average visitor has the time to read between 2,500 to 4,000 words, which makes each and every one of these 32 tales of terror - from some of the best contemporary independent authors - within this anthology of horror the perfect, meticulously calculated length. Dare you take a walk to the small room from where inky shadows creep out to smother the light and solitude's siren call beckons you?

Dare you take a quiet, lonely walk into... The Toilet Zone

Invasive Species

A monster has come to Maldus, Arkansas, and the residents of the small mountain town are too busy to notice. With the monster comes something even more terrifying and threatening than gnashing teeth or razor-sharp claws. The monster has brought change. The residents of the small mountain town are too busy to notice at first. Busy with things such as addiction, racism, work, or land deals. Unnoticed, the change the monster brings in its insidious wake spreads like wildfire. Unnoticed, the town of Maldus falls prey to an Invasive Species.

**A HellBound Books LLC
Publication**

http://www.hellboundbookspublishing.com

Printed in the United States of America